DRAGONS & DINOSAURS

Pater's Crystal

TIMOTHY MARTIN

Order this book online at www.trafford.com
or email orders@trafford.com

Most Trafford titles are also available at major online book retailers.

Print information available on the last page.

ISBN: 978-1-6987-0300-8 (sc)
ISBN: 978-1-6987-0302-2 (hc)
ISBN: 978-1-6987-0301-5 (e)

Library of Congress Control Number: 2020916522

Trafford rev. 09/09/2020

www.trafford.com
North America & international
toll-free: 844-688-6899 (USA & Canada)
fax: 812 355 4082

CONTENTS

I suffer from Post-Traumatic Stress Disorder after working 25 years with the Royal Canadian Mounted Police. Without all the love and care I receive, I would not have been able to be an author or even be here in this world. I dedicate this book to Citadel Canine Society who brought me together with Hunter, my medical service dog, who is always by my side, silently supporting me in the down times.

A portion of the money received from the sale of this book will be dedicated to a non-profit organization which trains and provides service dogs.

PROLOGUE

The Continuing Story of The Dragon Mage:

I am known here as the Dragon Mage Jim, or Kai by the dragons. I am accompanied in my adventures by my loyal companions and warriors, which include dwarves, elves and even the Yeti, or Snow People (also known as the Ice People).

I must search out the Pater crystal, which was hidden by the father of all dragons. Its magical energies were too powerful to be left in any hands or claws at the time of the dragon father.

This is the continuing journal of my life since I have entered this strange new world, where dragons are intelligent, and all sorts of magical creatures inhabit the land.

It is amazing how quickly you can learn magic when you need it to survive.

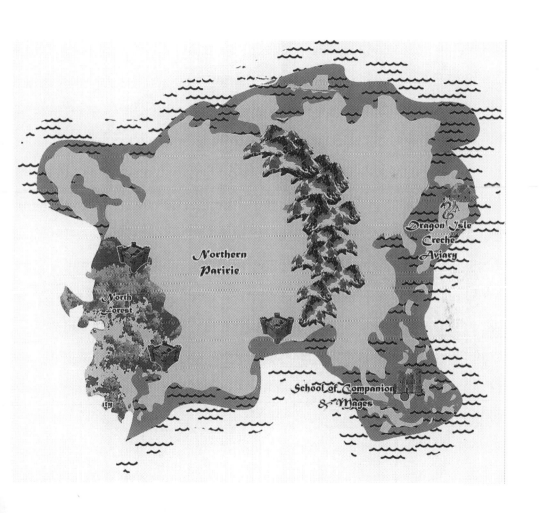

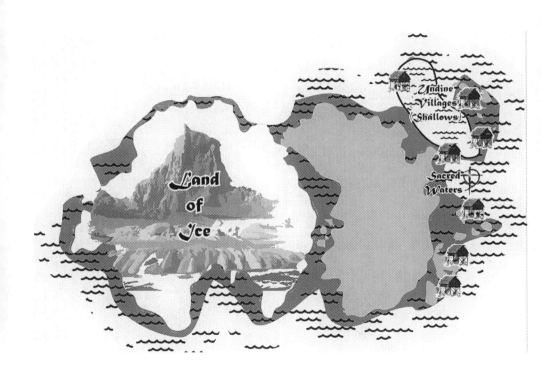

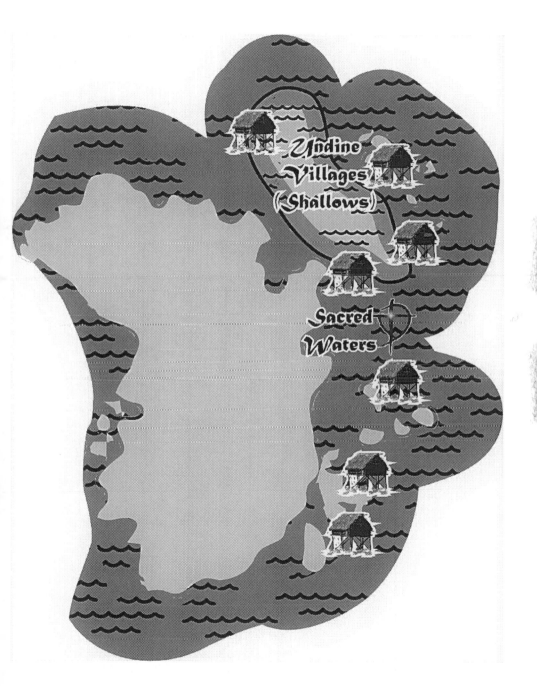

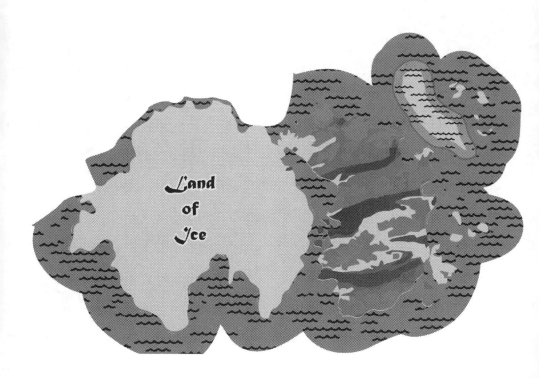

ONE

Time to take to the Road

I stood there on the road under the heat of the sun, with a couple of my team leaders and a trio of Drakes. We intently watched the approaching caravan.

I am known as Kai by the dragons, and I am also known as the Dragon Mage, Lord Jim. With me were Ice Storm, a large white Yeti, and Tomar, a Dark Elf, who until recently was the head assassin of the Guild, and the most deadly man known to all races.

The drakes were ready for battle. They were Matilda, who was the oldest and the Alpha female of the pack; also Bonnie and Clyde, a matched pair who were younger but not afraid to get into a fight.

The caravan was made up of Orcs transporting prisoners to the mines, where they would spend the rest of their lives in heavy work. The outriders approached the group without fear, riding large raptors to clear the path and get the strangers to stand aside or be arrested.

The orc outrider yelled brazenly, "State who you are, and by what right you are blocking this caravan's path!"

"I am here on behalf of the dragons, who will no longer tolerate your slavery trade that condemns these people to a life of servitude," I replied angrily.

The orc soldiers drew their weapons and told us to stand aside or die. The two raptors were dead within seconds; Matilda took out one raptor and Bonnie and Clyde took out the other raptor. As their mounts fell out from below them, Ice Storm used his claws on one orc, disemboweling him in an instant. The other orc was dead with an arrow through his throat—shot by Tomar before he could even flinch.

"Orcs have never been ones for long conversation, have they?" I said morbidly, but with a grin on my face.

Tomar replied, "They are better known for knocking heads. Let us see what the rest of the caravan is like."

When the rest of the caravan showed up to our position, they were also less than polite. The caravan leader stepped out from his shelter and approached the trio, while making loud demands.

"What makes you think that your three pets and you could beat my one-hundred-man caravan?"

I put my fingers to my lips, and with a quick breath, released a high-pitched whistle. About fifty fully-armoured dwarves on each side of the road stepped out, ready for battle. The caravan master stood counting heads, calculating how many dwarf soldiers were surrounding his caravan.

The caravan master said, with a sneer on his face, "It appears to be an even fight, as we have the same amount of warriors on the ground."

"I don't think so," I said, holding out my arm. Lady Gizmo landed on my shoulder. The caravan master looked like he was going to say something rude. Then a sudden rush of wings made him look around, and he turned very pale. Six fully-grown dragons in battle armor were standing strategically around the caravan.

"It is your choice; surrender or perish in the ensuing battle," I said, gazing deeply into the caravan master's eyes.

"I have no choice. I am strongly outnumbered, so therefore I surrender this caravan to you. What are your demands?" The orc caravan leader looked like he had eaten something very sour. He spoke quietly, and seemed to have a hard time swallowing.

"Leave the prisoners and wagons and start walking back the way you came from. We will give you enough rations to reach the nearest orc fortress. We will give you some personal weapons for defence, but if we find anyone following us, they will be killed outright, and their bodies left for the scavengers," I said in a commanding tone.

A couple of the orc warriors got out of line while they were preparing to depart. They did not last long before being quickly dispatched by the dwarf warriors.

As I walked slowly down through the caravan, my attention was drawn to an unusual cage on top of one of the trailers. As I looked closer, I noticed two Undines in tubs of brackish sea water; the smell was atrocious. I had a harness fashioned out of leather straps to carry the cage.

I called the last two dragons from the end of the caravan.

"Great Ones, please carry this cage to the ocean, so these creatures can return to where they belong," I asked gently of my brother dragons.

Both dragons nodded, indicating they understood and would do as I asked. I called Mercury down, mounting up with Lady Gizmo, and flew in tandem with the dragons carrying the cage.

When they landed the cage on the shore, I jumped down and sprung the lock so that the door was left ajar. I took to the air immediately with Mercury and circled the area at a high altitude, while still watching the cage. It was not long before the two prisoners opened the door and slowly walked into the sea.

We flew together back to the caravan's current location, several miles from where it originally was. The dragons were rotating patrols in the air to ensure that the orcs did not double back to attack the caravan.

Once I got Mercury unsaddled and settled in to his special bed in my modified transport, I had time to relax and reflect on the past year. A lot had changed, and if you had suggested any of the things that I had been through, I would have laughed at you.

I was a police officer and former marine, who had crossed the portal into this world and found dragons and dinosaurs, just for starters. In no time I had met and got to know elves dark and light, dwarves, orcs, ogres and even a powerful Dark Wizard.

The People who populated this plane of existence were slightly shorter in stature, but the Yeti was larger. Throw in a bat-like creature who was supposedly once a dark dragon, but who had changed over the centuries, and the whole thing made for a dangerous, exciting, and amazing world. Nothing mechanical that I could find on this world worked, with the exception of my pistol, which never ran out of bullets. In the last few months, I have learned more magic than I ever dreamed possible.

I spent several months in a wheelchair after being picked up by a flying dinosaur and dropped a great distance, which broke my back. The dragons performed a magical miracle, and fused part of a dead fledgling dragon's spine with mine, thus making it possible for me to walk again.

I was welcomed into the clan before, but by the grafting of spinal tissue into my body I was even more so now. I could talk to all dragons now without having to go through the sharing of blood magical ceremony.

The mother of all of the breeding females had named me 'Kai', after the name of the fledgling dragon who had passed away. As a result, I was now considered a proper dragon. I am bonded to two females, the first being Sylvia, a Dwarven widow who was barren before I was able to gift her with a child. The unborn child was killed in an attack on Lady Sylvia, which was almost fatal to Sylvia herself.

The other female I was bonded to was Rose, a princess of the Elves. The two of them were aware of each other, and participated in a ceremony bonding all three of us together.

James came into the great room of the transport to report on what was found in the caravan's lock boxes and general cargo.

"Other than the two sea creatures you returned to the ocean, Dragon Mage, there was not much in the way of anything unusual in the caravan master's accommodation.

"The surprising thing is that all the rest of the prisoners were dark elves," James said calmly, showing no trace of emotion.

"Ensure that tomorrow the caravan is escorted to the dark elf stronghold, where these people will be safe. Please send Tomar to speak with me," I directed James.

Tomar came into the room, with Neb shadowing him closely.

"If you have not done so already, I would like you to talk to the elders in this group of dark elves and reassure them that they are being taken to a safe place. Also, about Neb's training; how is it progressing so far?" I said to Tomar.

"I have reassured the elders of this group. They are naturally hesitant, considering the history between the elves and dwarves. It would do a lot if you could talk to them and make them sure that things have changed. Neb, step outside please," Tomar said in a concerned tone.

Neb bowed his head and quietly exited the room.

Tomar continued talking, saying, "Neb is doing excellently. I do not want to admit it, but he is trained as much as he is going to be. I would appreciate it if I can turn him over to your care as a companion. I will explain it to him for you."

"I will speak to the elders tomorrow. Neb will be welcome as a companion in our ranks," I said, eyeing the door where James went out of the great room. Neb returned later and stood silently with James until they were dismissed later in the evening. Neb was initially to room with James until I decided what to do with him.

* * * * *

I rose with the dawn, and walked over to the elder dark elves who were in the caravan. I spoke with them at length about where they were being taken and what they could look forward to.

As the caravan was setting out, I asked Mercury to take Tomar and one of the elders who was brave enough to ride him. They were going to the stronghold so that the elder could see for himself what was happening. They left as soon as Mercury was able to be saddled, and they returned the next day by mid-morning. The elder dark elf was wide-eyed with excitement at what he had seen. He had a long discussion with me about the marvelous new accommodation they would be taking over.

* * * * *

Within a week we arrived at the village, which had been set up as a cover to hide the secret portal to the rear of the dark elf stronghold. I had arranged for a fully functioning village of the People and the dwarves to maintain the place and provide a cover for the portal. There was also a secret entrance to the Yeti caves nearby for reinforcements, if needed.

Once the dark elf clan was safely ensconced in the stronghold, I called Neb and James to my quarters to speak with them.

"I want you to disband the warriors, with the exception of enough to protect a small caravan enroute to the Diamond clan stronghold. That is the location we will be headed to. The rest of the warriors will make their way stealthily to the secret stronghold, where I will catch up with them," I said to Neb and James.

"You two will take turns watching over me and my family. I include you as well as part of my family, so do not throw your life away needlessly," I said, watching them both swell up with pride.

James left the room at a trot, with Neb standing silently behind.

"Yes, Neb. Is there something I can do for you?" I asked.

"I am honoured to be included as part of your family, to protect and be protected from harm," Neb said, holding back his tears, "especially since I treated you so harshly when you were a captive in the dark elf camp."

"That is why I had Tomar train you to the level that you are; he may not be around when I need a skilled assassin to watch my back," I said to Neb. Neb did not smile, but you could see him holding it back to keep honour in his clan.

"I think James can handle this during the daytime. Go say good-bye to your clan, as I do not know how long it will be 'til the next time you see them again," I said calmly to Neb.

I called a companion of the people clan and instructed him as to what I had done, and to inform James of this so that he could take appropriate action for the security shift.

TWO

Time for Open Warfare

The next morning, twenty-five dark elf warriors strode out of the secret portal to place themselves in front of my caravan. Each was wearing a different clan color. The dwarf warriors placed themselves in defensive positions, as did the elves, two dragons, and Mercury.

The drakes came out of the carrier and strode alongside the dark elf warriors, sniffing each one as they passed. Neb must have briefed the dark elves, because they did not move a muscle as the drakes passed by each of them.

"Neb, is there some meaning to this gathering? Or should I be worried about an attack on my personal caravan?" I asked.

"We represent the twenty-five clans of the dark elves. We have pledged our lives to yours to show our trust in you completely. Since Tomar cannot be in two places at once, I will represent his clan, to show honour is kept in full," Neb said.

I nodded to James, because like the little dragons, I could sense their intent to fulfill their promise. The dragons and all others dispersed, leaving the dark elf warriors in place in front of my caravan.

"Neb, you have brought me these fine warriors, but my army is getting too large for me to control alone. I want you to take over these members of the clans, because one from another race would have a tough time when it came to hesitate or act," I directed Neb.

I said to him, "Have James come and see me at his leisure."

James came into my quarters to talk to me and said, "Why do you wish to talk to me in your quarters, Dragon Mage Jim?"

"You can count, James. I want exactly that many of the People warriors gathered here at your earliest possible time. No more, no less, but exactly twenty-five warriors to balance out the numbers," I said.

The dwarves and elves were called in with the same numbers. The dragons were reduced to Mercury and two full-grown dragons, as well as the only two small dragons, Isaac and Gizmo. They were great counsel, and I would not give up their guidance for the entire dragon clans' hoard of treasure and gold.

By the time we reached the Diamond clan stronghold, we had over one hundred warriors from the four races who had aligned themselves with the dragon clans. As usual, I did not have to wait for an audience with Elijah. The minute I entered the stronghold, anyone with Elijah was ushered out and I took priority as a member of the Dragon Clan.

"Elijah, I seek guidance on stepping up the battle against Chavez a notch. I do not know what his limitations or the extent of his powers are," I said.

Elijah replied. "I do not know what his limitations are, but the Keeper of the Crèche may have some inkling as to what steps to take, to steal the wind from under his wings. Talk to Neela and she will guide you. She has more insight than I in regards to keeping her little Kai safe and sound."

I smiled briefly to myself, and then called Mercury to be saddled up. Once Mercury was ready, I saddled up with Gizmo and one aged dwarf who, as a reward for his long service, was being honoured by a trip to the Crèche to help with hatching of the eggs. He was also to help with teaching history to the fledglings.

I left the dwarf with his people to show him around and get him acquainted with his duties.

"Greetings Great Mother, it is good to see you again," I said warmly.

Neela answered, "It is good to see you, my little Kai. How can I help you, or are you just here for a visit?" she asked jovially.

"Great Mother, I have come to bathe in your beauty," I said, smiling broadly.

"You flatter me, Little One," Neela said, as she stretched out to her full twelve feet of length, which included her tail. Neela flexed her huge, sleek wings, while a glimmer of light from the window caught the metallic red of her scales.

"I am also seeking information in relation to the Great Wizard Chavez. Do you have any knowledge of his weaknesses that may be of use to me?" I asked Neela.

She responded, "You must search for the Pater Orb, which contains a crystal that will protect you in any magical battle, no matter how powerful or how many foes are attacking you. The crystal is believed to be at the bottom of the ocean somewhere, lost centuries ago by a careless fledgling."

"Obviously, the odds of finding the crystal are slim to none," I answered back, despondently.

"I did not say the task was easy; it will be difficult and time consuming. But I believe you are up to the task. It is written in the sacred books, prophesying that you will find the crystal," Neela said.

"Thank you, Great Mother; I will do my best to find the crystal. Do you have any idea where I can begin my search?" I asked.

"There are more clues to be found somewhere between the crèche and the Diamond clan stronghold on the mainland," Neela said.

"So you are not really sure where the crystal may be; on the land or in the ocean," I said, frustrated.

"That is correct, Little One," Neela said fondly. "The ancient tome does not tell where the crystal was lost. It only tells that the dragon mage will find what has been lost; all others will search but fail."

"I hope that I am as successful as you feel I will be," I said, still having at this moment lots of doubts about my own ability.

I could feel Neela chuckling in my head, as I decided to take a few days of rest and recuperation. I sought out the dragon clan historian, asking him to search out any mention in the tomes of the dragon mage and the crystal of Pater. The sacred books could not leave the island, and they were under heavy guard.

During the time the historians were searching the sacred books, I wandered the island to learn more about the dragon clans and those that served them. The dragons, as they learned to fly, moved about the islands. The companions had been there for generations serving their masters. It was very rare that anyone left. Those who did leave understood that they could not return with any information that may have tainted what the fledglings were being taught.

As I was considered a part of the clan, I was allowed to come and go as I pleased, with a reminder of what information I may pass along to the companion instructors. Rumours must be avoided at all costs, so that information was straightforward and true when it was passed on to the fledglings and future teachers.

After a week of lounging around, I was called to see the great historian of the clan.

"Good day, Historian. I hope that you have good news for me," I said, paying respect by bowing my head slightly.

"I have been able to find bits and pieces of information; unfortunately not much and strangely disorganized. The tomes speak of the Stone People and the Sea People," the historian said, giving me notes that had been transcribed from the clan books.

"I have seen the sea people and have aided them a couple of times. But I have not seen these stone people. However, my people have a story of Gargoyles which would fit the description," I said to the historian.

"I recall seeing that name in the tomes; allow me a couple more days to research that name of Gargoyles," the historian said, frowning deep in thought.

"Of course. Find out what you can about those two types of species, and let me know what information you can find in regards to the two peoples," I said, acknowledging the historian's efforts in locating data for me.

The historical books had been searched. Other than references about the oceans for the Undines and the Land of Stone for the Gargoyles, there was very little information there.

I talked to some of the aged dragons to try to get information on the Undines or the Gargoyles. There was not much known about the Gargoyles, or if they might have information about the Pater crystal. The dragons had very little communication with the Undines, an aloof race who had little in the way of interaction with any other races.

I managed to find out that the Gargoyles were known to be around old sites similar to Mayan temples. I never had an opportunity to visit one of the old temple sites, but would have to look closer to see if I could find one of these elusive creatures. I told Mercury to saddle up and get ready to travel back to the mainland. The Lady Gizmo was waiting patiently with Mercury to start our journey; a Dwarf was also waiting with my travelling companions.

THREE

Betrayal

"**M**y name is Cerebus. I have been directed by the dragons to return to the mainland to instruct others in dragon magic. I was told that you might give me a ride to the mainland if asked," Cerebus said, showing up as Gizmo and I were preparing to mount Mercury.

"Of course I do not mind giving you a ride, Cerebus. A little more notice would have been nice, but no problem," I said to the little dwarf.

I did not feel comfortable giving Cerebus a ride, but I did not think to question that he might be more than he seemed. I just presumed that, being where he was, he was a trusted person, and I left it at that.

The flight to the secret stronghold took the entire day. As usual, on arrival I was treated like a returning hero. The dwarf mage was accepted as a friend and given a room for the night. Cerebus advised that he would arrange for transport to where he was going the next day.

* * * * *

I awoke in a strange bed, dressed in nothing but a hospital gown. Looking out the window, I could see fog and what looked like a highway in the distance. I could see, by the fact of vehicles appearing to be driven on the wrong side of the road, that I was back on my old world or somewhere similar.

A doctor walked into the room and I could see a British bobby standing guard outside the door, so obviously I must be somewhere in Great Britain. The doctor said, "Good to see that you are up and around; the police and I have some questions as to how you got here."

"Well, for starters—where is here?" I said, and the doctor frowned, replying, "Liverpool Hospital. You were found on the shore near Holyhead. We took your fingerprints while you were asleep, which has been a nap of a couple of days."

"You know who I am, then; so the question is how I got to England from Northern Washington State," I said, looking at the doctor.

"Yes… well, I will get you a dressing gown and slippers; then you can answer some questions for some gents from Scotland Yard. I will not make you tell me once then have to tell it again," the doctor said.

Once the door closed behind the doctor, I stood looking out the window. I debated on how much to tell the doctor and the detectives from Scotland Yard. If I told the truth, they would think I was certifiable. If I lied, I didn't know what the results of that would be. It was hard to say how much I could get away with, until I could get back to Rose and Sylvia and everything I held dear. I didn't even know for sure if I was ever going to make it back to them.

A nurse returned with a housecoat and a pair of slippers, so at least I was not hanging out in the wind, so to speak. As I turned toward the open door, something black and tan moving by the window caught my eye, but when I looked again it was gone.

I prepared myself to spin the yarn of the century, knowing that if I told them the truth I would be locked up in the loony bin for a long time coming. I was escorted into a small room where the doctor and two plainclothes detectives, whose name tags read Rawlings and Smith, were sitting there waiting for me.

We went through the whole deal, including full name and address, what day of the week it was, and who was the U.S. President. The only questions I could not answer of course were those dealing with the current date, since the dragons did not keep track of dates, but rather just of seasons.

I went through my story, telling them that the last thing I remember was a car crash in the woods in Northern Washington State.

Detective Rawlings asked in a demanding voice, "If that is the case, Mr. Martin, where is the wreck of the vehicle? Also, why were you rambling on about dragons and all sorts of mythical creatures in your sleep?"

"I don't know what to say other than the truth; the vehicle was where I left it last. Maybe one of the creatures out of my dreams stole it and drove it away," I chuckled loudly.

"I don't believe you," Detective Rawlings said in a commanding tone.

"That's funny. If you can find a plausible excuse for how I was able to get overseas with nothing on but some nightclothes..." I said, looking directly at Rawlings and his partner.

"We have a court order here, Mr. Martin, holding you for a psychiatric evaluation, pending deportation back to your authorities in the United States," Rawlings said with an irritating smile.

FOUR

Gizmo Saves The Day—Again

I was escorted by a couple of burly male nurses to a secure room in the South wing and locked in a room with bars on the windows.

Late that night I heard scratching at the glass outside my room window. Looking out, I could see Gizmo fluttering around. I quietly opened the window as much as I could. A sturdy chain was wrapped around the window bars and attached to a dragon waiting nearby.

It was an old building and did not take much of a pull to open a very large hole in the side of it. Just as I was standing to step through the opening, a male nurse stepped in.

"Any chance of getting an extra blanket? With this large hole it is a little cool in here right now," I said jokingly to the male nurse.

The first sight of a dragon the male nurse got did him in, and he fainted away, dead to the world. Alarm bells were ringing in the hospital, as power must have been cut by the tearing out of the wall section.

As the doctor had given me something to sleep, I was feeling very unsteady on my feet. Lady Gizmo was prepared for this eventuality, and several dwarf warriors carried a stretcher for me.

Meanwhile, Gizmo was keeping up a mile-a-minute cursing streak about Cerebus and playing dirty tricks on master mages.

Gizmo said, "There are many portals in the area at this moment, and it is in enemy territory. We have set up inside of a large barn for you to rest and recover, while the dragon Kali was available to help for a few minutes. There is a large portal big enough for Kali a few miles out to sea."

"Who is here beside you, Lady Gizmo?" I asked.

"No one from our people. Elijah would only allow a certain few to offer themselves up to help; these dwarves knew this might be a one-way mission. So, all are volunteers. Some are from the dark elf prison to redeem their honour," Gizmo explained to me, sitting on the edge of the litter.

"And their honour has been redeemed, both in my eyes and the reigning council of dragons as soon as we get back home," I said proudly.

"We must wait here, as this portal only opens at sunrise. Our path has been muddy and clouded by rain, so we should be safe until it is time to leave," Gizmo explained.

It was to be a close call, though. The sun was rising and the police were showing up outside of the farm to hem us into their trap. Although all they had to go on was a gibbering male nurse and vague descriptions of little warriors, the police had tracked us down to this farm (I think they were tipped off).

"Let me know as soon as possible when the portal appears. It is getting very crowded out there in the pastureland, with police and military standing by. I am surprised I am considered much of a threat, considering that when they found me I was in my sleep attire," I said while watching out of the slightly ajar barn door.

"Speaking of which, here is your uniform and weapons. They may not be as powerful as on our plane of existence, but they are not without some use," Gizmo said, indicating a bundle that one of the dwarf warriors handed to him.

I could see the dry brittle grass of the pastureland, and the wind was blowing toward the welcoming party. Using some hay bales, I was able to get a fire lit at the front door. We pushed the burning bales out towards the pasture with pitchforks so we could not be seen.

As soon as the portal appeared in the side of the barn, I quickly ushered all but Gizmo and me through, pushing the bales of hay toward the field to give us some cover.

Once we were through the portal, we were greeted by four large dragons in battle armour and a Mage companion standing by to seal the gateway. I had the troops stand by in case anyone got through the portal before we could seal it from this side. Fortunately the barn was an old building and was quickly fully engulfed in flame.

I was feeling a little weak, but the dwarf warriors had thought this might be a possibility, so they had provided a small trailer for me to ride on.

"Lady Gizmo, come here. The first thing on my list is to find Cerebus and bring him in for justice. If that is too hard, or if he puts up too much of a fight—kill him! He is a danger to the dragons and a powerful ally to Chavez," I said as I rested on the wagon.

"Tomar is looking as we speak. It was just too convenient for the wizard to disappear at the same time that you did, right out of your bed in the middle of the night," the Lady Gizmo responded.

FIVE

Capture of Cerebus

Tomar came to me the next day to report what he had found out about Cerebus. As he did not have direct communication with all of the dragons, he asked Kali to make some enquiries about Cerebus escaping from the island chain and to find out if he was a danger. As it turned out, Cerebus was a prisoner of sorts; not a danger to the dragons, but to the rest of the clans he could be an ongoing concern.

Neela has requested that any dragon who detects Cerebus's energy signature tell her, and has directed that Cerebus be either killed or captured to protect the clans from his evil, and to keep Chavez from sharing Cerebus' knowledge of the dragons.

After a week of searching this plane of existence, it became obvious that Cerebus must be on another plane. One day a dragon appeared, wishing to speak with the Lord Dragon Mage.

The dragon introduced himself to me and said, "My name is Midnight. I am a seeker for the Great Mother Neela of things that are lost. It has taken awhile, but I have found this thing that is known as Cerebus."

"Are you sure that this is Cerebus that you have found, and if so— where is he now?" I asked, looking directly at Midnight.

"Mother has shown me her mind and the energy signature that Cerebus emits. He probably feels that he is safe, as he is more than one portal away from where he dropped you to be dealt with by the authorities there. They have that odd way of talking, just like at the first world where you were dropped off," Midnight explained.

Tomar interrupted with, "I can deal with this myself. No help will be needed other than Neb—perhaps. I had the opportunity to travel to different worlds when I was a member of the assassins guild. Now, on your behalf, it will be a pleasure, my Lord Dragon Mage," he explained with self-assurance.

"Thank you Tomar. If possible, bring him back alive to be judged by the dragon enclave. If you cannot bring him back alive, or if he puts up too much of a fight, you may kill him. But bring back proof of his death; his head would be ideal," I said angrily.

Midnight and Mercury set off immediately, as the portals in the air were easier to access than the ones on the ground. Tomar, Neb and a small dragon named Flit flew with Mercury. The sun was setting, so the group would be hard to see flying through the air at night. Before leaving, they shared the blood and potion mix for Flit so he could translate for them during their travels.

If they had walked, it would have taken several days. They would have to hide from prying eyes during the day. The pointed ears and pale skin color were a dead giveaway. Fortunately, by flying they were able to reach their destination within a couple of hours of starting off.

Midnight indicated with his nose and said (Flit translating), "This is the house of Cerebus. On this world he is a healer of sorts, making up different concoctions to fix what ails you. I can tell by the energy signature that Cerebus is not at home. You must be wary of possible traps set up to ensure his safety."

Mercury set the trio down on the roof next to Cerberus's house. Tomar and Neb quickly climbed down off Mercury and Flit started patrolling the block that Cerberus's home was located on. Mercury and Midnight flew off looking for a place to hide until they were needed.

To Tomar this was old hat. It was not the first time he had had to sneak into someone's home to take out a target and then get out again in one piece. Neb carried a small bag filled with tools and things Tomar might need to spring traps without getting hurt.

There must not be much in the way of magic on this plane of existence, as all the traps Tomar could find were simple and more mechanical in nature. Tomar was through the traps and making himself comfortable in Cerberus's living quarters in a matter of fifteen minutes—hardly any time at all.

Tomar and Neb waited patiently in the dark until Cerebus was due back from his night of carousing and visiting the local brothel. Apparently he was wooing a lovely lady that he would not have a chance with on the street in broad daylight.

When Cerebus arrived home, he had an entourage of six tough-looking individuals in tow to protect him. Tomar and Neb kept out of sight from the bodyguards while they searched the house for any interlopers. Then and only then did Cerebus leave the street to enter the house.

Tomar and Neb waited until the house settled down and four of the bodyguards had gone to bed before disposing of them in their sleep. Removing the bodies was easy, as Cerebus had a trap door hidden on the ground floor, which led to a small river feeding the main river the town was built around. The bodies were quietly slipped below the water and carried rapidly away.

The two bodyguards left in the house were positioned on the balcony and the entry to Cerebus's bedroom respectively. Neb had Flit fly near enough to the house to distract the balcony guard. A quick blow to the back of head and the balcony guard was out for the night.

Neb took up his position and donned the bodyguard's coat, just in case Cerebus decided to look out at his balcony. Tomar waited until the other bodyguard was looking away before silently dispatching him. When Tomar entered the bedroom, he grabbed Cerebus and trussed him up with sheets, ensuring he was tightly bound and gagged. Tomar lit a couple of lamps and opened the doors to the balcony. Neb helped him carry Cerebus out, and Flit called the dragons back.

Midnight gently took the bundle and flew off while they were climbing back onto Mercury. A couple of shots rang out as they were flying away.

Tomar said, looking at Neb with a disapproving glance, "You should have hit that guard a little harder. But, now that he has brought attention to himself, he will have a little difficulty explaining how his employer has disappeared, with one dead cohort and four others of his guild missing."

Neb did not comment. He knew no comment was expected from him. Neb was just expected to do a better job in the future. The rest of the trip back to where they came from was short and uneventful.

* * * * *

When I woke up to the rising sun, I was filled in by Tomar on what had transpired last night (minus Neb's mistake). Neb came to me later to explain that he should have done his job better, but since Cerebus had been brought back alive, it was not an issue.

Midnight had flown directly to Elijah with Cerebus, who had been placed in a special cell—one that would not let him use any dark magic or call for help. Cerebus was to be held in this cell until such time as the Dragon tribunal could gather and determine his fate.

SIX

Trial of a Traitor

I enjoyed a hearty breakfast, then walked down to the tunnels and entered the portal. In a heartbeat I was at the Diamond stronghold—prepared to deal with the upcoming meeting of the Tribunal.

"The rest of the dragon tribunal has arrived. We will be ready as soon as you show up to start the proceedings. We need to decide how to carry on with things in the future, as well as deal with Cerebus," Elijah called to my mind.

Once the tribunal had gathered, Cerebus was brought in front of the dragons.

Elijah looked at Cerebus narrowly and said to him, "Do you have anything to say for yourself, Cerebus, that might convince the tribunal to leave you with your head on your shoulders? You were showing great promise when you were younger."

Isaac interrupted Elijah. "I request an adjournment of the tribunal. Time must be taken to see if Cerebus will be forthcoming with information about his contacts. This information could save the crèche from danger."

Elijah responded in an exasperated tone, "Very well. We will await the outcome of your questions, and reconvene in two days."

The most skilled of the dragon companion interrogators were brought together. They worked on trying to get information from Cerebus, with no success. After spending so many years at the crèche, Cerebus was skilled at keeping his thoughts to himself, without anyone being wise to what he was thinking. After the two days had passed, Cerebus was brought again to face the dragon tribunal.

"I do not think that keeping Cerebus captive any longer is serving us any purpose. He is a threat and therefore must be disposed of immediately," I said when Cerebus was brought before the tribunal again.

There was a quick, silent vote amongst the dragon tribunal, to determine what Cerebus's fate would be.

"Since you have meddled in our affairs by kidnapping the dragon mage, I can see no other decision that we can make in regard to your fate. You will be taken out immediately and executed in the center of the stronghold. Your body will be left for the carnivorous wild life to dispose of outside the gates," Elijah directed loudly so all could hear.

I went with the large entourage of guards and little dragons to the center of the stronghold. The executioner was waiting patiently, wearing his hood and holding a large axe in his hands to do the job needed. Cerebus was not allowed any last words, as there were concerns that he may try to weave a spell over those present and escape.

The dragons were generally gentle in their punishment, but in the case of Cerebus there was no choice, as he had enough control and power that the little dragons could not read his mind to determine what he knew or did not know.

Since Cerebus was not forthcoming with his information, there was little option left but to terminate his life, to keep possible secrets out of the hands of the enemy.

Cerebus must have either been deathly afraid of Chavez, or was very faithful to his cause to stoically face the executioner the way he did. Security was tight around the execution block. I counted at least eight dragons, six little dragons, and over two hundred warriors of all clans and species.

As I detailed before, the dragons were loath to end any life, feeling that life was sacred. They only took this step when completely necessary, as in the case of Cerebus. The actual beheading took only a moment. It was the lead-up and thorough check of all those attending the execution that took the longest.

"Isaac, did you get any impressions from Cerebus' mind, leading up to the point where he lost his head?" I asked.

Isaac responded to me with a concerned tone, "No, he kept his mind closed right up to and including the point when he was executed."

I shrugged and wandered down to Elijah's chamber to speak with him prior to heading back to the secret stronghold.

"Greetings, Kai. I am glad that you are back in one piece and we have put the Cerebus matter behind us. Have you given any thought as to what you want to do? I think that we need to bring this battle out into the open," Elijah said, and I noted that the tribunal was still convened.

"I agree that the time for secrecy and hiding is over. Now we need to take the war and bring it to Chavez and the orcs to see if they want to fight or surrender. I have a rough idea about how to send our message to the orcs, but I need a couple of days to think it over," I said, deep in thought about the situation.

I bid Elijah good day and headed back to the secret stronghold to rest and formulate plans as to the next step in the ongoing conflict with the orcs. As usual, Rose and Sylvia were there with welcoming hugs and kisses to greet me. I spent a week of quality time with the ladies, broken only by thinking and wondering how best to present the dragons' ultimatum to the orcs.

SEVEN

Search for the City of Stone

One morning I was awakened early to hear that a special messenger from Elijah had arrived, requesting my presence to talk with him on an urgent matter. Elijah had left instructions that he be left undisturbed until after he had an opportunity to speak to me.

"Great One, how may I assist you on this urgent matter?" I asked.

"I have received word of a city of stone located near the coast. Midnight has been doing what he does best, searching this world as suggested by the great mother Neela. When you are ready, Midnight will direct you on the right path," Elijah said.

"I take it that this has something to do with the Pater crystal?" I asked, looking at Elijah.

"Exactly. We have been discussing it behind your back and feel that it would give you that much more protection in dealing with the dark forces," Elijah said.

"I appreciate your concern, but in the meantime I will make do with the powers I have, hoping they will do in dealing with the enemy. Tell Midnight to meet me at the secret stronghold," I said in response.

Leaving the meeting, I travelled down to the portals and was in the general room outside my private chambers in no time at all. I called James and Neb, and told them to gather the commanders for a council of war. When they arrived, I advised them to gather a force to travel to the city of stone. We would deal with any orc forces along our path of travel.

I spent the following week supplying and organizing a caravan to travel. My men were almost ready to go when the man in the watch tower called to announce he could see multiple dragons on the horizon, approaching the stronghold.

Midnight and six other dragons flew into the courtyard, landing lightly. I saw that each of the dragons was fully armoured and ready for battle.

"Greetings, Kai. We went to the Quartz clan and threw our weight around, so to speak. They made the armor right away, forestalling all other orders," Midnight advised. He showed off the armour, black and shiny, which now cloaked all the dragons. "The time has come to bring the war to the orcs and Chavez. Other dragon warriors are getting outfitted for battle and will come to us as they are ready," Midnight said with confidence.

"Good. We will leave tomorrow morning at first light in the direction set out by you. This information must be kept between Lady Gizmo, Lord Isaac, you, my companion commanders and me; is that understood?" I said to Midnight.

"Your commands are clear and concise and will be obeyed without hesitation," Midnight said, bowing his head slightly.

The caravan set out at the break of dawn, meeting a small group of dwarves waiting patiently along the road. It was Creditum and his caravan handlers, who had been standing and waiting for the caravan to arrive.

"I received word from a highly confidential and trustworthy source to await your presence here, and that you would be along in a short period of time. I felt that you needed someone to handle the beasts while you were busy with other things, My Lord," he said.

"I think I know who gave you the information. I will have to thank him for sending the appropriate help. You are welcome, my friend. As always, your assistance is gratefully accepted," I said warmly.

Creditum immediately took over the handling of the beasts and the kitchen staff. In no time at all he had the caravan working like clockwork, without any problems.

"I have done a headcount of the troops and dragons so that you can relegate the command structure. There are one hundred of each of the races led by one of your companion guardians, who will answer to you," Gizmo advised.

"What about the dragons? Who will be in charge of them to relay messages for me?" I asked, looking at Gizmo.

Lady Gizmo said, "Lord Isaac will command the little dragons and he will also answer to Midnight, who is the eldest dragon of the battle-ready."

"Good, then I will see them at mealtime to discuss what our plan of attack is, if we encounter any orcs during our travels," I said.

Gizmo nodded to me and flew off to ensure all the commanders were in place and had their orders to meet at mealtime to discuss things. I pulled out a copy of the world map that I had obtained from the scholars at the Diamond stronghold.

When all had arrived, I opened the wide door to allow Midnight and Mercury to look in and add comments on anything I had to say.

"I want—for starters—to thank you for coming to this meeting to plan an attack on the enemy forces. First priority is to ensure that all dragons at the strongholds be armoured for protection. Also, I want two adult dragons armoured and stationed at the Diamond stronghold to help with the protection of Elijah," I said. "I also want at least ten adult dragons armoured to protect the crèche. The young and the females are important to us, so we must ensure their safety."

"All the young drakes born this season will be sent to the crèche to be trained for the dragons' protection. We will be travelling to the city of stone; any orc forts or strongholds along the way will be disarmed and the soldiers disbanded. We will greet any new races in peace unless they show us that they cannot be trusted," I said, commanding the troop leaders.

"I will lead you to the city of stone, but I have seen no signs of life the few times I have flown over the city," Midnight stated.

EIGHT

Bringing The Battle to The Orcs

W ithin a week's time we were ready to head out. The caravan was broken up into three groups of mixed races spread out so that all of the groups could not be targeted at a single time. We already knew about the first hurdle to overcome; there was a large orc-held stronghold directly in our path. It had been a dragon-held stronghold that had been taken over by orcs in one of the many previous wars. I waited out of view of the stronghold, planning my attack, as this was the next in size to the capital and would be a formidable target.

I called a meeting and ensured that Godfrey was there as well, knowing that the rest of my commanders would not understand the concept or the history from my plane.

"I think it is time for the Trojan horse scenario," I said to Godfrey.

Godfrey replied, "I agree. I see no other recourse on how to sneak into the stronghold without being caught right away."

Godfrey explained history from our plane of existence, and how in our ancient mythology, the great and impenetrable city of Troy was offered a gift from the Greeks. An enormous sculpture of a horse was accepted and wheeled into Troy. What the Trojans didn't know was that the hollow horse housed Greek soldiers, who waited inside the horse until dark, when they opened the gates to the city to the Greek army, who then vanquished the city and its people.

In our case, we would clear out Mercury's resting area in our own "horse," a hidden area above the general living quarters platform on one of the Ankylosaurs carriers. We would hide inside and then our troops would let the animal loose around the gates of the orc stronghold, in the hopes they would be happy to benefit from our "lost" ankylosaurs.

Everything went off without a hitch, and the orcs were more than happy to rescue the animal and bring it inside their stronghold. There were a few tense moments when one of the orc warriors ordered to inspect this gift from above proved to be a little more thorough than expected, and came within a foot of discovering us hiding in Mercury's quarters.

As the sun went down in the sky, we entered the living space of the carrier and waited until it was time to lower ourselves down to the ground and silently steal out into the courtyard.

We quickly disabled the unsuspecting guards at the gate to the stronghold and unlocked the doors. The door was left open just enough for Yeti troops to come in and take out the guards on the walls. Once that was done, the dragons, as well as Elven archers, took to the walls.

"Well Isaac, what do you think? Should we give the commander something to capture his attention, or wait until daylight?" I said, smiling.

"I think, Kai, that we should light that large bonfire they have set up, obviously for an execution of someone in their cells," Isaac responded.

Taking his advice, I first had dwarf warriors secure the underground area where the portals and dragon residence would be if this were a dragon-controlled stronghold. Once I received word that all access to the stronghold was under our control, I sent a ball of fire to light the wooden structure ablaze.

As usual in the orc way of doing things, a very fat and slovenly looking orc (the stronghold commander) came out cursing loudly and demanding answers. He wound down as he approached the gate where I was waiting with Gizmo in her usual place of comfort—wrapped around my neck.

The orc commander was yelling, "Who are you? What do you think you are doing attacking my stronghold?"

"I am the dragon mage. The dragons want this stronghold back under their control. You are free to leave peaceably, or to die as loudly as you like," I responded calmly.

The orc commander yelled out in rage. He pulled out a long knife and ran forward towards me. He was dead within five feet of starting, with an arrow through his heart.

"So who is the new commander of this stronghold, now that this piece of dinosaur dung is gone? Gather everyone in the central courtyard so that I may speak with them when they are ready. I will be in the caravan resting until then. Find and free any slaves or captives for questioning first and foremost," I said.

Typically of the current orc-run regime, all of the cells were full of dwarfs, from warriors to shopkeepers and commercial dealers taken from caravans. Two cells were located that had been recently bricked up, sealing whatever or whomever inside.

NINE

Homecoming

I had a couple of engineers pry open a few of the bricks so that we could look inside the cells. Much to our surprise, we found a couple of female Yeti and about a dozen young. They had been sealed in their cells and left to die.

"Bring Ice Wind and a few of the Yeti warriors and healers here," I directed. "The occupants of these cells will not react with violence if freed by their own people."

Ice Wind and a dozen warriors stood by while the engineers cleared the brick and took the hinges off the doors to free the occupants. Both of the adult females leapt through the doors ready to attack whomever opened the door. But their battle stance turned to smiles and hugs when they saw Ice Wind and their own people.

"Ice Wind, please escort your people out to your encampment so that there is no conflict with the dwarfs, who are not aware we are teammates in dealing with the orcs," I directed.

Ice Wind responded, "As you wish, Dragon Mage. I will be back once these ones are welcomed back to my people."

The occupants of the stronghold were gathered together in the central area, where there was a lot of room. The orcs were disarmed and kept in a separate area to prevent any problems.

"I represent the dragon clans. They have decided it is time to step in and prevent the damage and torture that the orcs have caused to other races of this world. From this point on, all races will be bound by the same law. You are all free," I said, raising my voice so that all could hear me.

"We will set up a contingent of dwarf and elven leaders to maintain peace among the residents of this stronghold. Also, a dragon will arrive shortly to oversee everything here. Neb, let me know who the orcs pick as their new leader. Bring him to my quarters to discuss what is going to happen," I said to Neb, as I went to lie down.

I returned to my quarters and enjoyed a nice warm meal with Sylvia and Rose, relaxing until the new orc leader had been determined and brought into my quarters.

"My name is Otis. I have been selected by the ranks as a representative. The officer ranks want us to die fighting while they stand back. Since that is not a viable option, I was selected by the rank and file to talk with you for an option that will not involve any loss of life," Otis said with concern on his face.

"Well, I do not want to end any lives if I do not have to. I know that you are only a soldier and have no input in the garrison's overall actions. What is it that the rank and file orc want at the end of this day, before any decisions are made?" I asked.

Otis replied, "We simply wish to live in peace for a change, without someone ordering us to torture or kill captives that we were ordered to capture in the first place."

"I can do that, if your people agree to some screening with the little dragons and a dwarf interrogator, to ensure that your actions will match your words," I said.

Otis replied, "I am sure that we can accommodate you, Dragon Mage. We understand that you have some concerns, due to the centuries of bad will between our people and the dragon clans."

I arranged for a dragon mage to open up the portal system and get some more little dragons and dwarfs to question all the orcs and weed out the threats to their security.

It took about a week in total for the little dragons and interrogators to show up and complete the process. Only a few of the upper ranking officers were deemed a concern; the rest of the rank and file were allowed to go where they wanted to with their families. All chose to remain at the stronghold, continuing in their jobs.

The six remaining officers (who did not have family with them) were locked up in cells until such time as they could be sent back to the orcs with an escort. I did not trust letting them leave on their own, as the potential for them hanging around to cause trouble was always there.

Once our supplies were replenished, and after a couple of dragon lords came to supervise the stronghold, we headed out along the road again toward the City of Stone.

There was a fort near the valley we were headed to that caused me some concern. Although it was not on the direct path to the city of stone, it was close enough that the warriors could be a nuisance even to a party of our size.

I walked into the fort with a group of elves (light and dark). This confused the fort's commander, as he did not know that the dark elves had allied themselves with the dragon lords. I quickly assessed where the cells were and how many of the People were held there. I also saw a small group of dwarves cursing and calling the orcs by every name that they could think of.

"I am the dragon mage. You will surrender your fort or it will be burned down around your ears," I said, looking at the commander of the fort.

I sent a bolt of flame from my staff to the locks on cages holding all the prisoners. The dwarves quickly grabbed their weapons from where they were piled and gathered around us in a defensive circle, ready for a fight. The people stayed in their cages, not sure what to do, and waiting to see what happened next.

The fort commander growled at me, "Prepare to die then, so I can collect the bounty that the High Lord Chavez has placed on your head."

"I guess it's going to be really hard to apologize to Lord Chavez when you're dead, but it is your choice," I said in reply.

The commander called on all of his troops, and they came boiling out of the huts, ready for a fight. They slowed down when they noticed the number of full grown dragons, also ready to fight. No matter the amount of yelling from officers, the orc warriors did nothing.

"All those who wish to leave in peace may take their personal weapons only and head to your stronghold along this road. You will remain there for a period of time with your fellow orcs, but you will not be placed in cells. All of the remaining orcs will be dealt with harshly, with no quarter given," I yelled at the orc soldiers.

I stood there waiting as the majority of the orcs dropped most of their weapons and slowly walked out of the gate. Some of the remaining loyal orcs tried to throw spears into the backs of those who were leaving. I quickly put a stop to that by burning the spears and encircling the enemy in a wall of fire.

I gave the order to attack, and the sky was blackened by elf arrows, followed by heavily armoured Dwarven warriors on the ground. Between the arrows and the dwarves, the remaining orcs did not last long. I had my people quickly search the fort and release any captives, escorting them out of the danger area.

"My brother dragons: now that the area is clear, feel free to do some target practice and burn down this fort. I do not want to see any part of it left higher than a dwarf," I commanded the dragons.

"Consider it done little brother; as soon as your warriors are out of the way," one of the encircling dragons said.

The fort was nothing but rubble within an hour. We set up camp nearby, knowing that the bright flames would help to keep predators away from the area.

"The rest of the way to the city of stone is clear of any orc construction. There is one town of the People along the way where we can drop the ex-prisoners off for care and to get them help to go home," Midnight said to me.

"Thank you Midnight. It is good to have your eyes looking ahead for any possible danger that might hinder us," I said in reply.

The morning dawned bright and clear. The caravan was set up and ready to go with military proficiency. I had the caravan circle the small town, while a delegation approached the town with the captives seeking asylum.

TEN

City of Stone

We reached a point where I could see the city of stone built up and coming out of the mountain. I had our camp set up in sight of the city, and no closer. I wanted only a small group to take into the city, as I was unsure of what we would encounter. I did not think a large force would go over well if there were any occupants.

I sent Midnight and the other dragons to circle the city early the next morning, leaving Isaac with the rest of my soldiers just outside the city limits, waiting for my call if needed. I had that feeling in the back of my mind that this day was not going to end without at least some bloodshed.

The streets were clean, no debris or garbage anywhere. The buildings reminded me of Egypt back home, with a lot of rounded roofs, varying from single story to two or three stories, and a couple of towers that looked like lookout points. I did not hear any noise until I was well into the city and approaching where it touched up against the mountainside.

"You cannot enter the inner sanctum unless you are properly prepared and cleansed. It is obvious by your look and smell that you may never be allowed to enter here." What appeared to be a gargoyle was saying this to a group of orcs—one who I recognized.

"I am here by the command of our leader, the Great Chavez. You will either get out of my way or be destroyed by my troops," Morlack said to the gargoyle.

"Well, short dark and ugly, I see you are up to your old tricks again—threatening and trying to push your way around," I said, laughing at the orcs.

Morlack yelled at his troops, "Men! Attack these interlopers first— then we will deal with these others who are in our way!"

The orcs came running at us, and the first twenty men were dealt with in an instant. The rest of the group slowed down and attacked us at a slower pace; the results were the same. Morlack ended up standing alone, with his troop's bodies lying around him.

"Midnight, please seek out an orc encampment nearby. First tell Isaac where you are, and then destroy it. If you need help, the ground troops will take care of anyone trying to flee the encampment," I said, while watching Morlack just standing there taking in all the carnage around him.

"Kai, your wishes will be taken care of. We know where it is, and it is surrounded already by Lord Isaac and your ground troops. Do not think of it any longer; just as a bad dream already gone," Midnight replied.

"Take Morlack and tie him up for questioning later," I ordered the men in general.

When the orc commander was taken away to the troop encampment, I approached the figures standing at the entrance to what I had heard, in the conversation, was the inner sanctum.

"I am the dragon mage. The odorous interlopers have been taken care of and I wish to talk to you, man of stone," I said, while looking at the stone men.

"I am Malachi. We have heard of you and the legendary work you have done in ensuring the freedom of all races. What can we do to help you, Dragon Mage?"

"I have come in search of Pater's lost treasure. I was hoping that the treasure was here, or word of it might lead me in the right direction," I said, looking at the creature of stone.

He replied, "Dragons may enter the inner sanctum, but you must go through some cleansing before you can enter."

"What do you mean by cleansing, Malachi?" I asked hesitantly.

Malachi replied as if he was reading from a book of rules and regulations: "We require a cleansing by fire; there are very few that can survive to enter the inner sanctum."

I started a magical dragon fire around me, letting Malachi feel the heat as it burned what was left of the orc corpses, whose weapons had even started to melt with the heat.

Malachi nodded his head, and beckoned me to enter into the building, with Gizmo on my shoulder. The companions were told not to enter, and rather than start a fight, I directed them to stay outside.

I got a good look at Malachi as he was walking ahead of me. Gargoyle is the first word that comes to mind as to his description. But that would only apply to his body; he did not have the traditional ugly facial features meant to scare off evil demons or enemies. I could detect a slight, almost grinding sound of stone on stone as Malachi moved.

He was about five foot six inches in height; slim, with a large set of wings that even when folded gave him an overall height of six feet. He wore a single belt made of leather around his waist, with a small sword and hatchet hanging from it. Without the wings, he would have fit in perfectly as a work of art in one of the museums back in my world.

The women, when I saw them, were the same height, but with finer features than the males.

When we entered the inner sanctum, Malachi announced that we were not captive enemies, but new friends from the dragons. Malachi also introduced the dragon mage to the stone people. The crowd of people were murmuring amongst themselves at this new revelation.

Something amazing started to happen as I watched the crowd of stone people. The pale stone coloring was changing to flesh and clothing. Within seconds, there was a group of real live people with wings standing or sitting, and watching me.

In the middle of the meeting hall was a cairn built up with a staff and a glowing orb on top of it. At the bottom of the cairn were three thrones, all empty of occupants.

Malachi went to the centre throne and sat down in front of us.

"Now we can talk without interruption. Not only is this a place for meeting, but it is also a place of safety. We can seal this great room up and weather any attack for as long as we need to. I know you can communicate with your companions outside of the inner sanctum. They are free to enter any building in the city, with the exception of this one," Malachi said.

"I wish to talk to you about Pater's treasure," I said.

Malachi replied to me, "There will be time to discuss that tomorrow. In the meantime I suggest you get some rest this evening. Unfortunately, the lights in the city have not worked for over one hundred years."

I called Isaac and enquired about the orcs in the area.

Isaac advised me, "There are no orcs within eyesight; just debris that we are burning to ashes to keep predators away."

"Thank you. Have the men move to the other side of the city, away from the orc encampment—just in case," I directed.

As Gizmo and I walked out of the inner sanctum, the sun was starting to set in the western sky. Looking at the non-functioning lights that were spread around the city of stone, I recognized them as the same style as those used in the Yeti caverns.

Reaching out with my mind, I held Draco high in the air and incanted the appropriate spell. Slowly, each street light lit up, bringing back light where everything had been dark. Even in the buildings, you could see lights springing up and making the city look more inviting.

ELEVEN

The Task List

I saac had the caravan moved closer to this side of the city and directly opposite from the orc encampment, as directed. The troops were instructed that they could use the buildings as shelter.

"Isaac, it appears that the population of the gargoyle people has declined over the years; otherwise more of the buildings would be occupied," I said.

Isaac said, "I noticed that as well, Kai. There are a lot of residences inside the inner sanctum. You probably noticed that Malachi took up one of the three thrones in the meeting room. The other two thrones were deliberately left empty. That may mean there is only one clan represented instead of the three that were there when the sanctum was built."

A lot of questions were driving me, but they would have to wait until tomorrow.

Malachi was waiting outside in the sun in his human form, not stone as he was the first time I had met him. Malachi did not say anything, but just handed me a roll of parchment wrapped up in a piece of leather with a seal on it. Malachi then turned away and walked back into the inner sanctum. A large stone door that I did not see before closed quickly behind him.

I took the parchment back to my camp. Entering my quarters, I gently placed the parchment on the table. I carefully opened the aged document, spreading it out on the table, and using drinking mugs to hold down the four corners.

"Read this for me, Gizmo. I can make out the map and the indications that this is some sort of mine, but I cannot read the instructions, as they are written in the old dragon tongue, which I can only read part of," I said, while holding as much light as I could on the parchment.

Gizmo read the document and translated: "It says, 'Greetings, searcher. Attached is a series of tests that will bring you closer to your goal. The first step is to head to the mine and steal the talisman without getting caught. The second step is to free the miners who are forced to labour there. You cannot have help inside the mine until you complete their freedom. The goal of this task is not to get caught. With either of these tasks, if you have to kill any of the keepers of the mine, you must ensure their bodies are not found.'"

Along with the map and direction was a drawing of the talisman, which appeared to be a dragon on top of a key.

TWELVE

A Mine For The Taking

The mine had a large grass-clear zone, so that they could see clearly around the site. There was a ten foot high palisade surrounding the mine buildings, and two watch towers, which were unoccupied at night. The orcs' control of the mine had never been contested, and there had never been an attack on the mine site.

It took a couple of days for me to organize the troops and set them up, hidden in the woods surrounding the mine enclosure. The troops were expressly ordered not to interfere with any traveller to and from the mines, as well as not to be seen by any of them.

Someone had to teach the dwarves a little bit about stealth, as they were very brusque in nature; they did not have much experience when it came to hiding in the bushes.

I set up a position up in the hills, where I could observe the mine site for a couple of days. At night there were two guards near the gate, to ensure that there were no escapees from the cages. They never climbed into the watch towers, but took turns sleeping in a small guard shack near the gate.

I spoke to Isaac, Gizmo and Elijah, making sure to learn the strongest sleeping spell that had ever been thought of. On the day before I planned to steal the talisman back and free the prisoners, I walked onto the mine site in broad daylight.

I used the ring that I had taken from the Orc wizard Torlack, making me completely invisible to the guards lazily standing by the gate. It might have even been possible to sneak behind them, as they were paying more attention toward the mine site than they were to the outside.

I found a spot where the side of the mountain met with the fence protecting the mine site, and sat quietly watching the day and night habits of the orcs and their captive miners. I looked around for the talisman, only seeing it hung from the commander's neck as he stumbled on a piece of ore that had fallen from the trailers they were loading to send for smelting.

My resting place was only disturbed once, as an orc came down to my location to urinate. He came very close to hitting my boots, so I threw a small pebble behind one of the nearby buildings, and he went to investigate there.

There were six cages full of the People: men, women, and children. All of them, regardless of gender or age, were put to work in the mine; I later learned that anyone who could not walk was killed. So there were no babies or elders present in the cages. I did see one cage that had about a dozen engineer dwarves in it; they were loud and obnoxious to the guards on the way into and out of the cage. As the whip marks on their bodies indicated, this was an ongoing issue between dwarf and orc guards.

I waited for a few hours after dark before casting the sleep spell. As the orcs were sleeping, it would allow the spell to be stronger. Nothing short of an explosion or severe pain could wake the sleeper. I went into the commander's quarters and found the talisman in a pile on the floor with his clothes. I quickly pocketed the talisman and walked to the gate, ensuring that the two guards on duty were asleep.

I quietly lifted the crossbars on the gate and pushed it wide open. James and my companions were waiting just outside of the gate. I reminded them that to complete my task I had to free the prisoners alone. I also instructed them that they needed to bring up some Ankylosaurs to load the freed people on to get them out of the area as quickly as possible.

After that was done, I instructed them to take the two trailer loads of ore as well.

Walking back onto the mine site, I allowed myself to become visible again, and walked over to where the captive dwarves were. I unlocked the cage with the keys I had taken from the sleeping guard. I entered the cage and shook the first dwarf violently until he woke up. I had to hold my hand over his mouth so that he would not shout out.

I whispered quietly to the dwarf, "I am the dragon mage Jim. You will be silent while waking your fellow captives. You will help the People as I free them. There is a caravan outside the walls with dwarves and people warriors to help you. You will not kill or disturb any orcs, as I wish them to wake up tomorrow and try to figure out the mystery of losing all their miners and two trailers full of ore. Their leader will not be happy with them and will take vengeance on them for us. Nod if you understand and will comply with my order."

The dwarf nodded and proceeded to wake the other engineers quietly. It took me a good hour to unlock and start to wake up the occupants of the other five cages. Any children were left to sleep, and were carried by adults quietly through the gates. Once that was done, we had a couple of Ankylosaurs hook up to the ore trailers and leave.

I then closed the gate and put the crossbars back in place and ensured the keys were back on the guard's belt after I relocked the cages. Mercury flew down into a wide spot on the mine site and flew me up and out. I instructed the dwarf contingent and the people contingent of my army to escort the caravan to the nearest stronghold, which was two days' travel, to deposit the ore and then return to the city of stone. I had the light and dark elves set up their archers strategically placed to eliminate and hide any bodies of the inevitable search parties that would be set out from the mine to look for the missing captives.

I did not have to wait too long, as luck would have it. A small orc caravan came late the next day with supplies and empty trailers to pick up the ore. With the gates closed, the caravan leader was finally let in by the night guards. Very quickly thereafter, you could hear alarm bells ringing, and several groups of orcs came running out and heading off in different directions.

I nodded, and messengers ran ahead to advise troops to set up and dispose of the orc patrols, and hide the bodies. This would not be unusual. It was not uncommon for troops to be either eaten by predators or to desert their posts completely. The high number of men disappearing would be quite the mystery, as well as the trailers full of ore.

I watched until later in the day. Since no other troops left the mine site, I ordered the troops to withdraw back to the city of stone. The withdrawal was done as quickly and as quietly as possible, so as not to alarm those who were now manning the watch towers.

Without the caravan, we were able to make it back to the stone city in a short time. I spent the night in my quarters, which was carried by the only Ankylosaurs left with the troops. The others would be on their way back tomorrow, after depositing the detainees from the mine.

I was very tired from my mission to the mine, and slept until James came to wake me around lunch time. James advised that Malachi wanted to speak to me when I was ready, at the entrance to the inner sanctum.

I instructed James on what to do: "James, go tell Malachi that I will be along shortly. Also, where are Rose and Sylvia this afternoon?"

James replied, saying, "I do not know, Lord Jim; they went into the city of stone this morning and have not been seen since. Do you want me to send companions to check on them?"

"No, I want you to wait 'til someone sees their bodies decaying in the sun! Of course I want you to send the companions that should have remembered their jobs and gone with them in the first place! Find and protect them!" I yelled angrily at James.

James turned beet red, nodded his head and ran out of the quarters, yelling at the top of his lungs to locate and organize the companions. I called Midnight and sent the dragons airborne, looking as well.

In the meantime, I cleaned myself up and headed into the stone city toward the entrance to the inner sanctum. Matilda and the other drakes followed along with me; sensing my mood, they were hissing at anyone who got too close.

A couple of times warriors would approach me, ignoring the hisses of the drakes, to ask a question. I was in a bad mood and held up my hand to stop them from talking. By the time I was approaching the outskirts of the city, everyone knew not to talk to me right now.

Malachi was waiting at the entrance to the inner sanctum. I went to hand him the talisman, but he refused to take it.

Malachi stated to me, "No, you keep it, dragon mage. You will need it for your quest. You have successfully completed all of the tests put before you up to this point. The staff you were seeking from the inner sanctum has been placed on the other side of the city."

"Thank you. I will be back to talk to you after I acquire the staff," I replied quietly, then headed off to where Malachi had been pointing.

Malachi just nodded as I headed in the direction he had indicated. There was a cairn with the staff placed on top of it. I saw the women that I cared so deeply for standing with their backs to a building. As I got closer, a large group of orc warriors came out of the brush, dividing into two groups. One group headed toward the ladies and the other group headed toward the cairn and the staff on top of it.

I only had seconds to decide in which direction to head first. I knew that I would be unable to recover the staff and protect the ladies at the same time. I did not hesitate, heading to protect the ladies with a battle cry and my pistol drawn.

When I reached Sylvia and Rose, everything started to shimmer like a highway on a hot summer's day. I blinked my eyes while everything disappeared: the cairn, the orcs, the ladies and the staff.

Midnight interrupted my confused state, saying, "The ladies have been located at the south end of the city, and their companions are just arriving to watch over them."

"Thank you, my brother," I replied to Midnight.

"It is the least we can do for you, Kai. If you need any more assistance you have but to ask," Midnight stated modestly.

I walked back to the entrance of the inner sanctum and Malachi was still standing there, waiting for me.

Malachi stated sadly, "I am sorry, but that was the final test. We had to know if you would sacrifice lives to achieve your goal. My people cherish all life. If you had chosen the staff, you would have failed."

"What happens now?" I asked, looking deeply into Malachi's eyes.

He replied, "Now you can come into the inner sanctum and take the staff that you have rightfully earned. But know this: it does not contain Pater's crystal. It is merely another tool to use as you search out the crystal.

THIRTEEN

The Air Staff

I walked behind Malachi into the inner sanctum of the gargoyle people, entering into the area where the staff was still locked into its place of honour. As I entered the meeting area, all of the gargoyle people stood and gave me a standing ovation.

Malachi said, with a hint of pride in his voice, "This is the first time in many years that someone has passed the tests and come to claim the Air staff."

"The Air staff?" I enquired, looking at the staff in its resting place.

"Yes, that is what it is called. It enables the user to generate a field of force, or air bubble, that will protect the user and any with him. You will be able to walk underwater or withstand a bombardment of any kind, protected behind your dome of air," Malachi stated, explaining the powers of the staff.

I walked over to the cairn holding the staff and inserted the key, turning it until I heard it click, freeing the staff into my hands. I examined the runes on the staff explaining how to activate the powers it held. I was going to have to learn the ancient tongues to be able to learn how to flush a toilet in some of these places.

Mind you, I was never alone; usually one of the small dragons was with me. With the exception of the bedroom, it was like they were keeping a closer eye on me to make sure that I did not make any finds that they were not aware of. Maybe I was getting a little paranoid as my power increased. You know what they say: 'Power corrupts, and absolute power corrupts absolutely.'

I slept alone that night, telling the girls that I needed the solitude. Part way through the night, I had a bad dream of fighting off a horde of orcs—single handed. Poor James tried to rouse me from my dreams, and in my disoriented state I threw him into the wall of my room before waking up enough to realize what I had done.

James did not say a word, just bowed at me and strode out of the room. When I went to bed the next night, I noticed a small container of water set up with some pulley and rope arrangement to douse me in water should I awake with more nightmares again.

I said, "Now that is using your brain, James. It is an excellent idea."

James just smiled and said, "It is better than bearing the bruising from last night, Lord Jim."

Rousing myself out of my very comfortable bed was exceptionally hard this morning. James actually had to come in and check on me a couple of times before I caught the hint. I got dressed and went out into the common room, where a delicious breakfast awaited—as well as a surprise visitor.

Malachi was standing by the table, and waited patiently while I was served. "Do you have any questions of me, now that your quest is partially complete?" Malachi asked gently.

"Now that you mention it, I do have a few questions to be able to understand your people better," I said, looking at Malachi. "Please have a seat so that we can talk and learn from each other."

Someone brought Malachi a stool without a back so that he could be comfortable with his wings hanging down behind him. I explained to him where I had come from and the way that my society was structured there.

This seemed to confuse Malachi, who finally shook his head and said, "I am not sure I would understand or feel comfortable in the world that you come from."

I laughed loudly and said, "There are a lot of people in my world that would say the same. They do not feel comfortable with the way things are either."

Malachi explained that his people once had been too numerous to count, but for some reason the birth rate had suddenly declined, thereby reducing the population to the point where it had stood stagnant for the last century. The people of stone did not deal with the rest of this world often, and were too proud to ask for help from others.

Their healers were unable to determine what caused the sudden drop in the birth rate.

I advised Malachi that I would get some of the expert healers from the dragon clans to see if they could research the cause and find a solution, if possible.

Isaac said, "I have already spoken to Elijah about this, and he is in full agreement with you. He will send out the best healers, with protectors to escort them to the city of stone. In the meantime, our historians will search the books to determine if there is any historical knowledge on this matter."

"Any help that the dragons can offer to my people will be greatly appreciated," Malachi replied, and bowed deeply at Isaac and me.

FOURTEEN

The Easter Bunny?

I awaited the return of the rest of the caravan, leaving the troops in the hands of my companions, whom I felt were very capable at this point of working on their own. I instructed them that I wanted them to drill the troops by themselves until they were comfortable with the way they could work together. Then they were to contact one or more of the companion guardians to make sure the troops could work well with the other warrior races.

My reason for this was twofold: one – to make sure the troops could respond quickly together or apart; and two – to help eliminate any prejudices they might have of one of the other races.

The next morning, as soon as the rest of the caravan showed up, we were ready to head out. As usual, the camp was taken down with precision, and we were soon on the road travelling back to the Diamond Stronghold and Elijah's council.

I spent long hours deciphering the inscription on the handle of the air staff to determine how to activate it. I did not want to use it until I thoroughly understood the limitations, if any, of the staff.

On the second day of travelling, Gizmo called me to the front of the caravan. We had stopped at the top of a hill leading into a valley with grassy fields. Gizmo called my attention to something moving in the grass, approaching two Tyrannosaurus, who were fighting for territory. I pulled out my binoculars and looked at the grass until the creature popped out of the tall grass to an area where the grass had been eaten down.

I could not believe my eyes; I was looking at a giant jackrabbit. It stood about four feet tall and looked exactly like a jackrabbit in all other ways. I noticed that the rabbit had what appeared to be a bag or satchel of some sort hanging from its side.

I could see it headed toward the two fighting tyrannosaurus. As it came into their sight, everything stopped. The two dinosaurs just stood there staring at the rabbit as it walked past them. One roared and raced towards the rabbit, but was thrown back fifty feet. It happened so fast that I did not see what happened; the rabbit continued on past the dinosaurs as if nothing had happened.

I looked at Gizmo with a questioning look on my face and asked, "What was that, and how did it do that to the dinosaur?"

Gizmo gave an almost human shrug and said, "There are times when Portals open up to other worlds and someone or something wanders through. It is the job of the little dragons to watch over those that enter our world and try to get them back to where they belong."

Gizmo continued, "There are occasions when the great dragon Elijah can feel when and roughly where they will come from. He will then dispatch one or more of the little dragons to watch for their arrival."

I called Elijah and said, "I think that you need to watch over this creature to see where it goes, although by the looks of things I don't think it needs protection, from what we just witnessed."

Elijah replied, "Yes Kai, it sounds very intriguing. I don't recall ever seeing or hearing of such a creature in my long life."

I laughed and said, "It almost reminds me of stories when I was little about the Easter Bunny travelling and hiding eggs for children to find."

Elijah responded, "The world that you come from has many legends and stories of what you call mythical creatures, where, in fact, they do exist in other worlds. I believe that in the past, these creatures did live in your world, and left via openings into other worlds when man became more numerous and aggressive."

"Midnight!" I called. "Follow that creature, but keep your distance until another dragon comes along to monitor it."

Midnight responded, "As you wish, Kai. I will watch this new beast from a distance and not interfere with it. If the incident with the dinosaurs is an example, it does not need protection from me."

I laughed, saying, "I agree with you, my brother. I have a sense of powerful magic around this new creature. I wonder if it is lost or knows where it is going."

As I turned away and headed back to the caravan, I doubted that I would ever see this creature close up or even from a distance again.

The caravan made good time, arriving at Elijah's stronghold after a week of travel. As usual, I walked down to talk to Elijah immediately upon entering the gates.

Elijah looked up and dismissed his companions so that he and I could talk in private. Elijah said, "I see that you have had quite the adventures of late, my boy. Midnight lost track of the creature he was following. It appeared that he opened his own portal into another world and disappeared. The opening closed before Midnight could examine it and follow."

"That does not surprise me," I responded, "especially after seeing what it did to that Tyrannosaurus that tried to attack."

"Yes," Elijah said. "The creature seems to be a very powerful magic wielder who would make a formidable ally—or enemy, as the case may be, if it returns to this world.

I thanked Elijah for his counsel and headed to my rooms in the Diamond Keep. I wondered to myself if any of this creature's relatives had visited my old world, which would have given rise to the legend of the Easter Bunny. It was a possibility, as stranger things had happened during the past year that I had been living here.

My ladies were waiting in our rooms with a sumptuous dinner for just the three of us. I felt drowsy after the meal. Since it was still too early to turn in for the night, we all went for a stroll around the stronghold, with Matilda in tow.

I saw the merchant that I had trouble with when I rescued Fred from false imprisonment. When our eyes made contact he turned pale, and quickly disappeared into the crowd in the marketplace. I chuckled loudly as the merchant fled, and I got some strange looks from people in the market wondering what was so amusing.

FIFTEEN

The Plot Thickens

As we were walking back to the keep, I saw the merchant talking to a couple of large ugly types. Right off the bat, I labelled them as muscle, or thugs for hire. The merchant was talking to them, and was very animated when he saw me. The muscles looked at me and were pointing at Matilda and my companions. They then laughed, slapped the merchant on the back, and walked away. The merchant was very upset, and when he saw me looking, disappeared into the crowd again.

I instructed Ice Wind to locate the merchant with some fortress guards and arrest him on conspiracy to murder the dragon mage or one of his people.

When the guards and Ice Wind came back with the merchant in tow, he was howling like a banshee. The Diamond clan chief showed up as the guards were escorting the merchant to the dungeon.

The Diamond clan chief yelled at me, "You have overstepped your authority this time! I am going to talk to the eldest dragon Elijah about you. In the meantime I want you out of my stronghold and my friend the merchant out of the dungeon—right now!"

I nodded to the chief. "Very well. I will be out of this stronghold within the hour. Blade, gather the ladies and the companions and escort them home. Ice Wind, release the prisoner from the dungeon and escort him to my home and a cell there."

I thought the chief was going to have a heart attack, he was turning so many different shades of red. I instructed Isaac to take some companions and find the thugs that the merchant was trying to hire and bring them to my stronghold as well, blindfolded and under heavy guard.

Isaac said, "It will be as you wish Kai. I will have them at the stronghold within an hour." Isaac flew off with a dozen companion warriors following him at a run.

As we headed down the tunnels to the portal room, we were met by two dozen Diamond stronghold guards blocking our path.

The guard captain addressed us gruffly: "Dragon Mage, I have been ordered to arrest you for offences against the Diamond Clan. You are to be escorted to the dungeons, and I am to free your prisoner."

I looked around at the guards, and said, "It will be a sad time for the Diamond Clan if I have to kill all of you." The guards behind the captain started to fidget and draw their weapons. Of course, the companions drew their weapons as well. Matilda, Bonny and Clyde pushed through the companions and looked like they were prepared to fight at a moment's notice.

Just when it looked like I was going to have to kill some warriors, Gizmo and Isaac flew into the room and ordered all the combatants to stand down.

Gizmo said, "Kai is the dragon mage; he is considered a dragon in all but form. Would you challenge a dragon this way? It is within his rights to sweep you aside as one would dust."

The guards looked down in shame, and cleared the room without looking up at all. Isaac ordered, "Captain, report the results of our little meeting to the clan chief, and advise him that we will talk to him as soon as Elijah is ready to hear his complaint."

Once through the portal, I was greeted by a couple of my guards watching the portal room. I said to them, "Run ahead and have the stronghold commander bring twelve warriors to protect this room, and a mage to seal the entryway until I come back in the morning. Also, I want each of the prisoners in separate cells, with two guards on each cell to ensure they do not come to harm."

The guard bowed and ran off down the tunnels, headed to the surface to advise his commander of my orders. It was only a matter of twenty minutes before the prisoners were secure. The portal room was sealed, with a dozen guardians armed to the teeth. Fred remained with Bonnie and Clyde to assist in case of attack. Fred's mother ensured that a healthy meal was prepared for the warriors in the portal room, as well as cots and blankets so they could sleep in shifts.

I took the ladies and headed up to my rooms to try to get some sleep; needless to say, my adrenalin was still pumping from the disputes earlier. I finally managed to fall asleep as the sun was just starting to crest on the horizon. The ladies ensured I was able to sleep until midday, and prepared a delicious meal for me, keeping me company but not talking. They knew that I had a lot on my mind and would talk to them if I felt the need to.

Gizmo flew into the room through an open window and landed on her perch. Gizmo said to me, "We finished interrogating the two toughs that the merchant tried to hire. The merchant wanted you or one of your close associates beaten up in revenge for the embarrassment that he suffered when he falsely accused Fred of stealing a piece of jewelry that he was going to give to his mistress."

Gizmo continued, "When the toughs saw you and the drakes, they laughed at the merchant and walked away. I scanned their minds and they were telling the truth; there was no sense of deception at all."

"Tell them that they will be released after we talk to the great dragon Elijah this afternoon. I want double the companions with me for protection from stupid people, so I do not have to kill someone," I said, instructing Gizmo.

"Arrangements will be made and the warriors will be ready within ten minutes," Gizmo replied.

As we walked down to the portal room, I looked at my companions, pondering the assortment of races I had watching over me. Not only that, but Matilda the drake would not leave my side, sensing my anxiety level rising. When we walked through the portal to the Diamond clan to talk to Elijah, we found the tunnel lined with warriors. The warriors fell into an escort formation around my group, causing a lot of friction between my companions and the Diamond Clan warriors.

The clan chief was waiting at the entrance to Elijah's chambers. He looked like he had not slept at all last night. I ignored him and escorted all three of my captives in front of Elijah. There were two other dragons in the chamber to hold judgement over the merchant.

I knew I was biased, so I allowed Isaac to present the evidence to Elijah. Elijah questioned the two the merchant had tried to hire, at length. When he was finished, he had his companions escort the two safely out of the chambers.

The merchant denied everything, stating that the two thugs were lying about everything. Elijah finally stated, "Shut up. Your mind is like an open book to me, and I can see the hatred that emanates from you toward the Dragon Mage."

Elijah continued, "The only thing that remains is to determine the penalty for plotting to injure or kill a dragon—because the Dragon

Mage is a dragon, recognized by the clans. You will be escorted to a secure but comfortable room, under guard, until a decision can be made."

Elijah's companions escorted the merchant, ensuring that there was less conflict, as no one in the stronghold dared interfere with Elijah. They would remain guarding the merchant as a matter of honour, keeping him safe and preventing him from escaping custody.

Elijah said to me, "We will reconvene tomorrow morning. In the meantime, I would like you to consider and have input into the penalty for this person. Especially since it was you and your companions this so-called merchant was targeting."

I bowed to Elijah and slowly walked out of his chambers, then headed to the rooms I had occupied previously when I was in the Diamond stronghold. The guards at the door to the keep refused to let my party and I enter, as they were under orders from the Diamond clan chief that I was not allowed accommodation in the stronghold. Isaac started to berate the guards, but I held up my hand and stopped him, saying, "We will address this tomorrow when we talk to Elijah again. Let us go back to our stronghold through the portal. That way, I know we will be safe."

Isaac kept quiet until we were in my stronghold, then he asked, "What was that about? You should have let me talk to the guards, and we would be sleeping in the Diamond clan keep."

I replied, "Yes, you could have, but I am worried about the consequences of such action and keeping safe throughout the night. This way, I can sleep peacefully, without a large entourage of guards watching over me."

Isaac looked at me for a minute, mulling over what I had said to him. He then nodded, and flew off to check on the stronghold guards.

I sat in the common room, watching the fire blazing away in the fireplace, sitting in a big comfy chair with a glass of what passed for brandy in this world. I watched the flames, and sat thinking deeply about what to do with the merchant without causing too much turmoil in the Diamond clan. With the clan chief being best friends with the merchant, there appeared to be nothing I could do as far as penalties went, that would not affect my relationship with the clan.

I fell asleep, waking a few hours later when one of the companions was stoking the fire. Someone had thrown a blanket over me, and I was so comfortable that I fell asleep again within a few minutes. I woke up in the early morning, with Gizmo sitting on the arm of the chair, watching me intently.

Gizmo said "Do you know, Kai, you snore quite loudly. If you are out alone in the wild, you could draw in some predators with all that noise."

"You know that you can be a real pain in the ass at times, Gizmo?" I said with a smile on my face.

"I am ready to deal with the merchant and his powerful ally, the chief of the clan here," I said, cleaning up and getting ready to meet with Elijah. "Bring the merchant and the clan chief to Elijah's chambers, where he will be sentenced." Gizmo nodded and flew off to make the arrangements.

I got my formal garments out, and Sylvia came and braided my hair with a golden dragon hair clip in it. I smiled and said to Sylvia, "Wish me luck." She smiled and gave me a great big hug and kiss.

I gathered my usual entourage of drakes and companions and headed down to the portal. We were in the Diamond stronghold in a matter of minutes, and found the portal room to be swarming with guards. The captain there tried to tell my companions that they were not welcome in the stronghold. The guards were only going to allow Gizmo and me to enter; they would not listen to anything I said about my companions.

I looked at Blade and nodded. The stronghold guards were quickly disabled by my companions and the drakes in a moment. I looked at Blade and said, "Disarm them, and I will seal the entryway so that they cannot come up behind us."

I looked at Isaac and said to him in my mind, "Fly back through the portal. I want at least double the amount of guards here to take custody of these and escort them to Elijah's chambers when I am ready to deal with them." Isaac nodded and flew back through the portal to my stronghold.

After the companions finished disarming the guards, they placed all their weapons outside of the main entrance, which I resealed, knowing that they would have to wait for a mage to come along and unseal the doorway.

Elijah contacted me as I entered the stronghold. "You will never guess who is here ranting and raving about this travesty of justice! He want you in chains and your authority removed. I have just let him finish until he starts to wind down."

I explained to Elijah what I had to do, and that after we dealt with the merchant, we would deal with the guards from the portal room. I said, "If the clan chief is mad now, wait 'til he finds out that I have his guards in custody as well." I felt Elijah chuckle in my mind.

I entered the chamber, and his companions stood to one side, bowing to me as I passed. I noticed that Elijah's companion warriors were present in force, to ensure things did not get out of hand. I thought that they also wanted to see what transpired, as there was no love lost between the companions and the Diamond Clan. Most of the guards had come from Elijah's last home up north.

"There he is! I demand that he be put in chains and put in the deepest, darkest cell. He has overstepped his authority one too many times!" The Diamond Clan chief yelled. He was so worked up he was spitting as he yelled, and was frothing at the mouth.

Elijah roared, "Shut up and sit down! I want you to listen to what is going on. If I do not like the answers I get, you may not be the clan chief at the end of this meeting!"

The clan chief was visibly pale and shaking as he sat down on a bench in the room.

The merchant was brought in to stand in front of Elijah. Elijah asked him, "Do you have anything to say before sentence is imposed for planning to attack the dragon mage and or one of his companions?"

The merchant went into a tale of how he was a victim of dragon mage targeting ever since he had mistakenly claimed young Fred had stolen something valuable from him. He also stated that the two thug types were in cahoots with the dragon mage and had made up this tale of threatening to have him killed or injured.

Elijah let him ramble on until he ran out of breath and lies. Elijah looked at me and said, "Dragon Mage. Do you have anything to add in regard to his sentencing? I leave the decision to you, as you were the one wronged by this man."

I looked at the merchant and said, "I know that you have a wife and children who help you run the business. I do not wish to penalize them for your pettiness and vindictive nature. If I levy a fine, you will just pay it and not learn your lesson. Your wife may divorce you, since you are going to spend the next ten years in prison in another stronghold, working in a subservient position. You will be forbidden from returning to this stronghold for this time period."

Elijah said, "You will be placed in a cell here until the paperwork is done. Then you will be transported to a random stronghold to be kept there for the next ten years. I feel that you are getting off lightly; in years past, you would have been sentenced to death."

The merchant was escorted out of the room by a couple of Elijah's warrior companions. I looked at Elijah, and sent him a message mind-to-mind about the guards in the portal room, who were in the process of being escorted into the room.

The look on the clan chief's face was perfect. He was finally at a loss for words, standing there with his mouth open, not knowing what to say.

I explained to Elijah about the incident in the portal room, and how the warriors, acting under orders, attempted to interfere with my passage, and to prevent my companion guards from entering the stronghold. This would put me at a disadvantage if the clan chief decided to do something drastic—not that I could not handle a large amount of enemies at one time. But it was always nice to have someone watching your back in case an assailant came out of the shadows.

Elijah spoke directly to my mind, saying, "I leave this as well to your judgement. Just let me pave the way so the chief understands that you are the same authority as any dragon lord."

Elijah proceeded to chew out the clan chief, initially explaining that his future was in the hands of the Dragon Mage. I looked at the clan chief and said, "Your future in charge of this clan is in jeopardy. If I do not like your answers, you will be replaced by another family head to lead the clan."

I looked at the guards and said to them, "You are now under my command, and will report for duty in my stronghold immediately. I will not punish you further, as you were simply following orders. You are dismissed."

I had the room cleared of everyone, with the exception of Elijah's companions and the clan chief. Looking at the chief, I said, "Now is your chance to explain your actions, and why you should remain in charge in this stronghold."

The clan chief spoke, while looking at Elijah and me: "My name is Adam, and my family has led this clan through good times and bad. I allowed my friendship with the merchant to cloud my judgement. I have been called to task because of these mistakes in my decisions. I ask that my family be allowed to continue leading the clan during these troubled times. I will submit to whatever punishment the dragon mage wishes to levy, but please do not punish my family for my mistakes."

I looked at Adam and said, "Well-spoken, clan chief. There is hope for you yet. I think with Elijah's agreement, we will leave you in place, with the understanding that if you decide to cross paths with the dragons, you can and will be removed without notice."

Adam bowed deeply to me, and then to Elijah, and walked out of the chamber. I looked at Elijah and said, "At least we have resolved this conflict. Now is the time to discuss my plans for escalating the war against the Orcs and their leader, Chavez."

I explained to Elijah my plans for the next step in our ongoing campaign against the orcs. I was not sure whether to have the dragons attack the fortresses with fire, or whether a ground attack, burning the forts down, would be better. We decided that the second option was better, as it would not directly point towards the dragons initially. All the races had mages of some sort, from the basic Firestarter up to ones that could wield more powerful attacks and healing magic.

I spoke to Isaac, and had him gather representatives from each race to discuss a plan of attack, hitting the wooden forts that the orcs occupied.

I wanted to hit as many forts as possible on the same night. I explained to Isaac what I had in mind and we gathered as many Firestarters or mages as possible. In all, we were able to gather fifty, including guards to accompany them to their locations. I decided that we were going to hit twenty-five forts at the same time in one night. That way, two mages or Firestarters could attack a fort at one time, increasing the odds of success.

This was to be the largest mobilization of dwarves, elves, and people, in the known history of dragon lore. It would take a week for the furthest group to reach the designated fort for them to attack. I sent a small dragon with each group to ensure communication and perfect timing. If one group was delayed, then all the others could stand by and wait one more day, so that the attack was simultaneous, which was a strategy the dragon lords had never considered before.

But maybe that was why fate had caused me to enter into this world: to bring together both new and old ideas, from a different historical background and perspective.

I had Mercury fly from my stronghold to Elijah's as quickly as possible. I wanted to monitor the attack against the largest fort in the area, as well as to possibly participate in some way, depending upon whether my assistance was needed. It took two weeks to organize: one week for all the troops to gather, and another week to get into position, so that all of the attacks could take place at the same time all over the continent.

I climbed aboard Mercury and we flew to where the troops waited, a short distance from the orc fort. Like all of the forts built by the Orcs, this fort had been standing for several years. The wood was old and dry as a bone. The troops got as close to the fort as the underbrush allowed, waiting for the signal to begin.

We waited until the moons were starting to set, making it darker. The archers moved in first, firing arrows at the few guards left on duty to watch the perimeter. They did not stand a chance. They were not even paying attention, since the last time any attacks had been made on any orc forts was at least a generation before.

I called to Elijah to spread the word and attack the forts immediately.

Elijah said, "It will be as you ask, young Kai. The troops are moving in as we speak, and there is no sign of interference on the part of the orcs."

The archers were skilled, ensuring that the bodies of the orc guards fell out of the fort's palisades onto the ground, so not to attract any attention inside. The mages quickly moved into place onto either side of the fort and rapidly kindled flames, helping them spread faster than they would normally.

The troops withdrew to watch the fire start rapidly, soon waking the orcs, who tried to put out the flames, with little or no luck. I passed on word that if possible, captives in the forts were to be protected. If the protectors were seen, the orcs were to be killed.

I sat in the dark, watching the flames quickly destroy the fort. By the time the sun rose over the horizon, the walls of the fort were totally destroyed. After putting out the fire, the orcs could find no one to vent their frustration on. They gathered all of their prisoners, separating them into work parties, and headed into the woods to cut trees. The prisoners were kept under close watch by armed guards. My forces were spread out in the woods to dispatch the guards as quietly as possible.

The orcs were taken care of rapidly, and the prisoners were escorted to safety. I was advised by Elijah that, with the exception of one fort, everything went according to plan. To ensure secrecy, the fort that caused so much trouble had to be destroyed completely. No orcs were left alive, and all the prisoners were ushered to the nearest friendly village.

All the troops were ordered to return to their strongholds or villages, and would be called again if needed. I returned to Elijah's stronghold, to rest and plan the next phase of our escalating war against Chavez.

I spent the next week relaxing with Sylvia and Rose, enjoying the meaningful time spent in their company.

At the end of the week, I went to speak with Elijah. I said to him, "Can you send out your spies to determine what reaction, if any, Chavez and his people have had to these attacks on the forts, and if he is aware of who instigated the attacks?"

Elijah responded, "It will be done right away, and I will call you as soon as I have details of any rumours or information that Chavez has. In the meantime, I suggest you return to your stronghold and plan for the next stage against Chavez."

SIXTEEN

Repercussions

The destruction of the forts caused a lot of consternation at the capital. Chavez was fit to be tied. He strode around his palace ranting at anyone who got in his way. A few of his minions did not move fast enough, and the palace guards had to haul their bodies away to be disposed of.

I knew that Chavez would lash out soon, so I sent word to have all the villages evacuated, and the people moved to the nearest stronghold. They started working on the gardens surrounding the strongholds, under the protection of a good-sized group of guardians. Scouts were kept out roving to ensure that any orc force would be spotted, with lots of time to alert the people and get them safely into the stronghold.

Chavez left the capital city and went to converse with the Malum to seek advice and direction. The minute that he left the capital city, we sent forces out to burn down the forts as close to the capital as possible. This was done as quickly as possible. I realized that reinforcements would head out from the capital as soon as they heard word of the fire or saw smoke rising over the horizon.

I waited on the side of the main road. As soon as backup headed out of the capital past us, we stepped in behind the orc troops. As I was planning on leaving no survivors behind, secrecy was not an option to be concerned about right now.

It was a large group of orc warriors—close to one thousand strong. It was a little larger than I had expected, but not too large to deal with. I had dragons waiting a short distance away and all I had to do was call them with my mind and they would come running.

Once the orcs reached the next area of prairie, all the warriors set themselves up between the prairie and the forest, to cut off any avenue of escape. I called with my mind, and within moments, fourteen dragons appeared on the horizon. They immediately started to attack the large orc contingent.

The Elven archers closely monitored the situation, and shot down any of the orcs who were trying to hit the dragons. The dragons targeted any large siege weapons and transport animals first. They then laid down a ring of fire to contain the orc warriors from escape.

The dragons laid down fire, killing fifty warriors at a time. Those lucky enough to escape the flames were rapidly dispatched by the warriors surrounding the area. At the end of the battle, all that remained were dead orc bodies littering the field. No dragon or dragon warriors were injured in the altercation.

I thanked the dragons and sent them back to their strongholds. The elves and dwarves entered the field briefly to recover any arrows left after an orc was shot. Once that was completed, we all left the area to leave the bodies for this world's version of vultures and other carnivorous dinosaurs. By the time nature was done with the bodies, there would only be inedible bits of uniform and weapons left behind.

Everyone headed back to their own homes, so I headed to the Diamond stronghold to update the Great Dragon Elijah about how things were progressing with the battle against the orcs.

As I entered his chambers, Elijah said, "It is good to see you alive and well, Kai. One of the dragons from the attack has already advised me of how things transpired. So unless you have something to add, I am up to date on how our escalating endeavours are going against Chavez and the orcs."

"I think that we need to beef up our security at the strongholds. It's likely that Chavez will catch on soon that it was warriors of the dragon clans who caused the damage to the forts," I said quietly.

"Yes, I think it is just a matter of time before Chavez realizes that no one else could be capable of pulling this organized attack off," Elijah responded.

SEVENTEEN

Liar, Liar

Before long, there was a large contingent of orcs camped out near the main gates of the Diamond clan stronghold. A small group approached the gates and asked to have a meeting with Elijah. This surprised me, as they did not demand entry, as would be their usual procedure.

While the group was waiting at the gates, I spoke to Elijah. "I think they must be running scared. They have never had to deal with this level of devastation in their long history. So I think at this point we lie through our teeth and misdirect the orcs as much as we can. I will wait in the shadows and listen, trusting the great dragon Elijah to know what to say."

Elijah responded, "This is not the first time that I have had to deal with giving false information to an enemy, but I may be a little rusty." Elijah laughed out loud.

I had Matilda and the two other drakes, Bonnie and Clyde, with me as I watched Elijah direct one of his companions to escort the orc envoy into his presence. The envoy had an entourage of ten bodyguards, all of whom looked to me to be the type of toughs meant for battle and not for talking.

The envoy started off politely questioning Elijah about his knowledge of the fires to all of the orc forts. Elijah, of course, denied knowing anything and said so to the envoy. The orc envoy flew into a fit of rage, calling Elijah a liar, and at a command, his entourage rushed towards Elijah with the obvious intent of doing harm or killing him.

The drakes needed no commands, and attacked the orcs who were rushing towards Elijah, before his companions could even react. I stepped forward and started shooting the orcs that were not being attacked by the drakes. The brief-but-bloody battle was over in a matter of moments; Clyde had a sword cut across his face, but it looked superficial.

I looked at Elijah and enquired, "What do you wish to do with the remaining forces that are waiting outside our front gate?"

Elijah responded, "They have tried to kill me, so therefore their lives are forfeit."

I called Isaac and called for every nearby dragon to attack the Orc warriors and their siege weapons. Isaac replied, "There will be ten dragon warriors in the area within ten minutes, and as we speak, warriors are coming through the portals too, and forming up in the main courtyard of the stronghold."

I left Elijah with his companions, as more were running down after hearing the gunshots. I knew that Elijah was in good hands now that his companions were alerted, and more were coming down the tunnel to assist those who were already there.

The dwarves were forming up as I walked out of Elijah's quarters. Any elves who were available were climbing onto the walkways in the walls of the stronghold. As they were noted as the most accurate marksmen, so they were the best choice on the walls, to be able to pick their targets when it came to the upcoming battle.

I walked up to the wall and viewed the amassed legion of orcs, who were starting to get restless waiting for their commander to return. I gathered the Yeti companions and the drakes and stepped outside of the gates. One of the officers approached me and started to demand information about the commander and his bodyguard.

I said "Your commander attempted to attack the great dragon Elijah, and has paid for his foolishness with his life and the lives of his bodyguards. You have ten minutes to vacate this area or we will take it as an overt act of aggression and respond in kind."

I walked calmly back through the gates and into the stronghold. I could hear the orcs gearing up to attack. I just shook my head on the closing gates being locked and secured against the upcoming storm. As I walked back up to the wall, I could see the dragons approaching from afar. Blaze came to advise that there were one thousand dwarves standing by to engage the enemy.

Once the ten minutes were up, I called the dragons to destroy the orc siege equipment by laying down fire. And then I instructed them to lay down another wall of fire to cut off any retreat. The archers began firing, picking their targets carefully. While that was happening, the gates to the stronghold opened up and the dwarf troops marched out and began attacking the orcs.

The orcs were overwhelmed, as the archers were picking off any orc that looked like he was giving orders. The dwarves plowed into the disorganized force with little resistance; the orcs did not stand a chance against the well-prepared dwarves. The battle took about one hour, with the majority of time cleaning up the little groups of orcs who had managed to form into small knots of resistance.

Once the dwarf troops withdrew, I asked the dragons to lay down fire again, incinerating the remains of orcs and their siege equipment. This would cut down on the predators that would show up to the smell of decaying flesh.

By the time the dragons were done, there was nothing left but a field of ash, which would act as fertilizer for a new field of grass within a couple of months. I knew that time was limited and I had to step up my search for Pater's Crystal. Chavez would be stepping up his attacks against the dragons and those allied with them.

EIGHTEEN

Search for Knowledge

I returned to my stronghold to contemplate the next move we were going to take in the continuing escalation of the war against Chavez. I felt that I should be able to save some of the Orcs, so that the race did not go extinct in this world. I knew that Chavez was the driving force behind the orcs taking on the dragons in a war that did not have much chance of success. It was not something they would normally do on their own accord.

I spent a week trying to relax in the company of Rose and Sylvia. Then I climbed aboard Mercury and we flew to the Dragon Isle to study the ancient volumes. It was my hope that I could gather more information on where to look for the Orb of Pater; I felt that surely there must be some sort of notation of the area, at least, in which it was lost.

I took command of all the historians in the dragon aviary, getting them to do research work; looking through old tomes to find any reference to Pater's crystal. After three weeks of searching, all the information we found consisted merely of little tidbits. There was no detailed reference to the crystal, other than the occasional comment in some old books; only sentences in random places. They only mentioned the crystal in passing; nothing about its power or how it was wielded.

After three weeks, I was feeling despondent, as there was nothing I could use to find the crystal. I was led to believe that the crystal was the only thing that would help me defeat Chavez. I asked for an audience with Neela, the oldest breeding female in the dragon clan, and who was in charge of the dragon crèche and aviary.

As usual, with my preferred status as the Dragon Mage and being part dragon, being called Kai by most of the dragons (Kai being the name of the deceased fledgling that made it possible for me to walk again), I did not have to wait long before the invitation was given to see Neela.

As I walked into Neela's chamber, two drakes came storming up to me as if to attack. I just stood there and watched as they skidded to a halt in front of me and rolled onto their backs so that I could scratch their stomachs.

Neela said, "Greetings Kai. As always, it is a pleasure to see you, and as you can see by the drakes' reception, you were greatly missed!"

I responded, "They are very sensitive to a person's emotions, and knowing that I bear you no ill will, they are happy to play. As usual, I have come to bask in the beauty of the great dragon mistress."

Neel said, "Flattery will get you whatever you want, my little Kai!" She flexed her wings, showing her beauty, and then resettled in the comfortable nest in the middle of her chamber. I said, "I have come to ask if you have any knowledge of where I might search for Pater's crystal. There appears to be no mention of it in the ancient books of knowledge."

Neela sat silently for ten minutes and then slowly said, "There is a rumour that the Undines have knowledge of where the crystal was lost and where it is now, but as the conclave has decided to let them develop on their own, no one has the authority to search for more information. But I have a favour to ask of you while you are here. There seems to be a leak of confidential or secret data getting to the Wizard Chavez. Do you have any suggestions as to how we can rout out the spy or spies who are sending this information out of the island?"

NINETEEN

Spy Hunt

"**Y**ou have the tools right here to solve that problem, Great One," I said; pointing to the drakes, who were wandering around the chamber, checking infants and eggs. I continued, "As the drakes are naturally empathic, they instantly sense someone who bears ill-will toward the aviary or dragons in general. With your permission, I will take these two and wander the tunnels with some guards to find and interrogate suspected spies."

Neela looked at the drakes and did not hesitate, saying, "That is why you are so dear to me, Kai. You are always thinking of new and innovative ideas to solve problems. Take these little ones, and I will assign you a contingent of guards who will be directed to obey you without hesitation, and arrest anyone that you point out, regardless of rank or standing!"

It was late in the day, so I took the two drakes to my room to get acquainted. Examining the female, I noticed that she appeared to be pregnant. I had a messenger let Neela know the good news and suggested she arrange for someone to care for the pups when they arrived.

Early in the morning, the guards showed up wearing uniforms that indicated they were from Neela's personal companions. This would reduce any conflict from anyone we had to deal with. The drakes—right off the bat—were growling and hissing at two of the companions. I directed that they be taken into custody and escorted somewhere to be interrogated.

We set off rambling through the halls and chambers, following the drakes and waiting patiently as they sniffed at the workers in each area. All told, there were a total of twelve dwarves taken into custody, including various crèche workers, a knowledge-keeper (librarian), and several others.

That still left one important question: how was the information able to get off the island and into the hands of Chavez? I left the captives to be interrogated by trained dwarves, with the assistance of small dragons to read their minds and determine if the reason the drakes did not like them was because they should not be trusted completely; or if they were, in fact, spies.

The captives were submitted to the most extreme questioning that the dragons could think of. Since this entailed the security of the crèche and the dragons as a whole, they could not risk any further information being leaked out. Neela had assumed that the dwarves were hand-picked for their honesty and willingness to give their hearts and lives in service of the great dragons.

After a lengthy interrogation, it was determined that half of the twelve dwarves were somehow involved in gathering information to pass on to Chavez. Gizmo and Godfrey attended the island to question the captives for information. This was a unique situation, since Godfrey had never before been invited to the dragon island.

I met them at the main entrance as they flew in with Mercury. Godfrey was beaming as he climbed down off Mercury, and said, "I can now cross off one more item of the things I want to do and see before I die!"

I let Isaac and Godfrey in on what was happening with the information leak occurring here and possibly in other dragon strongholds. "I want nothing held back, and as is the case with spies, you are at liberty to use whatever means exist—no holds barred—as to what you use to get the information needed."

I arranged for Godfrey to have an escorted tour of the aviary and crèche, after he finished dealing with the potential spies. Godfrey and Isaac spent one day with each of the six suspects, breaking past any mind-shields, and gathering intelligence from each of them. At the end of the week Godfrey approached me and said, "It appears that five out of the six spies would report anything of interest to the sixth spy, who would in turn pass the information along to a small dragon. No one knew the little dragon's name, and relied on the head spy to relay the information to the appropriate source."

I took Godfrey to meet with the great dragon mother Neela. She said to him, "It is good to meet you, Godfrey, especially learning that Kai is from your lineage. He must have inherited his amazing traits from you."

Godfrey replied, "Thank you, Great One, but I think a lot of the credit should go to his parents. They raised him correctly, so that when he is faced with a choice, he makes the right decision."

Neela said, "Now, the next step is to identify the little dragon who has betrayed his or her people by sharing secure information with Chavez or his forces."

I said to Neela, "I have a plan on how we can identify the little dragon who is the betrayer. It will be interesting to see what Chavez has offered up that would tempt a dragon to betray his own species."

I knew that the head spy was a keeper of knowledge, or librarian, as he would be known in my home world. He had provided information to the little dragon contact the day he was arrested, so the dragon was not expected to make contact for almost a week. Since my powers to talk to the dragons via my mind was not yet as powerful as that of other dragons, I escorted the subject to one of the young adults and had him scrutinize the dwarf closely. He then broadcast the picture in his mind to dragon lords only, who would select a replacement they could trust.

Within a couple of days, a dwarf was found who looked very much like the knowledge-keeper in custody. As we dressed him in the other dwarf's clothing and stationed him in the hatchery, I explained to him what he was supposed to do. The knowledge-keeper had the habit of walking around the hatchery at a certain time of the day—every day. So this was obviously where the dwarf in custody would meet up with the little dragon to pass on the information he had learned since they had last spoken.

TWENTY

Fishing for Dragons

I t was almost a week before the little dragon showed up to pump his information source for more data. He realized immediately that the person he was looking for was not there, and he attempted to fly out of the hatchery.

It was at that time that Neela's companions dropped a net on the little dragon, and then wrestled him to the ground, binding his wings and his mouth so that he could not burn them with a breath of flame.

I learned later that his name was Raphael, not that I really cared what he was called. I was more concerned with getting him secured somewhere he could not escape from or call for help. I kept thinking of him as the Judas dragon. There was no historical reference for an appropriate punishment. This was the first time since the dragons had fought with their original masters that they differed in beliefs from each other.

I immediately went to see Neela, and was let into her presence instantly.

I told her, "We have rounded up all the suspects involved in the release of information to the enemy."

Neela responded, "That is excellent, Kai. Have you found out why the little dragon decided to betray us?"

"No. All I can get from him is a string of curse words, some of which I have never heard before," I responded, chuckling. "I am going to arrange for a large escort to follow me to the mainland to ensure that we are not intercepted by anyone or anything. I will bring him in front of the eldest dragon Elijah, and other elder dragons, to see if they can discern what information they can from him."

When the dragons showed up, I was amazed. Twenty four dragons, all in battle armour, showed up just as the sun was starting to set. This night was going to be dark, without any of the moons showing, so there was danger to the crèche from the Malum attacking during this time.

TWENTY-ONE

Battle for Dragon Island

I had Mercury organize the dragons to guard all the entrances to the caverns. Since Mercury was so much younger than the other dragon warriors, there were a few noses out of joint about being ordered around by some young pup. But since he was just relaying orders from me, the dragons kept quiet and followed the directions given.

I placed the trussed-up Raphael in Neela's chamber, with four dwarf companions watching over him. I instructed them to remain with Raphael and to kill him if any enemies managed to get past the dragons or warriors, and enter Neela's chamber.

Godfrey and I positioned ourselves at the only entrance to get to Neela. That way, we should be able to stop anything that got this far into the caverns. Raphael must have been a valuable asset, as we did not have to wait too long before the island was under attack. The first indication of the attack was the dimming of the torches and lamps. I could feel the stifling ominous blackness, which seemed to overwhelm almost everything.

Neela directed the female dragons to withdraw into the hatchery to protect the fledglings and unhatched eggs. The Malum swarmed the entryways in numbers too large to count. A few got through on the first wave of attack. We were ready for them, and only two managed to reach my point. I used the air staff to capture the two in a bubble of force.

They were obviously ready for capture as a potential option, because as soon as they were captured, it appeared that they willed themselves to death by bursting into flame, until there was nothing but ashes left inside of the bubble.

It was a long night. Wave after wave of Malum swooped down, attacking the dragon island cave entrances. If I had not called upon the dragon warriors to come and help defend, we would have been overwhelmed in a matter of minutes. As the sun started to rise in the sky, the attacks stopped. The Malum could not stand the sunlight.

I sent all the troops to bed, leaving only a skeleton crew to watch over the entrances in case a daylight attack was attempted by Chavez's forces. This was unlikely, because the only way was by air, the seas being too rough for a ship. But I was leaving nothing to chance, as the Malum may have brought orc warriors in by air last night.

In the battle for the island, we lost two dragons and twenty dwarf warriors. After all the posts reported in, we estimated that one hundred Malum were killed. I say estimated because when they died, they burst into flame and nothing was left but ashes, like the two I had attempted to capture. For some reason, the Malum did not want us examining their bodies. Perhaps they were hiding some weakness that we could use to our advantage?

The next morning I saddled up Mercury and took Raphael—all trussed up in a bag—to head to the mainland. Two more dragons carried a cage holding the dwarf spies, as well as four dragons acting as an escort to ensure the safety of all. We flew directly to my stronghold on the mainland coast, where the spies and Raphael were drugged and escorted to the Diamond clan stronghold to appear before the eldest dragon, Elijah. Raphael was placed in a special cell designed to block him from any communication or cast any magical spells.

In case anyone was watching from afar, I made a big show of leaving with Raphael and the dwarf spies. There would be no reason to attack the island, since the enemy's information source would be gone from there.

TWENTY-TWO

Interrogation

We landed at the nearest dragon stronghold, blindfolded the dwarf captives, and carried Raphael in a burlap sack through the portals, ending up in the stronghold of Elijah the Eldest. I made sure that when the captives were placed in cells, they were guarded by dwarves who did not have any clan marking on them. There was no way they were able to determine where they were, since they were not spoken to by the guards.

The spies went through an intensive debriefing, and the results did not surprise me. The dwarves were under the impression that, since they were dealing with a little dragon, this was a test of the security of the aviary/crèche on the dragon island. I scheduled a meeting with Elijah after all the interviews were completed with the dwarf prisoners.

Elijah greeted me the moment I walked into his chambers. "Welcome, Kai. How do you think we should deal with this current issue?"

I responded, "The dwarves have been taught for so many centuries that the dragons large and small are to be obeyed without hesitation. I think that the blame needs to be focused on Raphael, and not the dwarves. As punishment, we will farm the dwarves out to different strongholds in security non-sensitive areas. The dragon Raphael is another matter. I want you to call the Tribunal to interrogate him, as he does not seem forthcoming with any information up to this point."

Elijah replied, "I will call the others. They should be here within a couple of days. I will let you know when we are ready to talk to Raphael."

While waiting for the other two elder dragons of the tribunal, I spent the time in conference with the great dragon Elijah.

Elijah took a long breath before speaking. "You try the patience of the dragons all the time, asking for more and more leeway. It is a good thing that we have grown to love and trust you." Elijah chuckled, "I will speak to the tribunal members and then we will seek any input from the other dragon lords and ladies."

The three dragon lords showed up within a couple of days. I was called upon to stand guard over the little dragon Raphael while he was being questioned and judged by Elijah and the tribunal. I brought the Drakes and the Yeti warriors to stand close by and deal with any escape or attack on the part of the little dragon. I chose them, as they would not hesitate to take out the little dragon if necessary, whereas the dwarves might falter, as they had been raised to obey the dragons large and small.

Raphael was shackled by two heavy chains and manacles holding him down, making him unable to fly away. We had him in a small cart so that we could handle Raphael and the weights as we took him down to Elijah's chambers, where the tribunal waited patiently. Once Raphael was brought in front of the dragons, there began an intensive search, probing the little dragon's mind intently.

I monitored the interaction that transpired, so by the end of the day I had a massive headache. But we were able to get a lot of information out of Raphael as to his contacts and his reasons for betraying his own people.

TWENTY-THREE

Raphael's Story

R aphael was born in the crèche on Dragon Island like all dragons were, cared for and taught by the companions, who were especially trained to impart their knowledge. Raphael always appeared to be a slow learner. He was not allowed to leave the island for a few extra years, compared to the others who were hatched at the same time.

He was barely fifty years old, but unlike Mercury, did not mature as quickly as other dragons. He was assigned simple tasks, like delivering messages to and from the dragon island. He felt that he was not appreciated by the others, and had a major inferiority complex.

On one flight several years ago, Raphael was not paying attention and was captured by an orc patrol. Raphael was kept unconscious until such time as he was delivered to Chavez for questioning. Chavez realized that Raphael was the perfect source of information, as he was unsatisfied with his lot in life.

Chavez treated him like royalty, and Raphael spent a week having the servants bowing to him and getting him whatever he craved. At the end of the week, Chavez promised him power and promised to teach him dark magic spells that would make him more dominant than any other dragon, large or small.

Raphael was drawn in to Chavez's side, even as far as eventually meeting with one of the Malum, who taught Raphael a cloaking spell he would not normally even get an indication of while being a loyal member of the dragon clans.

So at the end of it all, Raphael pledged his service to Chavez and the Malum. It was unknown as to how much information Raphael had delivered into Chavez's hands. But I was assured by Elijah that the sources of information that Raphael had access to were very limited. Most of the information was historical, so Raphael would not have been able to help Chavez in his plans for world domination.

The reason Raphael was so valuable to the dragon tribunal now was the amount of detail he was able to provide about the time spent with Chavez, being wined and dined and treated like royalty. Raphael had access to all areas of the palace in the capital city, as well as the caves of the Malum, which he also had free admittance to while they were trying to woo him to their side.

The four full-size dragons pressed the information out of Raphael like a sponge. At one point, there were three dwarven scribes making notes in the chamber while Elijah and the others questioned Raphael.

Raphael was escorted under heavy guard back to his special cell in the underground. Elijah looked at me as Raphael was shepherded out of the chamber, and said, "We must decide what to do with him, now that we have all the information that he held in his mind."

I replied, "There can be no other penalty for Raphael than would be done with any traitor. He must be executed. I feel, though, that we should do it quietly—in the underground—with only a few people aware of his demise. This will delay any repercussions on Chavez's part, as long as he feels Raphael is holding out against interrogation and might be rescued."

I walked slowly to the special cell that had been prepared for Raphael. Isaac and Gizmo joined me to keep me company, and to be witnesses for the execution and destruction of his body.

Raphael looked up at me from his perch and said, "There is no need for comment, Dragon Mage. I know what I have done, and I am prepared to pay the ultimate price for betraying my people." Raphael continued, "I only ask that I be allowed to end my life myself."

I looked at Isaac, who nodded his head in the affirmative. I said then to Raphael, "Very well. We will stand by, until you have passed on."

Raphael's breathing slowed, becoming inaudible, and then he slumped into himself. He slowly turned gray, which I was told later by Isaac was usual. Raphael first turned into a statue of himself, then his stone body began to crumble into itself, leaving only a pile of ashes in its place.

Isaac said, "Normally his ashes would be spread out on the winds, allowing his essence to be shared with the world. Since he is a traitor, his remains will be placed in a sealed jar and taken back to the dragon island. It will be stored in a chamber where there are a few other traitors in jars, dating back to the first time dragons chose to settle on this world. After an appropriate amount of time, the mother of the nest—Neela or her successor—will choose one dragon's remains to be repatriated with the earth."

The dragons obviously believed in reincarnation, but only if their ashes were shared with the earth. This would complete the cycle of life and death, allowing them to return and correct any mistakes that were made in their previous life.

I could not help comparing the death of Raphael to the death of the Malum. Both ended up being reduced to either dust or ashes. Once the dust was collected and placed in a sealed jar, it was given to Mercury to deliver to Neela on the dragon island.

Mercury was back the next day, being eager to take me anywhere I needed to go. Mercury was a typical youth, being only fifty years old (young for a dragon) and itching for action. Mercury was the grandson of the great and oldest dragon Elijah, so he desperately wanted to make a name for himself and impress his grandfather.

TWENTY-FOUR

The Undines

Neela had said that the information about Pater's crystal was with the Undines, the Sea People. The next issue was to open up trust with the Undines, and to show these reserved people that they could be friends with the dragons. They had been left alone for many generations, to develop on their own without any outside stimulus.

I decided to take a week off, and see if I could come up with a plan on how to introduce myself to the Undines with a minimum amount of confusion to them. During my brief encounters with them in the past, there was never any conversation exchanged. I did a lot of talking in the first instance, but the Undine I spoke with never replied to my attempts at communication.

That was when fate stepped in again and helped me out when I was running out of ideas. I was walking the wall of the fortress overlooking the sea, when I noticed a figure lying on the beach apparently with little or no clothing. I immediately yelled for a group of guards and headed down to the shore a quickly as we could. The figure lying in the sand was six-and-a-half feet long, with webbed fingers and toes, and was wearing a loin cloth. The being had an elongated snout, and a blow hole on top of its head. The resemblance to a dolphin was uncanny—almost as if this were the next step in dolphin evolution.

The undine appeared to be sick, although there were no visible injuries when we encountered him. The healers had no idea of what to do with the 'dolphin man.' It was up to Godfrey and me to treat him. We alone had some idea of what the creature might be. There was a room in the stronghold with a large pool, which I arranged to be filled with salt water. A table was set up with various types of fresh fruit, breads, and fish for our guest to eat. We treated our guest, and then let him rest to heal on his own time.

I visited this amazing creature every day, spending time talking to him, telling him my story. But the creature only watched me, not replying to any of my comments. When the creature was healthy enough to leave, the doors leading to the water were left open. I watched as my guest slowly walked down to the ocean, disappearing under the waves.

This entrance was then locked up so that the guest, if he wished to return, would have to knock. A guard was stationed at this entrance, with instructions to allow the visitor to return if he wished.

We had found a huge machine on the beach at the time that we found the Undine. The engineers had been examining the machine we had found on the beach. They had found the entrance hatch, but could not figure how to open it. The machine finally measured out to be four hundred feet long and thirty feet wide. Closely scrutinizing the hatch, I could see some sort of a shell design. However, without a key or a proper opening spell, entry was not going to be gained without difficulty.

I had the machine towed along the beachfront until we could store it in the one cave entrance that was accessible to the water. We had left the gate off the stronghold where the submarine was moored (I could think of nothing else this could have been, other than a submarine). The Undines came and took their property back within a couple of nights. I hoped at the time that this was an act of good faith that could possibly open up a dialogue with these silent creatures.

During my training with Elijah the great dragon, I learned that the Undines and the Snow People (Yeti) were the two races that were not brought over into this world by the dragons. According to their history, openings had appeared for long periods of time into other worlds, and the Yeti and the Undines had come into this world on their own, settling before the portals closed.

The leader of the Yeti and I had one thing in common; it appeared that we came from the same world at different times. He was very intelligent, joining with the Yeti that were already here when he arrived. They had come from another alternate reality where they were hunted for sport, and for their coat of fur. The leader became The Voice of the Yeti, which was the title given to him after he taught the snow people how to defend themselves and become formidable warriors.

TWENTY-FIVE

History Revisited

H aving no luck with the dragon historians, I decided I would check with the Snow People and see if they had any written books imparting understanding of how they had come to this world. I also hoped that they might have some information on the Undines, since both races were here on this world before the dragons escaped their masters, battling for their freedom.

During my time on this world, I had learned from the dragons that they had been servants of powerful magicians before they found a portal leading to this world. There was a great war, spanning decades, between the free dragons and the ones who were still servants of the magicians. It was during these wars that the races of dwarf, elf, and the people (humans of slightly shorter stature) were brought over to serve the dragons.

Of course, the longer the races were here in this world, the more independent they became over the years. The dark elves were a product of magical genetic gene-splicing to make them more capable of fighting in the dark. They were totally self-governing, refusing to take orders from the dragons, so they were treated like criminals and most were locked up when located.

The dwarves were the only ones that still served with honour, building the strongholds and protecting the dragons. Seeking their counsel on all subjects, and obeying without reservation their suggestions, or orders, on all matters. The people still obeyed the dragons, and helped in whatever limited manner they could. The people were primarily content with being farmers and herders, selling their goods to the dwarves and others who wished to purchase them.

The dragons held to light magic, seldom using dark magic in any matter to deal with their problems. Instead, they relied on the dwarves as their enforcement arm when justice needed to be dealt out. The second great war was between the dragons themselves, one side sticking to light magic, and the other using dark magic to control or destroy things in their way.

It was during this second war that the Orcs were brought over by the dark magic dragons. The details of this were a little sketchy; a lot of information was lost during the war. The war ended with the dark magic dragons fleeing. They hid out in caves in a mountain range in South. Over the following centuries, they mutated into a bat-like creature the dragons now call the Malum.

The Malum rarely left the dark caves, except on the darkest nights, which were rare. They preferred to use spies and intermediaries to do their dirty work for them. No one had seen the Malum, and they ensured it stayed that way, blinding those servants that served in their caves so that no one on the outside truly knew what they looked like to this day.

Chavez was an enigma. He came across from an unknown world, and turned down the dragons' offer to train him in light and dragon magic. Chavez instead set himself up, slowly climbing the ladder of the ruling clans of the Orcs. Eventually, through treachery and intrigue, he was in complete control of the orcs. They were afraid of the magic he wielded, and Chavez became the first person to go to the Malum and return, after being instructed in matters of dark magic.

I wanted to find out if there was any more information on the Undines; I had exhausted any knowledge that the dragons held. This was not surprising, since the dragons had decreed that the Undines were to be left alone to develop. The truth of the matter was that most of the information they had was from my brief encounters with the Undines.

TWENTY-SIX

The Voice

I arose early in the morning. With Gizmo resting on my shoulders, and followed by three drakes, we made our way to the portals to enter Elijah's old stronghold in the North. The guards in the portal room quickly snapped to attention when we entered the chamber through the gateway.

As a matter of respect, Gizmo and I paid a brief visit to the lord and lady dragon who oversaw this stronghold. We then walked down the underground hall to the doorway leading into the caves of the Yeti. I pounded on the huge door with my staff, waiting patiently as a man door opened and a Yeti guard stepped through.

The Yeti looked at me and quietly bowed, indicating the open door that he held until my party stepped through.

He then stepped in behind me, and secured the gate again, saying, "Greetings, Dragon Mage. The Voice was expecting you some time in the next couple of days." A young Yeti led the way to the chambers of the Voice, the leader of the snow people.

The last time I had visited the Voice in his chamber, I had a little difficulty getting past the guards at his door. They wanted me to leave all my weapons and magical staff outside of his chambers. The Voice scolded them, and they let me pass unhindered on that occasion. This time, the guards to his chamber simply announced me, bowed, and held the doors open for my party.

The Voice stood as I entered, and softly said, "Greetings, Dragon Mage. It has been a bit since last we had the occasion to speak to each other. Much has changed. With the increase of the lights you were able to recharge, our crops are growing extremely well, and all of the snow people are well-fed. We even have enough of a surplus that we are trading with the stronghold at the end of the tunnel. How may I aid you? I sense that this is not a social call on your part."

I replied, "I am searching for information on the Undines, and I thought your people may have information that the dragon clans do not."

The Voice was silent for a few minutes, contemplating my question. Then he replied, "If anyone else had asked that question, I would say there is no information available to share. That would be a lie; we have a book from the sea people, given to us for safekeeping many generations ago. They have updated it, adding pages every decade, so that their history would not be lost if something happened to their people."

The Voice continued, "I don't know why they would have a pessimistic attitude when it came to their possible extinction. But since I did not read their history, I don't know much about them."

I asked him, "Why did you not read it, since you are so knowledgeable in other areas?"

The Voice lowered his head, appearing deep in thought for a minute. He then looked up into my eyes and said, "I have never learned to read. I found that in most cases there is no need to understand the written word. There are others that write down and research important matters for me. The fact that I cannot read is a well-kept secret of the people of the snow."

The Voice called his attendant to send for the keeper of knowledge to come and see him. The knowledge-keeper was obviously aware that his presence was going to be needed at this time, and so was in the chamber within moments.

The Voice looked at him and said, "Get the book of the sea people, and give it to the dragon mage for his use."

The knowledge-keeper started sputtering as he spoke in return, "But no one is allowed—"

The Voice held up his hand, stopping him, and said, "If we cannot trust the dragon mage, then there is no point in continuing on. We need allies who we know will not betray us."

The knowledge-keeper handed a thick binder, which appeared to be bound in some sort of scales, to me. I felt like I was taking a favorite toy from a child; I had to almost pry his hands open to get the book.

The Voice said, "To keep my knowledge-keeper happy about his precious books, I am going to assign two warriors, whose sole job will be to protect the book from unauthorized hands."

I smiled, and said, "I hope that does not include me!"

The Voice laughed out loud and said, "You will have control of the book, but at least one of these warriors will remain with the book. That is, unless you have one of your snow people guarding the book. It must be protected at all times."

I replied, "I will protect the book, keeping it in a well-guarded location at all times."

I told Gizmo to call my stronghold, and have all of my snow people warriors meet us at the underground city to escort the book to my stronghold. They arrived before the end of the day, and I gave them permission to visit family. I told them I would wait two days to return to my stronghold with the book. I spent the next two days relaxing and enjoying the hospitality of the snow people.

The whole entourage left, with the book carefully wrapped in a decorated chest that had held the book protected for many generations. We walked to the Diamond stronghold and entered the portal to my stronghold on the coast.

I had a special room set up to house the book, with a small room off it for the snow people guards to rest. The door locked securely on the inside. Entry was not possible without someone opening it from the interior of the room.

I sat down at the large desk in the room and opened up the book, to read what the Undines felt important enough to pass on in case they disappeared off the face of this world.

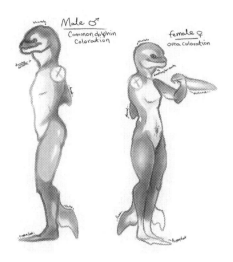

Male ♂
Common dolphin
Coloration

female ♀
orca coloration

TWENTY-SEVEN

History of the Sea People (Undines)

M y name is Tleec of the Sea People. As the most skilled of writers, I have been asked by the elders to document some of our story. That way, those who follow will understand why we had to travel to this world.

We shared our world with the people of the land, but in this world there was not much land. There was one large land mass, with the rest of the world covered by water of various depths. We lived in the shallows, venturing at times into the depths to hunt fish or harvest ore for smelting in the volcanic plumes of the deeps.

We lived in peace with the land people for centuries, without any problems arising between us. It was not uncommon for our people to rescue vessels in distress on the oceans, saving countless lives of the land people.

We co-existed with the land people, having close contact; trading fish, sea plants, and smelted metals for finished material such as cloth and certain types of machinery. Anything mechanical in nature had to be waterproof, of course.

We watched as the people on the land grew great in number, and began to fight over what space was available to them. There were several wars on the land, destroying farmland and killing millions of people. Fertile farmland became rare, causing the land people to build towns on stilts above the shallow water, and freeing up the land for farming.

With the encroaching of the land people into the shallows around the land mass, the sea people were forced to move to other shallow areas that were farther away. The sea people broke off trade with those on the land, as we realized how violent they were. We did not want to be drawn into some war between factions over what was left of the farmable land.

It took many centuries, but eventually we saw that all of the land people who survived the wars were at peace. By this time they all lived in the shallows, farming the land that was still viable, and living off the sea, as we did. As the land dwellers began to progress with their technologies, they got better and better at catching seafood in the shallows, forcing us to go deeper to harvest fish.

With the land people living in the shallows, their waste was dumped into the ocean, without thought of long-term consequences. They had platforms in areas of the ocean to pump out the black blood of the world, using it to run their machines, which bellowed black smoke into the sky. They did not care when the pipes broke and the black blood flowed into the ocean, killing or making sick those of us who were too close to it.

We tried communicating with the land people, to let them know the damage they were causing to this world. The ocean became thick with pollutants, and the temperature of the world became warmer. We could no longer see the stars at night because of the thick layer of smoke that covered the world.

We were a peaceful people, but the land dwellers blamed us as the polar ice caps melted and the water level kept rising over the years. The land people began to hunt us, forcing us to learn the ways of battle against them. Unlike the land people, we would only damage their ships, causing them to lose the ship but rarely ending in any deaths except our own, as they used weapons which shot out tiny spears.

We used magic to create undersea machines, as we could only hold our breath for so long before having to rise to the surface to breathe. It was at this time that we were most vulnerable to attack from the land people.

Using a combination of magic and some of the technology we learned from the land dwellers, we were able to create undersea cities, creating air spaces so that we could be safe from those others. We knew it was only a matter of time before the oceans were so poisoned that nothing would be left alive.

The land people were not satisfied with the fact that we were not around interfering with the way they wanted to do things. They still felt that we were the cause of the global warming and the rising of the ocean level. This was slowly destroying their farms, which were located on the shores.

They built machines that could run underwater, and began hunting us, searching out our communities. We lost a lot of people, as the land dwellers would find us and systematically kill everyone, including women and children.

It was at that time that Reee, who was a great thinker and explorer, was searching for a solution to the genocide that the land dwellers were imposing on us. Reee had a small undersea vessel he travelled around the oceans in, looking for something that would end these terrible attacks from the land people.

It was during this search that Reee stumbled across a large distortion deep in the ocean that transported him to another world— this world, in fact. Reee was amazed how pristine the oceans were, but he saw huge voracious sea creatures that dwarfed his little undersea vessel. Fortunately, the creatures did not have a taste for the metal hull of Reee's machine.

Reee searched the oceans of this world, and the various shorelines, looking to see if this world was populated or not. Reee was unable to find any intelligent life, but he only searched at the points where the land met the ocean. All he could catch were glimpses of prehistoric animals that were gigantic in size.

Our people need moisture almost continually to survive. Reee was able to find one island chain that was devoid of any large life. There were small flying dinosaurs in the area, though. Reee determined that this would be an ideal location to resettle the sea people.

Reee found the portal, as it had some unique geography which highlighted the area, almost as if it was predetermined for the sea people to escape the slow death on their world. Reee went to the capital of the sea people with the amazing discovery of an escape route.

The sea people went into high gear to build some large undersea vessels to carry as many as possible to safety, even though they knew that with the limited resources that were on hand, they would only be able to build a few of these large vessels.

The sea people held a lottery, making it fair, picking the first few families, as they knew that their greatest enemy, other than the land dwellers, was time. The first trip was made following Reee's underwater boat, as no one had taken this path other than Reee. In the boats were a few families and a contingent of sea people warriors to ensure their safety. Reee's boat was filled to capacity with books of knowledge to guide the people to rebuild in their new homeland.

Only two elders went with the first load—just in case. The others remained, organizing the exodus to the new world. They knew there was a chance they might not make it, but they were willing to make the ultimate sacrifice for their people.

The land dwellers did not appreciate initially that those they hunted were escaping from their grasp. It was not until they found a couple of sea people communities empty that they realized the sea people must be going somewhere. They stepped up their search to try to figure out where the enemy they blamed all their problems on was escaping to.

The sea people and their underwater boats kept up a steady run, going back and forth to the new world. Fortunately our boats were able to go deeper than the boats of the land dwellers, so we were able to avoid their patrols of the ocean. It was not until the absolute last trip that we were spotted, and the land dwellers gave chase to find where we had gone. They hoped to destroy us, feeling that if we were no longer there, all of their problems somehow would be solved.

It was a close call. Our little fleet did all it could to lead the land dwellers' vessels on a merry chase. Again, with the advantage of our underwater boats being able to go deeper than those of the land dwellers, we were able to escape their attacks. Once we were through the portal, we were safe. The odds of the land dwellers finding the portal, even if they had a vessel that could reach that depth, were astronomical.

Now came the time to start anew, building our new civilization from the sea bed up. The last boats were greeted with welcome arms.

The last of the elders were in those boats, in case there was some reason that they could not come to the new world due to the interference of the land dwellers.

That is the reason for this book: to write down the memories of the elders. Knowledge would then be kept for centuries to come and not be lost. With the example of how our old world was dying, we were concerned that there might come a day when we have to flee this world or die with it. The knowledge we gathered over the centuries could not be lost, and the lessons learned about how fragile the world truly is were very important to us.

The rest was followed by hundreds of pages describing cultural ceremonies and traditions dating back generations of the Undine.

We decided to make up two books: one of which ended up in the hands of the snow people, who promised to guard it with the lives of their warriors. The other book was kept in the secure area of the library, so that we could teach our young about protecting the environment in the future; and to learn some of the history of our race in this world.

Every ten years we sent a mission to our home world to see how things were going. It did not take more than fifty years before the land dwellers had killed themselves off. From what we could gather, they not only ignored our warnings about pollution and protecting the ocean, but they increased their production tenfold, rapidly destroying their environment.

We continued to check every ten years to see if the world was able to cure itself of the killing pollutants. It was not until one hundred years had passed that we began to see changes in the sea bed and shallows, as the world began to heal itself from the damage done.

There was no sign of the land dwellers. It appeared they had disappeared into the annals of history. The only thing our people could find was what was left of the land dweller cities, but there were no signs of intelligent life.

The land dwellers as a people had paid the ultimate price for not listening to the sea people. Our explorers who checked out the old world found that the air was oppressive, but breathable. It would take many generations before the old world was livable again, but since we had found our new home, we could bide our time.

We found that the sea creatures in this world were enormous and dangerous. Fortunately they rarely ventured into the shallow waters that surrounded the island chain that the sea people claimed as their home. The only thing that kept our population down was the occasional sea monster that ventured into the shallows, killing many sea people before a defence could be raised to attack it.

Reee designed a machine that could travel on land, and still supply enough moisture to keep sea people alive. Otherwise, without water, we would die. We need constant supplies of water to keep our skin moist.

It was during the time of searching out the land that we found the snow people. We did not know how long the snow people had been in this world; they had not kept a calendar system to keep track of days. There was also no documented history to indicate where the snow people came from. What history they did have was lost in what appeared to be a violent run for survival from their home world.

We watched as the world started to get busy; a war broke out between the dragons and wizards, with other dragons to assist them. We waited to see if these battles would affect our way of life, but nothing changed for us. A few centuries later, there was a great war between the dragons. We watched the skies as dragon fought dragon. After a few months, things settled down again. It still did not affect us. It appeared that whoever had won the war was going out of their way to leave our people in isolation.

It was like we were alone in this world. There was no interaction with us. The oceans on this world were rough and filled with voracious monsters of the oceans. Our civilization blossomed back to the level we had in the old world, prior to the land dwellers destroying the environment.

One day, a large male dragon flew into our main village, and was greeted by the elders of the sea people. The dragon did not remain long, only speaking to the elders for about one half hour. When he left, the elders had a crystal about the size of a child's toy.

The elders went to great efforts to hide the crystal, and its location was soon lost in the annals of history. Only select elders were aware of where the crystal was placed for safekeeping. This information was passed along from generation to generation as a valued secret. The details of the crystal were not shared with anyone else, and there was a great deal of speculation as to what it was, to where it was hidden.

One of our vessels found a furry looking individual (Yeti) struggling in the water, as he had been swept out to sea by a flash flood on the continent. As is our nature, we rescued the Yeti, who went by the name of Snow Warrior. We brought the warrior to our head village to meet with the elders, so that they could question him about this world we found ourselves in.

Snow Warrior gave us information about how the Yeti lived in their cave cities, only venturing out to hunt meat and help travellers in danger. The Yeti kept a close eye on traffic travelling through their area of control and shared any intelligence they gathered with us.

The Snow People, or Ice People, as they called themselves, were not involved in the dragon wars, but were merely uninterested observers. Snow Warrior explained to the elders about all the races of beings that had been brought into this world by the dragons, and what had happened since their arrival.

TWENTY-EIGHT

How Do We Make Contact?

As I read the book, most of the entries were in relation to births and deaths. Once the battles and fleeing to the new world were over, the majority of the book was dull and unexciting. There were no documents or notations in the book in relation to their deep sea vessels, which would have been very helpful in the long run.

Reading through the book from cover to cover, I found one reference which interested me greatly. The sea people actually refer to the crystal as Pater's legacy, and that again the elders were tasked with keeping it safe from harm or unworthy ownership.

The only hope I had of finding the crystal was to meet with the elders of the sea people, and get them to entrust the crystal into my possession. The question that now arose in my mind was how the sea people and the snow people maintained an open line of communication. The history of the sea people seemed to be written in ten year spans, or at least that is when pages were somehow delivered to the snow people.

I looked at the guardians of the book that came from the snow people, and I asked them, "Am I going to get any straight answers from you about how to contact the sea people?" They looked embarrassed and would not maintain eye contact.

Finally, one of the guardians said, "There are certain things we are not privy to. You must speak to The Voice, who may have that knowledge. We were not given that information, so that if the book were to be intercepted, we could not divulge anything about its contents. We are not even allowed to read the book, in case we might accidentally share information that must be kept secret."

I knew that the only way I could possibly get in touch with the sea people was to go back and talk to The Voice again. My escort and I took the book to Elijah's stronghold, again securing it under the watchful eye of the snow people guardians. I explained to them that a copy was going to be made for the dragon archives, and kept there securely.

The guardians were a little hesitant about letting anyone else copy any of the pages of the sacred book. I calmed them by saying I would get permission from The Voice before I allowed anyone else to read or copy pages of the book.

I spoke to Elijah, explaining the book and its contents. I said, "In order to keep a good working relationship with the snow people, I have promised that no one else will be allowed to read or copy any pages of the book without the express permission of The Voice."

Elijah replied, "I would like to know what it says. However, our relationship with the snow people must be maintained as the first priority."

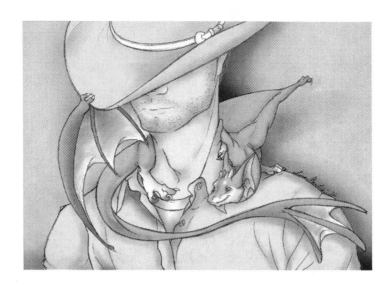

TWENTY-NINE

The Voice Makes it Happen

I travelled again to see The Voice in the caves of his people. Gizmo took up her place wrapped around my neck, and off we went. It took us a better part of a day to walk to the underground city where The Voice lived. When we arrived at his chambers, we did not have to wait long, and were escorted into his presence.

The Voice quickly dismissed his bodyguards and instructed them to bring a meal for himself and his guests. We sat silently until the food was brought in and mostly consumed.

The Voice broke the silence by saying, "I know why you are here. There is a copy of the sea people history book here that you may take with you, entrusting Elijah to keep it secure."

The Voice continued, "The next question is how to introduce you to the sea people. It is not going to be easy, but it can be done."

I looked at the Voice and said, "I appreciate any help you can provide to smooth the way in my introduction with the sea people."

The Voice called a group of warriors into the chambers, and had them take the original book into secure hands, transporting it back to the secure room. Another group took the duplicate book, and left to escort it to Elijah's stronghold.

The Voice slowly came to his feet, and had to have an attendant assist him as he headed out the doorway. He slowly ambled down toward the hall, leading me to the secure room where the book of the sea people was kept. The Voice turned down a side hallway just before the book room, unlocking another well-guarded door and opening it up. The room was devoid of furniture, with the exception of a large cabinet, which stood against the wall.

The Voice walked over to the cabinet and unlocked it, opening it up to display a map of the underground maze of tunnels that made up the cities and causeways of the kingdom of the snow people. The Voice said, "This is the only copy of our kingdom. Our people are taught when it is time for them to learn the different pathways that they need to travel, depending on their jobs. You may look at it, and memorize what you need to, showing the path that you must take to meet the sea people. There is a doorway marked on this map that you must open with your magic."

The Voice continued, "I will give you this talisman that will show the sea people elders that you are a person who may be trusted. From my understanding of the land dwellers they dealt with in the past, you do not look at all like them. You are taller, and your appearance is more defined than the land dwellers."

The Voice introduced a member of the snow people, whose name was Envoy—which also described his job. "The job is conferred by heredity, and is passed down carefully and with great honour. The information is closely guarded, and not shared outside of myself and the family who holds the secret."

I replied, "I need to prepare myself for this meeting, and I will get back to Envoy to arrange our encounter with the sea people within a week."

The Voice replied, "Envoy will travel with you, so that he has a better understanding of who you are when he speaks to the sea people on your behalf."

I thought to myself that with the addition of Envoy, I was gathering quite the supportive entourage. During my travels back to my stronghold, I first paid a brief visit to Elijah's stronghold, and introduced him to Envoy. I left him with Elijah, so that he could explain the writings in the book of the sea people and answer any questions that Elijah may have.

On my way back to my stronghold, I explained to the guards on either side of the portal about Envoy, so that they could show him the way at both ends.

When I arrived at my chamber, a sumptuous meal had been prepared. Lady Sylvia and Rose were talking in hushed tones, which ended suddenly when I entered the room. I looked at my girls, sensing that something was up just from the looks on their faces.

I sat down and both women served me with smiles on their faces, which made me feel that something was up.

I put my fork down and said, "Okay, I'll bite. What is the big news that you are just dying to tell me? I can see that it is eating you up."

The ladies were absolutely glowing as they both said in unison, "We are pregnant!"

I just sat there with my mouth open. One pregnancy I could understand, but both of them pregnant at the same time was amazing and exciting news. I got up and hugged both of them tightly.

I said, "That is fantastic! We will soon have the patter of little feet in the stronghold. I am overwhelmed by the good news, and could not be happier!"

After dinner, I called James in and spoke with him at length. I said, "I want a contingent of ten dwarves for the Lady Sylvia's bodyguard, and of course the same amount of elven warriors to act as Princess Rose's bodyguard." James just nodded, with a look on his face that showed he did not understand the reason for this new order.

I continued, "Both of the ladies are with child, and I do not want anything to happen to them or their unborn children."

James smiled ear to ear and said, "I am sure that I will have no lack of volunteers to protect them." With that, James left the room, headed out to the barracks area of the stronghold, softly whistling a cheery tune as he quickly exited the room.

James was back within a couple of hours to advise that all had been arranged. Needless to say, the women were a little upset about suddenly having an entourage around them all the time when they left the keep. I calmed them and ended any argument by saying, "You are both precious to me, and the unborn children more so because they were created by our love."

Both Lady Sylvia and Princess Rose closed in with me and we three shared a group hug for a good solid five minutes. My girls were crying, and I was starting to tear up, so I said, "I must continue my search for Pater's crystal, so by delegating bodyguards for you, I know that you will be safe while I am gone."

I spent a quiet evening with the ladies, but had a hard time sleeping. Thoughts of what might happen or things that had to be done kept flowing through my mind.

I spent the next few days with Envoy, sharing my life story with him. This way, Envoy had a better understanding of the world that I came from, as well as the pollution and global warming that was currently plaguing my home world. Envoy explained that I would only be able to bring the snow people warriors with me, as the sea people had not had dealings with anyone else over the last few years, since coming to this world.

It would be bad enough that I would be a bit of a shock to the sea people, with my appearance. If I brought a group of warrior companions, the sea people would think of this as an attack on their homes. Envoy and I headed into the underground of the snow people, accompanied by about ten of my guardian snow warriors.

After stopping and speaking briefly to The Voice, we travelled down tunnels that had not seen footprints for at least a decade. The one exception that Envoy allowed was Gizmo, who took up her position, wrapped around my neck.

The tunnel led us on a meandering course up and down, winding everywhere into the darkness. As we got closer to the portal leading to the islands of the sea people, the more hazardous it became, with unexpected attacks from giant spiders and giant rats.

Envoy said, "Normally, if it was just me, I would not have much in the way of problems, as I can travel quietly so as not to arouse any of the denizens in the caverns."

After a while, I reached a point where I was fed up with the constant attacks on our group. I unleashed some dragon fire down the corridors, thereby sealing the holes the monsters were coming out of, and reducing those that were in the tunnels to piles of ash.

As we approached the portal, I looked at Envoy and asked, "Is the opening on the other side above or under the water?"

Envoy replied, smiling, "Above the water, Dragon Mage, near the top of the island chain—well above the water level. Why? Can't you swim?" I stood by patiently, while Envoy performed the ritual movements and words that unsealed the portal.

I replied "Yes, but I do not relish having to hold my breath for an unknown period of time."

We stepped through the portal, entering into a gloomy and dark cave. I created a light and cast it about, lighting globes in the room and bringing light to the darkness. I could detect movement from large pools of water in the cave, and we were soon surrounded by a dozen warriors of the sea people. Envoy pushed through our group to meet with the leader of the sea people warriors.

"I am Envoy. I have come to introduce the dragon mage Kai to the elders, in the hopes that some help can be gained for either side. We have come to fight the evil that is slowing growing across this world."

The sea people warrior introduced himself. "I am Kleet. I am a guard captain for our people, keeping them safe from harm and fear." I could hear his voice in my head, which meant that they communicated mind-to-mind like the dragons when talking to other species. Except that there was no magic potion needed to make it possible.

There was another large door leading from the portal cave out to the island. Kleet waved his arms and made some whistling noises in his original tongue, causing the doorway to slowly open. Once everyone was through the doorway, Kleet sealed the doorway again behind them.

I looked out at the ocean and the lush growth that lined the path leading down to the shoreline. The sea people were tilling the fields, or lounging in small pools that were stretched out among the growths for the sea people to use to get moisture and not dry out. The sea people stopped what they were doing and watched our group as we walked past them down the path.

I saw a difference in Kleet as I followed him down the path towards the ocean. My dealings with the sea people in the past year had been with the average person resembling a dolphin from my own world. The average appearance of the sea people was: six-and-a-half feet long, with webbed fingers and toes, and wearing a loin cloth. The being had an elongated snout, and a blow hole on the top of its head. They resembled eerily an ancestor or descendent of a dolphin.

Kleet, on the other hand, had to be at least seven feet tall. His colored markings were more like the killer whales or Orcas from my home world. He was black and white, making him stand out from the other sea people, but the elongated snout and blow hole were still visible on the top of his head. I scanned the hillside looking for more of his kind, finding only a few standing guard in pools at strategic locations.

As we approached the beach, all heads turned to the ocean, where there was some sort of disturbance within the shallow water area. Kleet excused himself, racing for the water and jumping in, with at least a half dozen of the larger sea people quickly following behind him. I asked Gizmo to look at what was going on in the water from the air, sharing her vision with me.

I focused on Gizmo, watching through her eyes at what was going on in the shallow waters. What I saw amazed me! There was a huge sea creature trying to get at some young children. I could also see that there was a break in what appeared to be an artificial reef built to protect the shallow water.

The warriors approached the creature from behind, and began jabbing their spears at it to get its attention away from the children. I could see through Gizmo's eyes that there were not enough warriors to defeat the sea creature, but definitely enough to make it angry at the source of the sharp pain that was being inflicted on it.

The end result was obviously inevitable, with the warriors ultimately being defeated. Since I was being ignored at the time, I decided to lend a magical hand. I reached out with my mind and the air crystal, creating a ball of air around the sea monster, and lifted it out of the ocean. I was able to bring the creature to a bare spot on the beach, releasing the bubble and watching as the creature struggled to breathe.

I walked over to the sea creature and put some bullets in its head until it stopped moving. I then created a huge flame and cooked the creature where it lay. The sea people gathered around the creature, looking at it in silence. It was at least sixteen feet in length. Its head was four feet, and the teeth were at least two feet long—enough to make a very quick meal of any one of the sea people.

The unusually-coloured warriors slowly walked out of the ocean, approaching the carcass of the sea creature.

Kleet approached me and said, "You have saved many lives today, wizard. For that, we are eternally grateful! Now is the time for you to talk to the elders, and I will speak to the elders on your behalf. You have saved many of our young ones today. If it were not for your help, there would have been quite a few family members mourning the loss of clan."

The sea people started to harvest the giant fish, while Kleet led my party away toward some huts located near the beach. The huts were a shell, leading underground toward damp tunnels, which branched out in numerous directions. I could feel the damp air and coolness as I stepped into the entryway of the largest hut on the beach.

Kleet walked up to a group of what appeared to be elders lounging in pools. Kleet walked over to one of the elders and touched his head to the elder's head, obviously communicating mind to mind. Kleet kept that stance, speaking at length.

When he was done, the elder stood up and looked at me directly. "My name is Shree, and I am the eldest of this clan. You must deal with me in all matters before you can progress on your quest of knowledge. I see by the amulet you are wearing that The Voice of the snow people supports your journey to us, but we must still deliberate before making a decision to aid you."

I looked at the elder Undine and said, "I am grateful for your time and consideration of my needs to help keep your people safe. Because if Chavez has his way, you will not be safe over the course of time. He has no compassion for anyone but himself. Other races are just tools for his continuing search for wealth and power."

Shree replied, "We will consider your request. I must speak with the elders of the other communities to make sure there is a consensus on what should be done. You may return to your home, and we will send a messenger to you, once our decision is made."

As my entourage and I walked back to the portal entrance, each of the large black and white warriors stepped out of the pools and bowed their heads. They crossed their spears across their chests, to honour me.

Kleet leaned down to me and said, "I am sorry a decision was not made immediately in your favour, but you have my word that the warrior clan recognizes a pure heart and strength of a fellow warrior, regardless of your race. I have already contacted our the warrior elders, and you have our complete support if it comes to a vote. Unfortunately, there are ill feelings about land dwellers from where we originated. The warrior clan was tasked with protecting what you are seeking. There is a chance that some of us will break away and disobey orders if necessary to complete your quest, if a vote goes against you."

I thanked him quietly, but otherwise I kept silent until we arrived at the tunnels of the snow people. I spoke to Envoy and told him that it might be a good idea for him to return to the sea people and speak on my behalf.

Envoy looked at me for a moment and said, "I would be honoured to speak on behalf of the dragon mage, who is a friend of the snow people." Envoy bowed briefly and turned back to the portal and again entered it, leaving me with my followers to slowly head back to the city of light, where I spoke briefly to The Voice, informing him of what had occurred on the island.

I spent a night resting in the city, before heading back to my stronghold to await whatever decision the Undines made in regard to my search for Pater's orb, which held the crystal of the same name, promising great power to its wielder. I knew that without the aid of the sea people, it would be awfully difficult, if not impossible, to retrieve the orb. I knew that, with the orb being under the care of the Undines, it was probably underwater somewhere.

I arrived back at my stronghold in the early afternoon of a hot and humid day. The breeze coming off the ocean made the temperature bearable. I looked around as I walked into the center courtyard of the stronghold. There appeared to be something going on! Warriors were running, grabbing armour and weapons, and setting up near the front gates to deploy.

I grabbed one of the dwarf warriors and loudly demanded, "What is going on?"

He started stammering and saying something about "overdue."

I interrupted him. "Never mind—find James and bring him to me right away!" The warrior nodded and ran off to find James.

It was not long before James came running up to me. He seemed to be avoiding looking directly into my eyes.

I said, "Spit it out James! What the hell is going on that we have all these warriors getting ready for battle?"

James looked scared, and said, "The ladies went out to pick mushrooms and berries for tonight's meal, knowing that you were on your way back to the stronghold. We expected them back about half an hour ago. It may be that they just lost track of time, but I called out the warriors just in case."

I nodded solemnly. "Get Fred and the drakes out here and ready to go in five minutes." James nodded and ran off. I looked at Gizmo and said, "Get Isaac and Mercury and search from the sky. Do not worry about saddling up Mercury—I want you out there right away!" The two little dragons and Mercury took off immediately, searching for the women.

Matilda came bounding up ahead of Bonnie and Clyde. She did not wag her tail or try for attention, sensing that I was not in the mood for anything but business. I immediately started to head for the gate, noting that all of my guardian warriors were pulling on armour and running to quickly catch up.

My well-trained warriors spread out in a search formation, with only hand gestures to guide them. They had no intention of alerting anyone, possibly an enemy, who might be around the stronghold without permission.

It was only a matter of ten minutes maximum before I got a call from Isaac and Gizmo, reporting that they had found something west of the Stronghold. I called my guardians and ran full-tilt toward the area Isaac had indicated.

We arrived in a clearing and found a scene of carnage; bodies of elves, dwarves and orcs were lying spread out all over the area. I yelled at the companions to search for the women or someone that might be still alive. We were desperate for some information as to what had happened here!

Gizmo also searched, with negative results. She came to me with the news that there was no sign of the women. This gave us hope they were still alive, and in custody of the orcs. There was one dwarf warrior missing from the women's bodyguard contingent.

I called Ice Wind over. "Take your people and track the orcs, and keep an eye out for the missing dwarf."

Ice Wind said, "It will be as you request. Once we find a definitive trail, we will let you know as soon as possible."

Ice Wind waved at his fellow snow people, and they quickly disappeared into the woods.

Twenty minutes later, two of the snow people showed up carrying a badly injured dwarf warrior into the clearing. Geoffrey and I began working major healing spells trying to keep him alive, so that we could get enough information from him to save the women.

While he was being worked on, I called Mercury to get saddled up and ready for battle. I called Elijah in my mind, asking for help.

Elijah said, "I have heard from Mercury about the situation that is unfolding, Kai. I have called the clan to assist you in finding your family and defeating your enemy. Twelve dragon warriors of the clan are enroute, and will be there shortly. There are also another ten coming to your stronghold to await your command to head in any direction you desire."

I walked over to where the wounded warrior was being treated by Geoffrey and a couple of healers, doing their best to keep him alive.

I looked at the dwarf warrior and said, "I know the party was attacked. What I want to know is which direction did they head in when the attack was over, and—are the ladies still safe."

The warrior whispered, "We were overwhelmed. They came out of the bushes surrounding us and the battle was over in moments. They thought I was dead. When they left, I tried to follow, but my injuries were too severe for me to keep up to the group of orcs. I am sorry I failed you, Dragon Mage; there were just too many of them for us to stop them."

I looked at the warrior and said, "Do not worry, my friend. You did what you could. We will find the ladies, rescue them, and exact revenge for your brother warriors. Rest and recover, my man, you have fulfilled your duty to the best of your ability."

The troops headed in the direction the wounded warrior pointed in. I gave the dragons an update on the possible path of trouble. I directed them to fan out on the other points of the compass in case the enemy had diverged from their original path of travel.

Isaac called in the twilight of the day. It would get difficult for the trackers if they were following a small group. But as Isaac called to indicate that he had found the orc encampment, the path that we were following widened out, showing that we were following a very large contingent.

Isaac said, "It is a huge group of orcs. There must be at least one thousand men and their equipment. They have set up in a large clearing, with little or no foliage around them, so as to prevent anyone from sneaking up on them."

I turned to James and said, "Get the dark elves and Tomar here immediately!" James nodded and ran off to the stronghold. "Isaac: find the nearest three clearings around the orc encampment and divide the dragons between each, so that we are prepared to attack on three fronts. Elijah, canvass the strongholds and send out what they can spare in warriors right away. We will place them once they have come through the portals. This will deal a great blow to the enemy, but first we must recover the captives."

Elijah responded, "It will be as you ask, Kai. Everyone has been told that they are under your command."

"Isaac, as soon as it is fully dark, fly over the camp so we can get an idea of the layout and where the women may be held."

Isaac responded in the affirmative, keeping his reply short, as he was obviously concentrating on the tasks that I had set for him.

It was not long before the sun set and Isaac flew over the orc camp, getting the lay of the land. I watched through his eyes and quickly drew a map, which included the little clearings that were at strategic locations, but far enough away that the enemy would not know we were deploying troops.

Isaac did a quick estimate, and thought the enemy forces numbered close to one thousand orcs, including transport animals, ogres and raptors. James kept a running commentary as our forces gathered and deployed to one of the three staging areas. By the look of things, the camp was laid out in a giant circle, and included two Ankylosaurs with closed and closely-guarded platforms on their backs.

As I stood around a table with the roughly laid out plan of the orc camp, I said, "We need to get the captives secured prior to attacking the camp, so there are no civilians injured in the battle. If we plan this right, we can attack with dragon fire and have the troops standing by to attack anyone fleeing or trying to attack the dragon forces."

I had to figure out how to get into the camp unseen, secure and protect the women, and then lay the wrath of the dragon clans on these orc warriors. The trick was to get to the women and secure their safety first and foremost. They had to be in one of the two Ankylosaurs in the center of the camp.

Tomar arrived, bowing briefly to me, and said, "Dragon Mage, the dark elves are here to assist you in any way possible. Intelligence reports from my most trustworthy sources tell me that the average orc does not know that we have allied ourselves with the dragon clans. It will be very easy to walk into the camp and throw my stature around as the head assassin of the Guild. There are few that are not deathly afraid of my skills."

I looked at Tomar and replied, "If we loaded up our special platform, and all of its secret compartments, with a lot of valuables, could we get close to the center of the camp and the other two platforms where the women would be held?''

Tomar said, "Of course! That would be a brilliant idea; the commander would be drooling over the goods. He would want to see if he could steal part of the contents of the platform without getting caught, but he would also be afraid of me—so violence would be unlikely on his part. The commander would be afraid of my reputation and of being taken down by me."

THIRTY

Rescue

Fortunately, with my specially-designed carrier and an Ankylosaurs in my stronghold, the setup of the goods took about one hour, and then was on its way—headed to the orc encampment. I packed all the secret compartments with as many warriors who would fit comfortably. Of course, Isaac and Gizmo demanded to go along, and of course I was not given the option of refusing.

Tomar had gathered the fifty dark elves who had presented themselves as part of my entourage from all of the septs of the dark elves previously, when they were rescued from incarceration by the dwarves. With a little magic and some makeup, I was able to pass as a dark elf, and fit right in with the group that Tomar was leading.

Once the Ankylosaur was ready and brought out to us, we headed out towards the orc camp. We arrived at the camp around the middle of the night, which was perfect because the orc guards were tired and only half-awake as we approached the camp.

I followed closely behind Tomar as we approached the orc camp. Gizmo was curled up around my neck. I used the invisibility ring to hide Gizmo so that no one would accidentally see her, but I was able to give her direction to communicate with the main groups of dragons better.

As the group approached the camp with the Ankylosaur, we were immediately challenged. Tomar stood his ground, demanding to see the camp commander. The guards were a little hesitant at first until Tomar introduced himself, then they were scrambling over each other to answer his beck and call. No one wanted to be on the wrong side of the head assassin of the Guild.

The commander finally showed up disheveled and irate, putting on a fake smile so as not to make Tomar angry. Tomar took the commander inside and showed him all the valuable items and jewels, knowing that the chance of getting some valuable items was enough to drive the commander crazy with greed.

Tomar gave the commander some trinkets, and immediately a path was opened to the center of the camp, so that troops were all around the Ankylosaurs. The commander placed our group in beside the others who were in the centre of the camp, protected (but at the same time close), where the commander could watch over it. If he could get away with it, I knew he would take as much as he could. If it had been anyone else but Tomar, the commander would have killed the escort and claimed to Chavez that he had brought him a great gift.

I could see by the look on his face that the commander was giving it some thought. The only thing keeping him from attacking the whole group was Tomar, and his reputation. The commander came to his senses and was taking out his frustrations on his troops——yelling and kicking a few of them out of his way.

I waited a few hours until just before daybreak, slipping into the enclosures on top of the other two ankylosaurs, and killing all of the orc guards in and around the enclosures. Both women were locked in a room together, but other than a few bumps and bruises, they appeared fine.

We spent a minute holding each other until Neb came into the enclosure and said, "Dragon Mage, Tomar has found something in the other enclosure that he wants you to look at right away."

I looked at Neb and said, "I will be right there. First, ensure the ankylosaurs are blindfolded so they do not panic and hurt themselves or anyone else. I will use the air orb to create a protective bubble over our troops and the dinosaurs, and then the dragons can begin the attack." Neb nodded and ran off to accomplish his task.

I walked to the centre area of the three ankylosaurs, planting the staff firmly in the ground and creating a dome over our troops and equipment. I called to the dragons, and they began strafing the camp with fire. The orcs' other animals fled, trampling many of their warriors. The dragon troops were sitting on the outskirts of the encampment, taking out any warriors who tried to flee from the conflagration.

The dragons laid waste to the entire camp in a matter of minutes, as there were twenty-two of them laying down a field of fire that few could escape. I was later told that about one hundred warriors had broken free from the camp, only to be taken down by my troops.

Walking into the other enclosure, I was shocked to find a single large cage with an intricate padlock. Inside the cage was the creature that I had called the Easter Bunny when I saw it disable the two Tyrannosaurus. It may have been another creature of the same species, as I had not been close enough to get a good look at it before.

I was amazed that with its power, the Bunny (for lack of a better term) could be held in a cage. However as I approached the cage, I could feel an incredibly strong field of magic embedded in its bars, which would prevent escape by any magical creature.

Looking at the creature in the cage, I could see a major resemblance to a rabbit from my old world, with the exception that it stood on its hind legs and was about four feet tall. It was wearing a simple outfit that reminded me of a Greek robe. I touched the lock to examine it, and got a shock that threw me back ten feet.

Neb came running up and said, "Are you all right, Dragon Mage?"

I looked up as Neb helped me up, and said, "A few scrapes and bruises is all, Touching that padlock gave me quite the nasty shock. We need to find the key, because I do not think we have anything that will break that lock otherwise."

The large rabbit in the cage did not say a word. It just watched us silently, while standing in the center of the cage. I wondered if the sides were charged as well with magic, so that you could not touch it. But after the nasty shock I got when I tried to examine the lock, I was not prepared to touch the cage again.

It took the better part of the day to locate the commander's ashes, and of course he had been wearing the key around his neck. I moved the three ankylosaurs to my stronghold while the troops were scouring the camp for any of information that could explain why such a large force did not attack the stronghold when they had a chance.

I sat in a chair watching the creature in the cage, and spoke softly to it, explaining what was being done to free it from captivity. Once Tomar came rushing in with the key that had been found, I again approached the cage. The key seemed to negate the energy around the cage and I was able to unlock the door. Opening the door, the creature stepped out and walked over to where a large satchel was sitting on a table.

It looked at me and said, "My name is Peter. A favor is owed and I will return to discuss it with you when I have time." As soon as the last word left his mouth, the creature disappeared with a pop of displaced air.

I called Gizmo and Isaac to meet me in my rooms to discuss some topics I was concerned about. I also asked the dragons to scour the area where the orc encampment had been with fire, to reduce the remaining bodies to ash, to prevent attracting predators.

When we were all sitting at the table in the dining area of my rooms, I looked at Sylvia and Rose, and asked, "What were you thinking—going out, risking your lives and that of your unborn children?"

Rose looked at me defiantly and said, "We are not pets that you can lock up in a gilded cage. We need to be able to move around. We were out picking mushrooms to help with meal preparations."

I looked sternly at the women and said, "I am not challenging you about going out to pick mushrooms, but you wandered a little far from the stronghold, so help was not available when the attack came. I want you to recognize and honour those who gave their lives in an attempt to protect you. I want you each to take the task of writing to the families of those that have fallen. The letters will accompany a promise of a pension for them to be able to carry on with their lives."

I continued on. "Do not feel badly that as a commander of men, they were willing to lay down their lives for you without hesitation. It has turned out for the best; you are both safe, with minor injuries, and Godfrey will check you over to ensure both of you and the unborn children are healthy. If you must go out of the stronghold, there will be a larger contingent of troops to protect you. Also, the two drakes will come with you for added protection. The alternative is that you use the portals to travel to other strongholds and do your shopping there. It is not like we do not have the funds to buy our produce or whatever you need."

The ladies looked chastised as Fred came in with the drakes, and I instructed him on their new duties.

I said to them, "I have a lot on my mind right now, and need some quiet time to figure out what my next step is. I want both of you to stay at Elijah's stronghold for now, where you will be safer. I promise to visit you as much as I can during these trying times."

The ladies did not look happy, but Rose nodded and pulled Sylvia away to pack their belongings to prepare for their relocation to Elijah's stronghold. I called Elijah and explained to him all the details on what had happened.

Elijah responded, "We will ensure that security is tight in this stronghold and protect your loved ones for you. For what is yours is also ours as part of the dragon clan, and will be guarded closely."

I asked Elijah, "What about this magical cage that was holding our very short visitor?"

Elijah responded, "Lock it again once it is out in the courtyard of your stronghold. Your brother dragons will fly it to the deepest area of the oceans and drop it where it can do no more harm. As far as 'Peter' is concerned, I think that we have to wait for him to reappear and let us know what his story is."

I followed Elijah's directions, hauling the cage, which had no magic energy when it was unlocked, out into the courtyard. I then had ropes, secured by long lines, held in the air so that the dragons, when they took it, would not come into contact with the bars at all.

I tested the ropes to ensure that the dragons would not be shocked when they picked up the cage via the ropes tied to it. I called and a couple of young dragons landed in the courtyard to speak with me before taking the cage. They were like a couple of teenagers, eager to please and excited to meet me, telling me about themselves and how happy they were to assist their great brother Kai.

They reminded me so much of puppies, with the exception that they could talk, that it made me chuckle slightly as they flew off with the cage to dispose of it in the ocean. I received word from Elijah that they had completed the task within a couple of hours.

The Lady Sylvia and Princess Rose came to me and we hugged, holding each other tightly. They were a little teary-eyed as they walked down to the portal, entering it with the drakes and new bodyguards following closely behind them.

I was sitting in my rooms, reading and making notes. This was the first time in weeks that I did not feel I was rushed into doing other things.

Godfrey walked into the room and said, "I am sure that you guessed this, but the ladies and their unborn children are perfectly healthy."

I looked at him, smiling, and said, "I am sure that I would have heard from you earlier if this had not been the case."

Gizmo and Isaac flew into the room and Gizmo said, "We have a guest. Your giant—what did you call it— 'Rabbit,' has returned to speak with you." I walked down to the open area in the center of the stronghold, and there was Peter standing quietly there, looking around himself, silently taking in everything that was going on around him.

Peter looked up as I walked up and said, "Are you ready to come and see what I have to show you?"

I replied, "Can I bring one of the little dragons with me?"

Peter looked at Gizmo wrapped around my neck, and nodded his head in the affirmative, grabbing my arm.

I could feel my ears pop with displaced air and found myself, with Peter, in a large, park-like area. The trees and grass were more like what I was used to in my old world. There were no noticeably prehistoric plants around us. It was a matter of walking for five minutes before we came up to a path that led to what could only be called a train station. There was no engine visible, just little coaches with seats on each side of an aisle. Peter directed me into the first coach in line, and stepped in beside me, sitting on the padded bench opposite. He directed me to sit down.

A voice emanated from the air: "State destination, please."

Peter looked up and loudly said, "Central monitoring, please."

The voice announced: "Destination entered as central monitoring. If incorrect, please advise now or remain seated until coach reaches its destination."

I watched out of the window as the coach seemed to float along its pathway. I could see a huge city spread out ahead of us as we hurtled along the path.

When we finally came to a stop, we were in the centre of the city, in front of a huge building that appeared to be at least twenty stories high. There was a steady flow of beings who looked exactly like Peter, moving in and out of the building. They were all carrying a bag on their shoulders, and seemed focused on where they were going.

When the coach came to a smooth stop, Peter said to me, "Follow me; I wish to show you something important."

I followed Peter as he walked past the line of his people waiting to enter the building. I saw no guards or doors barring the way, as we walked to what appeared to be a bank of elevators. When the doors closed on the small elevator, light seemed to emanate from the walls all around us. There were no buttons on the panel. The box rose up and when it came to a stop, Peter led the way to a large room.

As we entered the room, I saw hundreds of screens in front of me. In my world they would have been television screens, but here they appeared to be something more. The colours onscreen were so vibrant and clear that you actually felt you were standing there in the scene, and not just watching it.

Peter waved his arm to encompass the entire room and said, "This is why my people travel to other worlds—to explore, and learn how things are. In centuries past, the monitors we left behind were found by people or seen when we were hiding them, leading to the story of the Easter Bunny."

Peter pulled what appeared to be an egg out of his satchel and said something to another person, who waved his hands over a panel.

Peter continued, "Now the monitors are not visible to others, and unless you know the proper spell, you cannot find them." I looked at the monitors and they showed a three-dimensional view of the entire room we were in, including Peter and the egg he was holding.

"Our people are the Watchers. We have been monitoring other worlds for centuries, getting better as each year passes and our skills improve. Our people deal in magic only; we do not have the skills to battle physically. That is how I got captured by those others. I had spent my magic on some animal that had tried to attack, and in a moment of weakness I was attacked and put in that cage," Peter said.

"Our strongest warriors are those with the magic staffs like yours. They are able to cast spells and expend more magical energies than any of us," Peter continued.

I said, "I appreciate the tour, but why did you decide to share this amazing world of yours with me?"

"This world that you find yourself in now is very dangerous, and we hoped that you would lay some of the monitors for us. Also, if one of our people finds themselves in trouble and needs aid, it is hoped that you would lend a hand," Peter responded.

I said, "Of course. I would never refuse you or any of your kind aid. I will lay the monitors in different locations, or get the dragons to drop them where I think they might provide you some entertainment." I smiled broadly at Peter.

Peter led the way out of the building. As we walked out into the street and headed towards the carriages, four slightly taller rabbits, carrying staffs, stepped in behind us. I looked back at them, and then at Peter, and asked, "Are we being escorted off the premises?"

Peter chuckled, saying, "No. They are another part of your entourage. They are going to travel your world, leaving monitors and setting up a station where you can see around your world. It is a gift from my people to you for saving my life, because as the people on your old world would say, I am older than I look. I am an elder of my people, having lived several centuries, watching. As a matter of fact, I have been watching you grow up and your maturation to the great dragon mage Kai."

I asked, "Do you have any suggestions as to what I should do now, Peter?"

Peter replied, "That is not how it works, Kai. We are Watchers only. We have sworn an oath not to interfere with any and all life that we have contact with. Our magic is defensive only; we will not kill or hurt another creature intentionally. It can happen occasionally, but our intent is protection and not aggression."

The coach that awaited us for the return trip was larger and more open, to accommodate the larger rabbits, Peter, Gizmo and I as we retraced our steps back to the forested area where we had come into this world. Once we returned to the stronghold, I suggested to Peter that his people would be better off at Elijah's stronghold. I escorted them past the guards through the portal, and the guards shook their heads, wondering what the wizard was going to bring through next.

I contacted Elijah, and had the greeting hall cleared out for the use of my new friends. Guards were placed at the door so that no one could enter unless they were invited into the new monitor sanctuary. It was not long before more of the rabbits were popping in and out of the central courtyard with crates that floated above the ground, and were directed to the monitor room.

They took over the entire floor of the keep, to use some rooms for storage and others for quarters. This caused some grumbling on the part of the dwarves, but Elijah quickly silenced them, advising that this was the best thing and they did not need to see what was being done, as Elijah trusted the dragon mage's word. Peter gave me six monitors to place as I saw fit, showing me how to activate them prior to placement.

They placed monitors in each of the strongholds, in a spot where you could see most of the area, including the zone around the front gates. Flit took on the task of putting the monitors in place in a couple of places in the capital city, as well as in a couple of larger enemy forts. Flit, being small and fast, was able to place the monitors where they would not be stumbled across, even though they were invisible.

THIRTY-ONE

Of Seashells and Submarines

I was with Lady Sylvia and Princess Rose in the monitor room in Elijah's stronghold, watching things all over this world. The women were ecstatic that they could watch what was going on and be an integral part of our information network by advising my people of anything suspicious going on. They were especially enamored of the fact that they could see everything in three dimensions, as if they were actually there.

One of the monitors came to me to advise that there was a messenger waiting at the door for me. When I left the hall, one of the dwarf guards from my stronghold came to advise that one of the underwater boats was seen cruising the coast near the stronghold. I sent him ahead to open the water doors so the boat could dock in the stronghold if it wanted to, and advising that no one was to interfere with the occupants if they came out of the boat.

I asked Peter if he wanted to join me, as there was the possibility that we would be taking a ride in a submarine, or underwater boat, as the sea people called it. Peter was very excited to join me in this adventure, stating that he would bring extra monitors so that they could see the ocean depths.

We traveled back to my stronghold, and I had to instruct the cooks on a vegetarian diet for Peter. Fortunately, he was not a judgemental person, letting me eat whatever I wanted to, as long as I did not force any on him. We waited a couple of days before the submarine finally pulled into the dock under the stronghold.

Kleet climbed out of the submarine and walked toward me.

"Greetings, Dragon Mage. I have come with good news and bad; we have an underwater boat, but we do not have the magical key that allows it to generate air and more than the basic power to run the boat."

I pulled out the seashell-shaped locket that I had found when I had first dealt with the sea people, saying, "Would this be the key that you were talking about?" I held it up for Kleet to get a good look at it.

Kleet's eyes grew a little wider and his hand was shaking with excitement as he took the key from me. He said, "How did you come to have this special key, Dragon Mage?" I explained in detail to him my dealings with the sea people when I first set up this stronghold, and how we had nursed one of their regular people back to health; also how we had found the submarine, and the key, which was left behind when the boat was recovered by his people.

Kleet said, "With this key, we now have full functions on the underwater boat. We can go anywhere that we want or need to. The council is stuck, discussing the matter of giving our trust to you. There are those who believe that land dwellers cannot be trusted at all. However, the warrior clans are all behind you, as we have seen what you are willing to do for us. You could have stood by and done nothing, and no one would have been the wiser, but instead, you killed that sea beast."

Kleet continued, "Would you like a tour of The Endeavour?"

I replied, "Of course," and Kleet directed Peter, Gizmo and me to the hatch leading into the darkness of the submarine. Gizmo sat in place around my neck, because she did not do ladders too well. There was lighting, as we climbed down into the submarine, but it was dimmer than the light had been outside.

"The basic key we had only allowed the turbines to go at a slower speed, which limits our depth in the water. We could not go where we wanted to, because of the limitations on the running of the boat." Kleet finished up.

"So, what you are telling me is that this is a magical key that allows the underwater boat to work at its maximum efficiency?" I asked.

Kleet answered excitedly, "Exactly, Dragon Mage! The other key only allows the boat to work at a basic level. This key is a master key, which will run the boat at its maximum level, taking us where we want!"

There were pipes running the length of the submarine. The deck surface at the level where I entered the submarine was a grating, allowing for any moisture from the sea people to drip down below the floor level. I asked Kleet what drove the underwater boat along the ocean, and he replied, "The key that you have given us causes the water to be heated. Then, the vapors push the turbines, allowing the boat to submerge and move along the ocean currents for longer periods, also providing air for us to breathe."

A closer look around the surface I found myself on revealed a further maze of pipes under my feet. The deck was grated, allowing moisture to drip down to the floor below. I could see about a foot of water on the deck below, indicating that the submarine appeared to only have two levels. We climbed down, after first looking at the steam-driven turbines and controls in the lower decks.

In the room where the turbines were located was a spot where the seashell key would go. I handed the key to Kleet, and he placed it the receptacle. Immediately, the lights brightened in the submarine and the turbines quickly began to turn. Kleet continued to walk through the submarine, showing me a pool with live fish it, and a bunk room with hammocks that sat in the water. This would allow the sea people to float on their bellies, with air holes exposed, allowing them to breath and relax at the same time.

Kleet said, "We must be going soon. If the elders rule against you we would be honour-bound to still take you, but we would be cast out of the warrior clans. But—if we go now while they are still deliberating, we may get away with a scolding and some censure!"

I quickly packed a small travel bag with food I might need, not knowing how long this journey would take. There were a couple of extra seats in the control area, with a large glassed-in front, allowing the pilot and crew to see where they were going. Peter placed one of his monitors above the watertight door to the control room, so that his people could see what was happening and record it.

It took us a day to reach the "Sacred Waters," an area that Kleet said was off-limits to all of the sea people, without permission of the elders. The area lay smack in the middle of the island chain where the sea people had built their homes. Kleet bottomed the underwater boat onto the ocean bed just outside of the sacred area.

Kleet said, "The warrior clans guard this area, patrolling in and out of a couple of other underwater boats. We will wait until tomorrow, when my clan begins to take its turn to guard this area for the next week. The boat captains know what is happening and will not challenge us as we travel through the area."

A couple of hammocks were set up in the upper deck area, where Peter and I could remain dry and above the water of the lower deck area. I sat for several hours, watching out of the control room window, as huge monsters swam by, as well as small fish. Even when nightfall overtook us, there was a glow at the ocean bottom from plants and certain types of smaller fish.

I was feeling a little claustrophobic. The air was warm and damp, making lying in the hammock a little uncomfortable. Once the lights were dimmed and the gentle glow from the viewing port in the control room reached where we were sleeping, I was finally able to doze off for a few hours, until the boat crew started to come awake. No matter how quietly they moved around us, I woke very quickly, being sensitive to my surroundings.

We were under way before any light filtered down from the surface even indicating that the day had begun. Kleet stood in his post as the captain of his vessel, and nodded at me as I walked into the control room. "My clan has taken over the guarding of the sacred waters for a period of a week, which is all the time we have to search out 'Pater's Crystal'. After that, we would not be able to search for several months, and I am sure you do not wish to wait that long."

I replied to Kleet, "I do not think this world can wait that long either. The evil is coming, and the darkness. If we were to wait, there is a chance without the crystal of Pater we might succeed; the odds are much better if we have it to help."

My ears began to pop as the underwater boat went deeper and deeper in the ocean. Kleet had the running lights on. When questioned, Kleet said there was a need for the light to keep the monsters at bay. Apparently, the deeper we went, the more light-sensitive the sea creatures were.

As we travelled to some point on the ocean floor, I noticed a glow that permeated a large area we were slowly approaching. As we reached a point, I saw that two more of the underwater boats had taken up position on either side of a large underwater archway. The light we could see was emanating from this archway. When our boat reached a point between the two other boats, Kleet turned off the running lights. The two vessels responded by turning their lights on and off slowly a couple of times.

Kleet said, "They are of my clan. They have signalled that the way is clear and they will watch at the portal, as is their responsibility. But they will let us pass, destroying anything else that comes through this entrance into another world, as is their duty."

I asked Kleet, "You hid the crystal back on your original plane of existence? Were you not worried that the land dwellers would get hold of it?"

Kleet responded, "There was always a chance of that, but we did not think they had the knowledge to do anything with it."

Peter handed one of the monitors to a crew member, who went outside briefly and deposited it so that the portal was visible.

Kleet said, "This is not like walking through a normal portal. It can be a little disorienting, as the entire boat has to go through the portal." Kleet was right. As the boat passed through the portal, it was as though the entire boat suddenly felt like it stretched for miles behind me, as we passed through the archway foot by foot.

When we entered the water on the other side, it looked like a graveyard. The water was lighter, indicating that we were closer to the surface on this side of the portal. What first came into sight was a mass of sunken ships, and even some submarines of a different type from the ones the sea people used.

I looked at Kleet with questions on my face, and he responded by saying, "There are some things that were not in the history that was shared with the snow people. This area is where several water battles took place over the years as the warrior clans attempted to protect all of the sea people."

Kleet continued, "As we progressed in our ability to protect ourselves, the land dwellers were usually ten years behind, and then they would jump ahead of us in new ways to kill us, but only for a short time. Our wise men and elders always were able to take what they were throwing at us and improve upon it to protect us."

"The portal was discovered while we were searching among the wrecks to find weapons that were being used by the land dwellers. We lost some warriors who went through the portal. You probably noticed that there is quite a difference in depth; with some of the monsters in the deep, anything could have happened to them. As you go through, it is possible to get disoriented and lose track of the entryway into another world. That is why we built the archway—to mark the portal's dimensions and location."

"We will travel in this direction for one half a day to clear from all the wrecks, before we head to the shrine where the Orb of Pater is kept." This was the first time I had heard Kleet refer to the orb that contained the magical crystal.

We could see some smaller fish, but the water was murky, limiting visibility to about one hundred feet ahead of the underwater boat. This reduced the speed of the boat to about half of what it was on the dragon world.

Kleet stood looking out through the control room window and said, "This is actually better than it was ten years ago. There are some species of fish coming back, and the water is twice as clear as it was then."

I told Kleet to call me when we got close to the shrine. In the meantime, I was going to lay down and rest in the hammock. I lay down, with Gizmo nestling on my chest. I closed my eyes, pretending to sleep, but instead speaking mind-to-mind with Gizmo. "I am a little worried about the sea people's cavalier attitude about the ignorance of the land people. One should not underestimate an enemy. I have a bad feeling about this. Looking at the wrecks, there are some really up-to-date submarines lying there near the portal."

Gizmo replied, "Seeing the things in your mind, I realize your concerns, Kai. We must wait and see what we find at the shrine before we make plans. Rest now Kai, and I will watch over you." Gizmo must have used some magic on me, as I had a very pleasant and relaxing nap.

* * * *

I awoke to a sudden flurry of movement, as the crew was squealing loudly in their home tongue. They were obviously excited by something! I jumped out of the hammock and strode past the crew into the control room. I believed this must be the shrine that Kleet was talking about. It appeared to be similar to a Mayan pyramid, only sitting in the ocean. By the looks of how light the area was, I figured that the water was relatively shallow—maybe one hundred feet deep.

The thing that surprised me was that the pyramid did not have a trace of sea life attached to it. It was glowing, even outshining the daylight that was drifting down from the surface. I know that a ship graveyard usually has coral growing on the vessels, and this was reputed to be ten times older than the oldest wreck.

Kleet said, looking through the control room window, "The pyramid was there before we started keeping a written history, and even in the stories passed down from the elders before that. Magic emanates from every stone, keeping sea creatures at bay and preventing the sea from taking over."

The underwater boat slowly approached the entrance to the shrine. Instead of stopping, it slowly entered the shrine, even though it barely fit through the opening. The boat came to rest at a dock that held air in the structure, and Kleet led the way, opening the entry port into fresh and clear air.

Kleet looked back at me and said, "It is always like this, or so I have been told. The air is always clear and regenerates itself regardless of how many are gathered here. During the wars, this structure has housed and protected hundreds of the sea people, while they waited for transport to the new world."

As we entered the main area inside the pyramid, there was natural light, grass growing on the floor and fruit trees in abundance. It appeared more like a park than the inside of a large structure, if it were not for the stone walls and roof showing through in spots.

Kleet led us toward a large entryway, leading deeper into the structure.

He said, "The orb is just inside this next room, which is a large hall."

I replied, "Have your men spread out—there is danger ahead! I can sense something in the next room; not evil, but not friendly either. There is a possibility that we may have a fight on our hands in a few moments!"

I could feel something moving in the great hall ahead of us, but could not place the feeling. I stopped Kleet and his men at the entrance and sat down, staring into the dark room.

I asked, "Is there normally light in this room ahead of us?"

Kleet responded, "Yes, but the light can be dimmed or the globes covered, to create darkness as we see before us."

I said to Gizmo, "Do you feel like taking a flight around the room to see what you can? I feel that there is someone or something in that room who is not expecting us. I would hate to go in without an idea of what lies ahead of us."

Gizmo responded, saying, "As you wish, Dragon Mage Kai. I will fly around this darkened room and observe for you through my eyes. This way, there will be no surprises and less danger to yourself and the sea people with you." I nodded at Gizmo, and she took off flying into the room. I sat away from the entryway, with my eyes closed, watching through her vision of the darkened hall.

There was a large cairn in the center of the room, but it was empty. I could feel a sinking feeling in the pit of my stomach, as I knew this was where the Orb of Pater was stored. Through Gizmo's vision, I was able to see several shapes huddling in the corners of the room. There did not appear to be young anywhere.

I called Gizmo back to me, and together we wove a strong sleep spell on all of the occupants of the great hall in the shrine. Once I was sure that the spell had taken effect, I directed Kleet and his men to move in, carrying some light globes to light up the hall.

When Kleet looked at the shrine, I could see that he was saddened, as his shoulders sagged and he turned to speak with me.

"I am truly sorry, Dragon Mage, but the orb is gone. It was on a staff in the center of this room. It would light up this whole hall with a beautiful radiant light and warmth. When under its light, you would feel calm and protected," Kleet said.

I approached the huddled men, who all appeared ancient. I had Gizmo read their minds after I woke them up. I did not allow them to wake fully, keeping them in a dream state so that they would not see the sea people and panic. It took longer to question them, but it definitely was safer and kept their minds clearer.

There were six ancient land people in the room. Apparently, when they initially were here, there had been eight, but two had passed away of old age. Kleet looked at the ancients, feeling nothing but pity for them.

Kleet said to me, "It is unknown how long they have been here, as we have not checked on the orb since it was first placed in the shrine. My knowledge of its effects and properties comes from the elders of the warrior clans, who were delegated to the placement and protection of the orb. We have failed you, Dragon Mage. We should have had the orb closer at hand, where it could be protected by strength of arms and a secure site where the enemy could not enter."

I responded to Kleet, "Mistakes are made, but to dwell on the past is useless. You must focus on the present moment, and we will search for the orb after I finish questioning these elders."

Kleet nodded, and he and his troops withdrew back to the entrance.

We questioned each of the land people gently, but firmly. They reminded me of a picture of a Neolithic man; more stooped in appearance, broader faces. But—these wore what appeared to be shreds of an old uniform.

The story that unfolded from them in regard to how they arrived at the shrine was relatively short. Their submarine had come to the shrine approximately fifty years ago; it was hard for them to track the passing days without the sun. Their captain ordered them to reconnoitre the interior of the shrine in detail. They examined every nook and cranny, and coming upon the entrance to the inner shrine, they were temporarily kept out by the sealed doors.

It took several days for the land people to breach the doors, entering into the inner shrine and finding the Orb of Pater in its cradle on top of the cairn in the middle of the room. The captain grabbed the staff containing the orb, and immediately headed back to the submarine. The eight others of the land dwellers were left behind as expendable. Maybe the captain did not want to share the glory of his new discovery, even though he did not appear to know what he had.

We searched their minds as much as possible due to their age, pushing past old memories that were long forgotten. We got an impression of what the submarine looked like and the markings on it, making it possible to search for the submarine in the ocean. The survivors almost enjoyed their lot, which included fresh fruit from the trees, and fish harvested from where the ocean came into the temple. They did not have to work hard to live, and would spend a lot of their time exchanging stories and mutual hatred of the captain who abandoned them. They had no weapons and were not a threat to anyone who might enter the shrine.

I said to Kleet, "They can do no one any harm. They possess no magic or weapons, and probably would die from shock and fright if they were to encounter a warrior of the sea people. We will leave them to enjoy their last years where they are happy. I am not sure what it is like on the surface, but if my understanding is correct, they can breathe easier and be safe here."

Kleet did not say a word, but nodded and directed the warriors to head back to the underwater boat. I told him that I would follow momentarily. I spent a moment with Gizmo, and wove a spell of false memories, so that the last days of these land dwellers would be peaceful and happy.

Gizmo asked, "Why did you do this Kai? They are enemies of our allies the sea people, and have assisted in the theft of something very valuable that we need."

I replied, "Yes, but these ones were abandoned by their own people. They did their duty right up to this time. They deserve to spend their last few days in peace; they are no longer a threat to the sea people."

I slowly walked back to the underwater boat, after taking a monitor egg from Peter and placing it on the top of the cairn which had held the staff and Orb of Pater. The crew was silent as we slowly closed the hatches and pulled out of the entryway into the pyramid temple.

I said, "We will go back through the portal and await your elders' wishes. If they do not wish to help us, we will find another way to search for the orb."

Kleet nodded, saying, "It will be as you ask, Dragon Mage. We will return to our people and put pressure on the council of elders to vote in favour of helping you."

The time seemed to drag as we headed to the portal back to the dragon world. I was frustrated, and it took time to fall asleep in the hammock. I spoke to Peter at length, asking him if he would be able to locate this world from the monitor world (Peter's home level).

Peter smiled, saying, "It is more than possible, Dragon Mage. The monitor I left in the shrine will send out a strong signal, which will help us on the home world to locate this level."

I asked Kleet to take his time when we reached the ship graveyard, so that we could examine the submarines for markings, to see if the one that was there when the orb was taken was there. As we slowly passed by all the ships on the ocean floor, I suddenly recognized one that had the marking on it that the elder land dwellers had remembered from their vessel. I got Kleet to bring his underwater boat as close as possible to the derelict submarine.

Kleet had a questioning look on his face, and said, "How does the dragon mage propose to swim from here to the other boat, which may not have any air in it still, after all of these years?"

I smiled and said, "You will just have to watch and learn, as we perform a feat of magic that will make it possible to walk over there without drowning."

I had Kleet position the underwater boat beside the derelict submarine. The hull of the submarine had the marking that the elders in the shrine remembered. Once the underwater boat was in place, I pulled out the air crystal, concentrating and creating a bubble of air that encompassed both of the vessels. I climbed the ladder and opened the hatch, ignoring Kleet's warning.

Kleet stood there with his mouth open, as no water came in through the hatch! Using a rope, I climbed down to the sandy bottom of the ocean floor, placing my staff between some rocks to steady it. I saw that there was little in the way of kelp or any other plant life in this area of the ocean bottom. I asked Kleet to have a warrior stand guard over the staff so that it was not disturbed, which may have interfered with the spell.

I walked around the submarine, looking to see if there was any damage that caused it to end up in the graveyard of boats, both surface and underwater. The hull was intact as far as I could see. We climbed up to one of the three hatches allowing access to the submarine. Opening the hatch, I noticed the foul odour of stale air. I directed to Kleet to open the other hatches. I told him we would leave the submarine for the day to vent the stale air and allow clean air in, to make searching the inside bearable.

We walked back to the underwater boat, where I spent a restless night tossing and turning. We did not know what we were going to find in the submarine. The next day, as the sun filtered down into the depth of water where we were located, we set out, quickly walking again towards the submarine. The bubble of air was holding quite well and did not seem to be changing size.

We walked back to the submarine, climbing up into the hatch, which still had a stale odour, but the air appeared breathable. Climbing down into the submarine, it appeared to be something out of World War II. This machine was an almost exact duplicate of a diesel submarine from that war, down to the batteries and fuel style.

I felt as though I were walking through a bit of history. The crew were still at their posts, but had obviously been dead for a very long time. The clothing appeared to be a type of uniform, but there was only mummified flesh underneath. Something had killed the entire crew without leaving a mark on their bodies.

I asked Kleet, "Do your elders have any magic that would explain this ability to kill them, without leaving a mark on the bodies?"

After a moment's hesitation, Kleet said, "I do not know. I do not think so, because we of the warrior clan would be told about this type of attack magic."

We searched all the nooks and crannies of the submarine, but could not find the orb anywhere. I believed that the orb must have been taken off the submarine before the crew died, or would it have been after? I searched for any clues that might lead us to the next step in our hunt for the orb, but there was nothing. It was if someone had scoured through the submarine before and cleaned everything up except the deceased crew.

Peter had a monitor out and was scanning the interior of the submarine to make a record for his people back on his home world.

I said, "Peter, I need to find another way to this world to continue searching."

Peter responded, "Yes, but first I must release a special monitor that will float up into the sky and travel with the winds to show where the land is. Otherwise, we could end up in the ocean and perish before we reached land. It is a little hard to transport and swim at the same time."

I laughed at Peter as we walked back to the underwater boat, thinking that this might be one of those unsolvable mysteries. That is, unless the elders were keeping something from the warrior clan, or the land dwellers kept a clean submarine and passed away from another cause.

It seemed to take a shorter amount of time to traverse the portal and end up back in the world of the dragons. I immediately contacted Elijah, and told him what we had found, and what we did not find in our search for the crystal.

Elijah said, "Do not give up hope, Kai. I believe you can still find it somewhere on that world. It is just not where you are initially looking. You must search harder, and in places you would not have looked before."

I travelled back to Elijah's stronghold to spend some time with Sylvia and Rose, who were beginning to show their baby bumps. The ladies in waiting in the stronghold were treating my girls like gold, and not letting them do much for themselves, lest they endanger the unborn babies.

I spent a week with the women, dining and walking through the market with them. To me, this was an important time, to bond and express my undying love for both of them and my unborn children. Gifts began to arrive from other clan lords: cribs, bedding and swaddling clothes. It seemed like a competition to garner favor in my eyes.

Chavez must have had spies nearby, because within the end of the week a large contingent of Orcs suddenly showed up, launching rocks and flaming pieces of tar and wood. Before any preparations were made to respond to the attack, Peter's warriors came up to the parapets with their staffs in hand and created a globe of force around the walls of the stronghold. Other than the first three missiles, everything else struck the shield and fell aimlessly to the ground.

Peter came out and went to talk to some of the warriors, where they had stationed themselves. Returning, he approached me and said, "If the weapons were magical, they might not have been able to maintain the defensive field for too long. But these weapons are just natural and non-magical. The warriors can keep up the fields for as long as they need to, before they get bored and go home.

I smiled at Peter, and said, "Let's see if we can speed that process up. I will just call a few dragons, and if we burn down a few catapults, that ought to hurry things up."

I called, and within a short time three dragons showed up and burnt the catapults to the ground. They left, flying back to their strongholds and leaving the Orcs in shock, because they were set up to protect their positions.

Peter and I looked at the orcs mingling around, and we both laughed. I wondered how long it would take them to realize we were not going to follow through with an attack on their troops.

Peter said, "Now that that issue is dealt with, I want you to come to my world, so that I can show you what has been found on the sea people's home world. Also, if your ladies wish, they can accompany you to my home world, which is a safe and welcoming environment. They will be my guests and will be escorted around our main city to show them our wonders that have been accumulated over the centuries."

I said, "Thank you, Peter. I am sure that Lady Sylvia and Princess Rose would be ecstatic to travel to your world, rather than being cooped up here in this stronghold."

Of course, the women were getting a little stir crazy, not being allowed to go out in the woods even to pick flowers without a large group of warriors to guard them. As soon as I broached the subject, I received my answer, which was a big "Yes!" The ladies then spent the next few hours gathering the essentials that they might need (which, of course, was more than any man would pack).

By later in the day, we were ready to go and gathered in the center of the stronghold. Peter and four of his warrior companions gathered around us. One moment we were in the stronghold, and then the next we were in Peter's world on a piece of grass, watching people wandering back and forth within ten feet of where we were standing.

We were escorted to the nearest transit center, and we boarded a very large and ornate car, which whisked us away toward our destination.

I asked Peter, "Pulling out all the stops and trying to impress the ladies?"

Peter laughed, and replied, "This is the largest car that we have, other than a troop carrier. I just felt this was more appropriate for ladies to ride in. This car is used for dignitaries from our world and the few worlds where we allow travel from other realms."

We travelled for a good ten minutes, coming to a stop in front of what appeared to be a fancy hotel in the world that I came from. Several of Peter's people seemingly came out of nowhere, and took the bags into one of their magical elevators. I explained to the women that there was no danger in these little boxes, and that we would be whisked up without having to climb the stairs several floors, like in the stronghold back home.

Rose said, "Sounds like a lazy way to do things, when walking helps to keep you fit and ready for battle."

I laughed, "I guess that is one of the penalties of progress, my dear."

When the elevator came to a halt, more attendants were waiting to show Rose and Sylvia the luxurious suite of rooms that was decorated with fantastic items that must have come from other worlds, picked up by the monitor people in their travels.

As darkness fell, the city lit up and created a beautiful glow, giving an appearance of a false twilight. We walked out on the balcony and stood admiring the city and the transportation below. What struck me most was the clean, clear air and the almost silent traffic. You could see the lights of moving vehicles, but they were almost silent because of the magical motive power for these vehicles, which did not cause any pollution.

Food, consisting mostly of vegetables and fruits, with some meat thrown in, was brought up to our suite of rooms. The meat was bland, hinting to me that the monitor people were strict vegetarians and the meat dish was just for us guests. This was confirmed more so for me when the vegetable and fruit dishes were done up with lots of flavor.

Peter showed up shortly after we finished dinner and said, "I want to take you to our Hall of Records, where we keep a history of all the levels we have visited or are monitoring. We can show you wonders like you have never seen before. We will go in the morning, Dragon Mage and ladies. Sleep well. You are well-guarded, and nothing will be allowed to enter these rooms without passing all of our safeguards and the lives of a dozen handpicked warriors."

THIRTY-TWO

The Hall of Secrets

The night was spent cuddling both of my girls in the giant bed that was in the main bedroom of the suite. Breakfast consisted of juices and fruits of unknown types that were delicious. After our servers left the room with the plates and glasses, Peter showed up as if he was waiting just outside the door for us to break our fast.

Peter said, "Are you ready for the grand tour, as you would call it?"

I smiled, "Of course, my friend. We are eager to see what you have to show us." Peter led us back to the elevators and the ladies were a little more relaxed this time, as nothing bad had happened yesterday when they rode the elevator for the first time.

This time when the door opened, it was obvious that we were underground. There were three cars waiting for us. Peter stepped into the middle car, and the warriors got into the cars in front of and behind us. Once everyone was inside of each of the cars, they took off right away, headed along the road in what appeared to me to be a different direction from the one we arrived in.

We travelled for more than ten minutes, eventually coming above ground outside of the city. The fields were ready for harvest, and the rabbit people were picking fruit from trees and cutting down what appeared to be wheat as we passed.

There was a large tower in the distance, surrounded by low-lying single level buildings. Everything was rounded out, flowing, and not square. It looked like a three dimensional work of art, and it appeared that this building and outbuildings were placed in this location deliberately

I asked Peter about the placement, and he said, "It is one of the blank spaces. It generates a field that cannot sustain a portal or the trans-dimensional movement of my people. The field is natural. When we began to travel from one world to another, we found a few places like this that can be protected without any enemies transporting in unseen."

This was the first time I had seen any type of tight security exhibited by the monitor people. One of the warriors at the entrance approached Peter and challenged him, asking him what his business was at this temple of knowledge. It took several minutes while Peter and the warrior were deep in conversation. The warrior stepped away for a few minutes and then returned. He apologized to Peter, and opened the door into the building.

Peter said, "The building is broken down to basic society and the more complex civilizations. We will start the tour with the more basic of worlds, and work our way up to the more complex." Peter led us through the building, pointing out the different worlds that were projected up on screens in the different rooms. Peter said, "It is nice to take a stroll through the hall, looking at the projections. Although we could stay in one room and call up all the projections, that is a little boring unless you are a student studying different planes of existence."

"For ease of use, each group is broken down to a similar level. The first ones you will see are those where life has not developed beyond the moss and lichen levels, and the seas are mostly algae, with seafood just starting to evolve," Peter carried on in a running commentary.

As we stepped into the next room, it was like stepping into another world. You could hear the wind and almost feel the warmth of the sun as shone down in the simulation.

Peter said, "If the world was toxic with anything that would hurt our people, we would know beforehand, as we send monitors through to survey the lay of the land, as your people would say, Dragon Mage."

I nodded and Peter continued, "That is not to say that we have not lost any of our travelers. If a traveler falls ill, they can send a message back to this world. Tests can be made by a special monitor to search for something that was perhaps missed in the first searches. When it is determined there is no danger to the home level, the traveler is directed to a special location, where they can be isolated. If a cause cannot be determined, then the traveler stays on that level until they get better or pass from this plane of existence.

I looked at Peter and said, "Obviously some sacrifices have to be made, and I am proud of your travelers that pay the ultimate cost. It is a difficult decision to make and some would not be able to do it. Peter,

I presume that you are very careful about screening those travelers who leave here."

Peter replied, "Yes, Dragon Mage; our guardians are able, with the right tools, to read the minds of candidates, Although we do not tell them, their first mission is false to see if they have the strength to make the right decision. When the choice is made, they wake up as from a dream. Depending on their skills, they may remain working with the monitors, but be unable to travel."

Peter continued, "As we go through these rooms, certain lights will flash briefly. If it is purple, it means that the world is dangerous for some invisible reason—mainly sickness. Usually, if a world does not appear to have any life, but has buildings or other signs of previous occupation, we will not allow one of our people to travel to that world, and only send remote monitors. Or a light will flash red, which means that a traveler has died and that no one else is allowed to that world without special permission."

Peter went on to advise the detail of the intensive investigation that would be done when a traveller died during a visit to another world. All steps would be taken if the traveller died of natural causes or was killed by an animal or inhabitant of that world, to bring him or her back for family mourning.

We spent the entire day viewing worlds of all types, prehistoric worlds and worlds that seemed to be far into the future. I saw worlds where the renaissance was still happening and worlds where cars were flying in the sky and the cities were spread over entire continents.

It was amazing the data that the travellers like Peter had gathered over the centuries and were still collecting. When we came to a series of worlds like mine, Peter made sure to focus on the previous world that I used to call home. We sat in the room and I pointed out things to Sylvia and Rose so that they could get an understanding of where I came from.

Peter then pulled up the world that the sea people had come from, and showed surveillance from airborne monitors that travelled over the land masses. As we were looking at the land flowing below the monitor, I saw a sparkle in the dark and twisted landscape. I asked Peter if we could look closer at the land below, where I had seen the glint. Peter advised that he and I would have to go to the main monitor station in the city, as these monitors did not have the ability of close-up views of the land and people below, because they were designed for students and teachers only, as learning tools.

The sun was starting to set in the sky when Peter and I escorted the women back to our accommodation for a small dinner party put on by Peter and his mate at our temporary residence at the visitors hotel where we were staying. I was surprised that vegetable dishes could be made so flavourful and savory. There was nothing bland except the two meat dishes that were provided for the guests alone.

The next day, Sylvia and Rose went shopping with Peter's mate, who guaranteed that they would be able to find things that appealed to them. The women quickly prepared for a day of shopping, while Peter and I went to the main monitoring station to see if we could enhance some of the pictures we found of the possible location for Pater's Crystal, which was located inside of an orb and staff that had been taken from the underwater temple sometime in the past.

The guardians at the entrance to the central monitoring station had obviously been briefed about my arrival with Peter. They barely gave us a glance, simply nodding and stepping aside so we could gain entry into the building. Once we reached the monitoring floor, Peter led me to a smaller room, with comfortable chairs.

Peter said, "This is one of the secondary monitoring rooms, where we can look closer at images we are receiving from the different monitors. It allows us to examine the worlds in detail, where in the main monitoring room, they do not have the time to scrutinize—other than the rudimentary particulars. We will pull up images from the original world of the sea people and see if we can locate the crystal, keeping in mind that we will only be able to see it if it is outdoors."

We sat for several hours, searching the landscape for any signs of Pater's orb and staff that held the crystal that I needed. The landscape was blighted; there was no grass, no flowers, and the few trees that were visible were stunted and looked desolate, being mere skeletons of what you would expect to see.

I could see in the monitor that there was no visible sign of animals or birds at all. Late in the afternoon, we found a village with a cairn in the centre of the community. There was no sign of movement in the village at all. It was almost as if all of the land dwellers on this world had died off, for some reason.

Using the equipment in the viewing room, we were able to zoom in to get a closer view of the village. The structures appeared to be made of mud. There did not appear to be any wood used in the construction process. Then, as we closely scanned the cairn at the centre of the village, we saw it! That had to be Pater's orb, situated in the top of the cairn on its staff.

I asked Peter, "Is there any way we can get an air sample to determine if there is anything toxic in the environment that might make it dangerous, if not impossible, to survive long enough to recover the staff and orb of Pater?"

Peter sat there for a few minutes thinking about my question and then replied, "It is possible, Dragon Mage, but it is something that we do not do on a regular basis, due to the potential danger to our world. I will have to discuss this with the guardians to determine if the quest outweighs the peril."

* * * * *

It took a couple of days before Peter was able to get back to me with an answer. Peter walked into the rooms I was sharing with my ladies and out to the balcony, where I was enjoying the fresh air and watching the nearly silent flow of traffic down on the streets below. Peter ears were drooping, and his demeanor told me it was not going to be good news.

Peter said, "I went up as far as I could in the leadership, as I was told that unless there was some way that you could ensure the safety of this or any other populated world, the answer would be no. They would not allow you to travel there and back, endangering any other life."

I stared at Peter silently for a short time. Finally, I spoke. "I think I have a solution in mind, but it will entail a lot of explanation and some education to make you understand." Peter looked at me with hope in his eyes. I asked, "Can you record images that we view, and edit them to make a presentation to your council?"

Peter said, "Of course. The images at the viewing library are all recordings. We would not want to scare the young ones with some traumatic event, like the death of someone into the jaws of a dinosaur."

I replied, "Good. Let's go to the monitoring tower and I will show you a few things from my old world and my new world, which might make things possible. We know that the oceans on that world are slowly healing. I surmise that the air is not breathable because of the land dwellers polluting the air and oceans, not realizing the danger to themselves until it was too late."

Peter replied, "I would love to be able to help you in any way that I can, as you have saved me from being someone's display item, perhaps stuffed and mounted on a wall."

I laughed at Peter as we entered the central monitoring station, and spent the next two days showing him what I had in mind and what we could do to reduce any risk to any of the worlds. As it turned out, once the proposal was formulated, Peter's people had contacts in one of the more advanced civilizations, and was able to procure the equipment needed.

We built a block house on a world that had never developed beyond the level of plant life, but the oceans were teeming with sea life. Nothing had ventured onto the land to develop further, the sea life was evolving, and some species seemed to have become intelligent. The block house was completely sealed, with a ventilation system that would force air into the portal that we would create, preventing anything from entering the world.

Peter had arranged for the materials, and we had custom-made environmental suits that were self-contained with six hours of air. That way, we did not have to risk breathing the air and risking any contamination.

Our party consisted of only four, to reduce the possibility of anyone getting infected by any bacteria in the air. The team consisted of Godfrey, Peter, a portal wizard (Lazarus) and me. The hardest part was finding a wizard who was willing to take the risk for this undertaking. Peter and his people had an innate sense of location, and were able to have the block house placed in a location just outside the village where Pater's crystal was located. We would not enter the world with the aid of Peter, as the displaced air from his travel might come with him. If it carried any bacteria, it could be incredibly dangerous.

We started off on Peter's world, where his contact explained the workings of the environmental suit and how to seal it. The suits were designed to start the air flow once they were sealed properly, and then we would only have six hours before the air ran out. They had done an excellent job customizing the suits for Peter and the rest of us; no small feat, since Peter's contact had four arms, was six feet tall, and had feathers.

Once we were all outfitted in our environmental suits, Peter had us all link hands as we travelled inside the block house, which had no doors or windows. It was designed to push air through the portal from this world to the next, and when the fans stopped, it sealed automatically. Nothing could enter or exit the block house without the use of magic.

Once the suits were sealed, Lazarus created an opening into the other world, where the crystal was. Lazarus was instructed that when his air got low, he was to seal the portal and remain in the block house. If we did not return, this was a one way trip with no hope of going home and possibly infecting others with some unknown disease. But knowing the risks, and with his loyalty to the dragon clans, Lazarus had volunteered to help the dragon mage in any way he could.

I strapped my gun and a sword outside of my suit, and carried my staff as we walked through the portal into a land of desolation and death. We could feel a strong breeze at our backs, as the powerful fans in the block house pushed air through the portal behind us. We were on top of a small hillside, looking down at the village and beach below.

The only sounds I could hear were my breathing and the occasional snap of a dead branch as one of my companions stepped on it as we walked toward the village. As noted in the monitoring station, there was no movement at all; no animals or insects could even be seen.

When we reached the outskirts of the village, we spread out so that if we were attacked, one of us would be able to help the other before being overwhelmed by an enemy. As it turned out, we did not need to worry. As we looked into the first dwelling, all that was visible were skeletal remains of the previous occupants.

We searched the entire village, with the same results; there was nothing alive in the village. I walked over to the cairn that held the staff of Pater, examining it closely to ensure that there were no booby traps. When I pulled the staff out of the cairn, I could suddenly feel a strong humming in the air which went down to my very core.

I looked around at my two companions and asked, "Do you feel or hear that humming?"

Both Godfrey and Peter nodded their agreement, and I said to them, "I think it is time that we left this area immediately. It seems to be some sort of alarm, and I do not want to see if there is anything living that is going to show up in response to it!"

As I said this I saw something crawl onto the beach and start heading towards the cairn. It almost defied description, being a combination of machine and something else. I momentarily froze, staring at this thing that looked like something out of a horror movie.

Godfrey and Peter ran for the portal. I placed my staff between the creature and me. I activated the air crystal and created a bubble around the creature, which was closing the distance between us rapidly. The creature came up to the barrier between us and I got a close look it. It was a combination of human body parts and mechanical features that sent a shiver down my spine. The eyes were definitely of a human type species, looking at me with anger and an unsatisfied hunger.

The teeth were razor sharp metal and the back was covered in plates that overlapped. Looking closely, I could see four sets of arms and hands that the creature used for locomotion. The arms had armour plate and some sort of protective gloves on each hand.

I had the tiger by the tail, so to speak, and I could not let it go, as it moved incredibly fast and may have been able to take all of my team, including me, out. I concentrated and created a fireball inside the sphere of force generated and surrounding the creature. Fortunately, the circle was very strong and the creature had no magic to break down the barrier, because the moment I started a spark inside with the creature, the air exploded.

The sphere held, although the ground shook beneath my feet, knocking me off my feet. I did not wait for the explosion to completely settle, as I did not want to light this world on fire. I slowly contracted the sphere to the size of a baseball and placed it into a pocket of the suit.

I walked to the entry of the portal and could feel the breeze blowing through the invisible opening. As we stepped through the portal, I heard Lazarus breathe a sigh of relief.

I said, "You weren't worried, Lazarus, that we would not make it back in time, and you would be stuck here—were you?"

I could see Lazarus blush bright red, as he tried to hide his face in shame, thinking I thought he might be a coward.

I placed my hand on his shoulder and said, "I do not dishonour you, my friend. I have a longer life span, and I could not bear to have to await death in this box either." Lazarus smiled slightly and bowed in reply to my comment.

We shed the environmental suits as the air continued to flow past us, kicking them to the floor near the portal entrance. I instructed

Lazarus to close the portal, but to stand as far away from it as possible. Lazarus was able to stand five feet back and enact the spell to close the portal. I had erected a magical barrier using the air crystal. The portal snapped shut and the air pressure started to build up before the fans stopped running.

I looked at Peter and said, "Take the others back, and I will incinerate the inside of this building to ensure that there is no bacteria, or anything harmful, left over. Give me ten minutes before returning, and land fifty feet away to ensure there is not enough heat to injure you when you return."

Peter nodded, signalled the others to link hands, and popped back to his world, with nothing but displaced air to show where he and the others had stood. I surrounded myself in flames and dropped the barrier that was blocking where the portal had been. I slowly increased the heat, and the environmental suits started to melt and burn. The air tanks were busy venting from the heat. I extended a shield, like an invisible umbrella, to protect my head. The walls and ceiling were turning to dust from the heat, as everything was consumed by the flames.

The block house crumbled around me, and the grass around it rapidly caught fire. I walked through the spreading flames quickly. As soon as I reached a spot that was not burning, I cast a spell enclosing the entire area of grass that was burning and the block house.

The fire was quickly extinguished, and I was able to close the sphere so that it just contained the heat around the block house. As I stood there watching over everything and the block house as it crumbled from the intense heat, I heard the pop of displaced air behind me.

I said, "This was the reason I wanted you to keep away from the block house. I was unsure about how much heat I could generate and what effect it would have to sterilize everything. Just about ready to head back, Peter, and relax for a couple of days before doing some more planning."

Peter said from behind me, "Whenever you are ready, Dragon Mage. I will just sit and relax in the shade of this nearby tree and await your command."

For the next few hours, I sat watching the glow of the block house dim. I closed the sphere and there was a little heat still radiating from where the block house had been. It was now safe, and I strolled up to the tree that Peter had sat down and subsequently fallen asleep under. Once he was awake, we travelled back to his world and I went to the apartments that had been set aside for my ladies and me.

I spent the next two days sleeping and eating, building up my energy. I did not realize how much energy I had expended destroying the creature and turning the block house to cinders to prevent any bacteria from spreading. I sent for a dragon clan small dragon to deliver a message to the sea people, that I had to meet with a representative as soon as possible. As it turned out, Flit flew into the rooms within thirty minutes. Once he had the message, he assured me that he would deliver it immediately and get back to me by the next day with an answer.

Peter came into the rooms the next morning and advised that Flit would meet me back at my stronghold, and that he had an answer for me already. The women had been busy, and it took a little extra help to pack and carry all their purchases down to the transition point where Peter ported us back to the Dragon world.

Flit was waiting patiently, sitting on a dwarf's shoulder, looking expectantly to talk to me. He said, "I have spoken to the sea people and advised them that you had urgent and important information that had to be relayed to them. They will have someone here with authority to speak to you by tomorrow."

I had the guards make sure that the sea entrance to the stronghold was open, as I knew that this would probably be the way that the sea people would visit the stronghold. Within a few hours I received a report of a submarine pulling into the dock with sea people disembarking, and asking for the dragon mage.

I walked down to the sea entrance and found Shree, with Kleet and a contingent of warriors as his bodyguard. I bowed deeply in greeting to Shree as the eldest in the group.

He bowed as well in reply to my greeting and said, "You called us, Dragon Mage, and we are eager to greet you and hear what you have to tell us."

I led them into a room that had been set up nearby so they did not have to travel too far in the dry air, which would be uncomfortable for the sea people. I had Peter with me, and I asked Shree and his followers to view the monitor to see the entire encounter on their old home world. I sat back and watched for any reaction on the part of the sea people, and was able to see them jump back when the creature came out of the ocean.

Shree asked, "Is this an accurate depiction of what occurred on our old world when you went to recover Pater's staff with the crystal that you wanted inside of it?"

I looked at him, positioning myself squarely in front of Shree and his bodyguard. I said, "Yes, I am the one who came face to face with the creature that you can see here. Nothing has been edited out of the monitoring of the village and the incident that happened. I can say that I was shocked and disgusted by the appearance of the creature that crawled out of the ocean. I wanted you to be aware that there may be others similar to this creature. We can assist you with closing the portal to your old world if you wish. Otherwise, I am not sure we can risk the potential threat to this world that the sea people have settled in."

Shree asked if there was some way the information and the visual display could be taken with them to show to the sea people council of elders.

I looked at Peter, who nodded his head yes, and said, "It will take a couple of days for us to get the equipment together and prepped to transport to where the other elders of the sea people can view it."

I indicated to Shree that there were several rooms with pools for the comfort of Shree and his bodyguards, if they wished to remain until the equipment was ready to load on the submarine to be transported to the sea people enclave.

Shree agreed to stay to wait for things to be ready. I guaranteed that his safety was paramount in my mind and I doubled the guard around the submarine and the sea gate to ensure the protection of our visitors.

It did not take as much time as Peter thought it would, and the equipment was loaded in the submarine within record time. I took Gizmo with me and went with Peter to join Shree and his bodyguards.

Entering the submarine, Kleet said to me, "I guarantee your safety on my life. If for any reason there is any threat, my warriors will stand in the way of danger to protect you."

I replied to Kleet, "My brother, I am overwhelmed by the offer of your warriors standing in place of me to take a fatal blow. There has only been one other so far in my time in this world who has put himself in danger and has died for me. His name was Joshua, and he will be remembered in my life and beyond for the sacrifice he placed himself in. If any of your warriors has to make the extreme sacrifice, he or she will be remembered in the annals of history as a hero who saved the life of the dragon mage."

Kleet said in reply, with awe in his voice, "Nothing greater could be asked for in our lives. The warrior clan lives for their names to be remembered down through history in the annals of our people."

We stepped into the submarine of the sea people and began the two day journey to the island where the elders were meeting. It was an uneventful journey, with no problems. We had only a few close encounters with some of the huge sea creatures, which gave us a wide berth as the submarine drifted by.

We arrived within two days, coming up to the dock and exiting the submarine with all of the equipment. The sea people directed us to place the apparatus in the appropriate place for the leaders to view the details of the incident in the village at their old world.

I waited in nearby lodging while the recording of the incident was played back to the elders of the sea people. I was told later that they reviewed the footage several times before they began deliberations. It took a couple of days before the elders came to a decision.

Shree came to me with his bodyguard in tow and said, "The decision is made that we will recall all our people from the ocean and close the portal to our old world. Kleet will take you and whoever is required to the portal and through to bring the other vessels back and close the portal behind you for the last time."

I took Kleet with me and headed to my stronghold as rapidly as we could in the submarine, which meant a journey of two days. Upon arrival at the stronghold, I arranged for Lazarus and Gizmo to join us to travel to the undersea portal to seal the entryway into the original world of the sea people and gather the submarines to return to their new homeland.

As we approached the area of the portal, I saw several of the creatures that I had dealt with on the old world of the sea people. These creatures were attacking one of the submarines, tearing it apart so that it could not ever be used again.

As we stood off from the submarine being attacked and the other sub standing by, unable to do anything to attack these sentinel creatures from the old world, I had Kleet signal the one sub to stand back and the one being attacked to abandon ship. As soon as the sea people were clear of the submarine and safely back at our ship I created an air bubble around each of the creatures and closed it. It was like a giant hand. I was able to crush the monster down to the size of a baseball and move on to the next one.

I could feel my energy level dropping, and I realized that I did not add Pater's crystal to the staff to make it whole completely. I looked at Gizmo briefly, not wanting to take my eyes off the enemy, and said "Take the globe out of my gear and smash it. Inside there will be a crystal. Hand the crystal to me so that I may add it to the staff to enhance the power to fight these creatures."

Gizmo flew off my shoulder and I could hear her searching through my gear and rolling the globe to the floor. I did not dare take my eyes off the creatures in the depths, but I could hear the shattering of the globe on the deck of the submarine. Gizmo could be heard scrabbling on the deck, and then she landed on my shoulder with something in her mouth.

I instructed Kleet to grab the other staff that was with my equipment. He came back rapidly and handed me the dragon staff. I reached out and smashed the globe on top of the air staff. I took Pater's crystal from Gizmo, and felt along the staff, placing it, too, in the appropriate recess that was obviously meant to hold the crystal. I could feel the surge of power along the staff; creatures seemed to suddenly realize that they were outgunned and started to head back through the portal.

I encapsulated the creatures that I could see as well as the submarine that they were demolishing, into a bubble of air. I was able to melt the creatures and the remnants of the submarine into a mass inside the bubble of air. I closed the circle around the two, crushing the creatures and sub into an object the size of a large world globe. I pushed the entire ball back through the portal, and Lazarus immediately began to close the portal with the appropriate spell. I could feel the power being cut off from my spell, weakening as the portal was closed. I could sense the closure of the opening like the slamming of a door.

I directed Kleet to signal the other submarine to search the area in case one of the sentinels was missed and may be still in this world's oceans. I had a bad feeling that there may have been one or two of the creatures left behind that were missed in the attack. They could cause a lot of damage if they were able to replicate more of the creatures and attack the sea people or others on the land, and I had witnessed their speed.

I now possessed the complete magical staff Draco with the Dragon crystal, the Air crystal and Pater's crystal, which made it the most powerful item of magic in the whole dragon world. I spent the next few days recuperating from my battle with the creatures from the sea people's home world; I felt exhausted down to my core.

Elijah advised that this was not unusual, as I was not attuned to Pater's staff. With all of crystals in place, it took more from me than it would once it was perfected to work with me.

THIRTY-THREE

Fire Bug?

About a week after returning to my stronghold and spending important time with my ladies, I received word that I was needed at the Diamond stronghold. I quickly rushed through the dungeon portals, entering into Elijah's presence within a few minutes of being summoned.

As I entered Elijah's room, he looked up and immediately dismissed everyone else from his presence. Elijah said, "There is something odd happening at an Orc fort located in the Northern prairie. We received intelligence from our sources advising that the fort has suddenly burnt to the ground for an unknown reason. However, there is still something there—glowing. It is generating so much heat that no one could get near to it. We think it might have a bit of sky material that sometimes falls to earth, but we are not sure."

I replied laughingly, "I presume you would like the dragon mage to look into it, as he is fireproof."

Elijah laughed, "Yes, that would be the gist of it, yes. Plus, it may be an item of power that the orcs have lost control over."

I called Mercury with my mind, and directed him to the nearest stronghold, to the location of this strange event. I told him that I would set out the next day and meet him when he was ready to investigate this area. My companion guardians showed up, and Ice Wind took his snow people out into the Northern prairie to scout the area ahead of us, to ensure there were no enemies hiding in the tall grass to ambush us.

When we arrived in the area where the orc fort had stood, we found a small contingent of orcs still in the area that was untouched by fire. My men spread out to search the surrounding prairie to determine just how many of the enemy were there.

Tomar the dark elf came to me and said, "We have located all of their sentries. There are only fifty orc warriors and a couple of dark wizards to deal with. You have but to say the word and we will start dispatching the enemy."

I replied, "Start now. Take out the sentries, and I will check out what they are doing in the centre where the glow is." Tomar nodded and ran off, and I tried to find a safe vantage point where I could see what was happening. There were a dozen orc warriors with long metal pikes, prodding at something that was down in a pit at the centre of the gutted fort.

I wanted to wait until my companion warriors had taken care of the other troops. I did not want to have to worry about someone coming up behind me while I was concentrating on what was going on. Tomar came back within a half-hour to advise that the rest of the orc contingent had been dealt with.

The sun had set by the time we were ready to challenge the orcs at the centre of the destroyed fort. I stepped into the torchlight, pulling my pistol out, and quickly dispatched the two orc dark wizards, killing them before they even realized I was there. My companions took care of the other ten orcs that were poking at something in the pit. I could feel the heat emanating from the pit, and looking down, all I could see initially was what looked like hot coals from a glowing fire. The heat was more than any of my companions could tolerate, and they had to step aside. Mercury had shown up to the devastated area, and was peering over my shoulder, looking down into the pit.

Mercury said, "Dragon Mage, there are few who have the opportunity to see such a sight in their lives. For down there is an extremely rare creature, a fire salamander. The orcs were probably hoping to use it as a weapon, but salamanders can be very quick to anger, and then it is better to just run. That is, unless you are a dragon or dragon mage, and can handle the heat—which would burn anyone else to cinders."

I smiled at Mercury, and slowly walked down the gentle slope of the pit to see this creature that I had not yet noticed. As I reached the bottom of the pit, I could see the salamander, which was a lizard about two feet in length. I grabbed the salamander gently and picked it up, placing it against my chest and cuddling it like a family pet. Initially it blazed out heat, but the longer I held the salamander against me the cooler it became, until it was a gentle heat, warming me.

I said, "I will call you Spirit, my little friend," as the salamander seemed to nuzzle me, digging itself into my chest and letting out a slight whine of pleasure. I walked out of the pit as the glow of the embers started to die down, leaving the site of the fort dark. The stars could be seen again as darkness encompassed the land.

As I walked out of the pit, Mercury said, "It looks like the dragon mage has a new pet to play with."

Once again I simply smiled at Mercury, and walked away from the site. I headed back to the portal at the nearest stronghold, to go home.

When I reached my stronghold, I stopped and talked to some artisans about building a box for my new pet. I instructed them that it had to be lined with something that would not burn, and had to be soft enough for the salamander to sleep in. The dwarf artisans were up for the task, building an ebony box that was made of something called dragon wood, which would not normally burn except at exceptionally high temperatures.

The box was lined with some sort of brick and some soft material that would normally line a dragons nest. The soft material, it turned out, was made from empty casings of dragon eggs. Like fibreglass, it was heat resistant, but could be used for a special material.

Once the ebony box was finished, the salamander that I named Spirit snuggled into it, making little sounds of pleasure while happily settling into his nest. I mused to myself that I was building an unusual entourage, and that nothing else would surprise me. Or would it?

I travelled to Elijah's old stronghold in the North with Spirit and brought him down to where the furnaces were kept running, to warm the stronghold. I placed Spirit into the furnace and he nestled into the fire, which immediately began to generate ample quantities of heat to warm the entire stronghold.

After greeting and having a meeting with the dragons of the household, I gathered my little Spirit into my arms and placed him in his comfortable box, where I left him sleeping. It only took me moments to return back to my stronghold, where I could rest.

I was incredibly tired after all the events of the last few days, so I planned on taking it easy for the next few days. I lay in bed, falling into a deep sleep.

I entered a dream state, where I found myself wandering in an open field of tall grass. The grass was moving against the wind, in different patterns that were not natural. Looking down at myself, I saw that I was clad only in my work uniform from before I left my home world, but I had no weapons of any kind or magical tools.

As I stood there in the dream, I could see the grass moving against the wind and headed in my direction. I watched in terror, unable to move or even scream as the creature I had seen at the old world of the sea people crawled out of the grass, creeping up on me. As I stood there, the creature lunged toward me, but stopped suddenly as a shadow came down from above, scaring the creature away.

I stood in silence, watching this new being float down in front of me. I saw the wings, the armour, and the blazing sword. I could not tell gender, but the name came to mind without any hesitation.

He turned to me after the sentinel creature fled, and said, "I Am Michael." I bent down on my knees, looking at the patron saint of police officers: Saint Michael, the Archangel and guardian angel of the gates of heaven.

I bolted awake, sitting up in bed, and listened to the early morning sounds that calmed my pounding heart. I could not perceive why I would have had that dream. I had never had a dream involving angels—only evil and the bearers of pain and suffering. I found my St. Michael medal in my hand when I woke up. I thought that I had lost the medal a long time ago, and never expected to find it again. The medal was hot in my hand.

I walked slowly down to Elijah's chambers, to discuss this unusual dream, which plagued me. I asked Elijah if he had any idea of what the dream meant.

Elijah replied, "I have shared your vision, and I do not know what you have seen. I have never seen this type of creature before. But then again, we have never had someone like you, who believes in a different god than those who have worshiped us. We have never claimed to be gods, but have only tried to lead the dwarves, and those who deal with them, with patience and understanding."

I did not know what the future held for my new family and I. As I walked out of the underground chambers that were the home of the great dragon Elijah, I was approached by Peter. He seemed to be concerned about something.

Peter said, "We have been monitoring the world, and we have found a large tear in the fabric of space. It is not a natural portal—it is something more than we have seen before."

We rushed to the keep and the monitor room, where Peter's people were trying to watch over this world. We could see a large group that appeared to have set up camp just this side of the tear. A closer examination of the group showed what appeared to be humans of normal stature in a group set up in a defensive perimeter.

I called Mercury with my mind, and spoke to a messenger to arrange for my troops to come to the nearest keep, to investigate the new arrivals to this land. Mercury would arrive by the end of the day, entering the stronghold through the dungeon portals. We were greeted, and the troops were quickly given food to eat and beds for the night. When Mercury arrived, he was shown down to the chambers near the resident dragon, a female who protected this stronghold, where he could rest.

We set out at first light, spreading out. I sent Mercury ahead to fly high above the new visitors. The dwarves were in marching formation, and making good time. The troops from the other races in my group of guardians could not be seen, as they were all skilled in stealthy movement.

As we grew close to this new group, Mercury called to me, "Hold off, Dragon Mage. There is a large group of something coming through the tear."

I asked him, "Can you give me any details on who or what they are? Are they interacting with the group that is already here, or just ignoring them?"

Mercury replied, "Stand by. They are pointing some sort of weapon at the existing group, and the group is pointing some sort of similar thing back at them, but nothing is happening. Both sides have dropped the weird weapons and the humans have drawn swords. The other creatures are attacking with claws."

Claws? I wondered what sort of creature these things were, but first I had to separate the combatants and see if I could calm things down. I signaled the troops to hold back and not get involved until I determined which side we might support if I could not broker a truce between the two groups on this field of battle.

I drove my staff Draco into the ground and concentrated, creating a bubble of force around the group of humans. Then I stood waiting for both sides to realize they could not reach each other. There were a few creatures inside the human lines, but they were dispatched quickly by the humans when more of their number did not enter the fray.

I got a closer look at the creatures as they worked their way around the perimeter of bubble. The word that came to mind was ant. The creatures had four legs, and had four arms, starting in the upper area of the thorax, and ending in claws that looked razor-sharp. The head had the typical compound eyes and sharp mandibles that could do severe damage to a foe.

I waited patiently for the ant people to notice me, and to see what their reaction would be. When they noticed me and my dwarf contingent, one of the creatures, wearing some sort of armor on its thorax, as well as some beads around its neck (which I presumed indicated rank), walked over to us. It was followed by twenty more of its compatriots. The rest of their horde held positions just outside of the field of force, facing the humans inside, ready to pounce the minute the wall of force went down.

The first words out of its face were a series of hisses and clicks.

I looked at it and stated, "I am sorry, but I do not understand what you are saying."

The creature stopped for a minute, looking at me and my group of guardian dwarves, then started again, then spoke again, saying, "I am (a series of clicks and hisses that I could not begin to spell or even hope to pronounce). You will kneel before us and submit to be our slaves or we will destroy you."

As I stood there contemplating my response to this request to surrender without even lifting an arm in defence, I suddenly felt the warmth of a mind that I had grown greatly attached to.

Gizmo landed on my shoulder and said to me, "They are a hive mind. They come and devour. They build a large nest on each world they encounter, and set up a queen to run the new empire. The others, the humans, are enemies from a level that worships one god. They have been able to hold their own up to this point. They are searching for allies in their battle to protect the home level."

I looked at the creature and said, "This is my answer," and I pulled my revolver out and shot it in the center of its head. I then ordered all troops, including Mercury, to engage the enemy. I told Mercury to focus on the rift where the creatures came through, to prevent any more reinforcements from entering this world. I laid down fire around the enclosed humans, and my troops made short work of the remaining creatures that had headed to attack us.

Locating the world that the tear was anchored in first, I then made the tear close and sealed it, to prevent any more of the creatures from crossing over. I walked to where Draco was implanted in the ground, dispersing the shield. I signalled my troops to step back, and they disappeared into the surrounding area.

I stood there as one of the humans approached. I recognized the symbol that historically indicated, in my world, the Templar Knights; an order of the catholic church. One of the knights approached, and spoke in a thick British accent.

He said, "I am Sir Justin, of the Order of the Templars, Protector of the Faith and His Holiness the Pope—Jason the Second. Thank you for your assistance in dealing with those devils, the horde. But now you must die, as you are a practitioner of the dark arts. If you hold still, I will make this as quick and painless as possible."

I replied to Sir Justin, "Unfortunately, I cannot allow you to take my life, as I am needed to help this world gain its freedom from someone truly evil." I signalled, and my guardians came out of hiding. They spread out to balance themselves, and were ready to attack the knight and his troops. Sir Justin drew his sword and prepared to engage me in battle.

All of a sudden, Sir Justin and all of his men went down on one knee, bowing their heads as if in prayer. I felt a breeze, and a shadow fell over me. I looked up, as an angel settled down on the ground between me and the Templars. I quickly signalled my troops to pull back and wait for the attack command. I recognized Michael the Archangel from my dream. He turned to me, nodded, and then turned his attention to the Templar troops.

Michael said to Sir Justin, "You shall not harm the dragon mage Jim. He has been marked for greatness, and is blessed. Whoever kills him, or tries to, will be condemned to hell, regardless of how pure of heart he is. I am setting the task of assisting the dragon mage and protecting him to you."

Sir Justin replied, looking confused, "But he is a wizard—a dealer in the dark arts. By the order of the Pope, he must be executed and his body burned!"

"Pope Jason will receive his orders from On High, when the time is right," Michael said. "Things are stable on this world at the moment. It is our wish that the dragon mage help rid your world of the horde, which is evil."

I looked at Michael with a smile on my face and said, "It appears that I have volunteered my help before even being asked."

Michael smiled at me in return, nodded his head in what seemed to be satisfaction, and then flew off—leaving me to deal with the Templars.

I invited Sir Justin to the nearest stronghold, where his men would be safe from roaming dinosaurs that could kill them, since they were unaware of the dangers of this world. They had two tank-like machines, as well as a possible siege engine for taking out large groups. These machines, like my police car, would rust away, not able to work here.

I arranged for a few large Ankylosaurs, hauling flat trailers, to come to this camp to load up the vehicles and haul them, along with the wounded, to the stronghold. Some of the dead ants were placed on another, because I wanted to examine the creatures to determine what we were facing as a threat.

I called out with my mind to Elijah, "We have a situation developing of unknown consequences. I don't yet know what it will grow into."

Elijah replied, "Yes, Gizmo has informed me of what has transpired, and I am intrigued. Especially since someone from your dreams showed up and stopped those men from trying to kill you."

Sir Justin talked with me over a delicious meal, which was served by Susan. I had to restrain him when the drakes entered the room, as Sir Justin called them hell hounds, and was ready to fight them with his sword. He was a little hesitant when Matilda walked over and started to make nice, licking his hand and wagging her rear end in happiness. He slowly began to become comfortable, petting Matilda and smiling as she lay against him.

Justin said, "It is an amazing creature. There is a description in the historical documents of the church, showing pictures and weak points of these beings. The holy church says these are atrocities of the devil, and must be destroyed if a warrior comes across one. Nothing has prepared us to study the animals and other creatures of our world. When we first arrived, there were many beasts that we had to battle to survive, so that may be why we do not trust them. As well, there were wizards and witches who tried to take advantage of us."

THIRTY-FOUR

Templar's World

J ustin settled comfortably in a deep chair, and began to tell me the story of his people. It was vaguely familiar to me, and may have initiated in my home world.

Justin explained that the Knights Templar were in the midst of a great injustice, in the Year of our Lord 1307. They gathered several villages in their area and fled through a gate that one of their holy missionaries had found in his search for God. The king of France was putting Templars on trial for heresy and witchcraft, seizing all their assets, and then burning them at the stake. Once they had settled the new land, his people picked volunteers to go back and scout out what was transpiring, but the spies could no longer find the gateway again. It had now been lost for hundreds of years.

Sir Justin explained that, aside from the strange creatures, they found a group of short-statured people in the new land, who were welcoming to their guidance and beliefs. They settled and built up the land, helping the people they conquered to till the land. After fifty years, the first pope was selected, and took the name John the First.

What surprised me most was the level of technology Sir Justin's people had reached, given the fact that the church was in control of scientific research and development. Justin explained that there were different branches of the brother monks that dealt with health, technology, and faith.

Each branch jealously guarded its secrets, and the monks in each group were the only ones allowed to work in their area of expertise. They started out as monks, working up to priest, and each wore a different colour to represent their field: blue for medical, red for machines, and black for the ecumenical and most powerful arm of the church. Members of the enforcement branch of the church wore a cross, positioned where their hearts would be, emblazoned over their tunics.

Justin was more than willing to go into detail about all of the arms of the church, with the exception of the enforcement arm. He advised that this was not a subject that was spoken of with strangers, as you never knew when you might be under investigation for heresy (this sounded a lot like the inquisition during the dark ages in my world).

As a nobleman, Justin had a vague understanding of the hierarchy. The church was in charge of teaching all of the noble families. The Templar Knights consisted of nobles who were already knighted. Their household armies answered to the knights, who answered to the holy church.

All Justin could say was that the power of their vehicles, weapons, and the power that ran the heat and light for the people was a holy power of the sun. I wondered if they had discovered nuclear power to run everything.

Justin explained that little was known about the horde, since they had showed up around ten years previously. Weapons and defences had to be developed to cope with the invasion of the horde. They had never captured one of the horde alive or dead, because they took their dead with them.

A messenger interrupted Justin's narration of the history of his people, to advise that Godfrey and some healers with him had finished examining several dead bodies of the horde creatures, and wished to speak with me to advise what they had found. We walked together to where Godfrey had set up a few tables covered with body parts of the horde creatures.

Godfrey looked up as we entered the room and motioned us over, saying, "From our limited experience with something as strange as this creature, we are able to make a few conclusions. The dragons have had more knowledge of general anatomy, and have been a great help. All of these creatures that we have recovered are without any sexual organs, which is typical of the ants that they appear to be.

"They have a poison gland and their mandibles are hollow, allowing a delivery of venom in a single bite. There do not appear to be any offensive weapons, other than their strength. They could probably tear a man apart, if given the opportunity. The point in our favour is that their weapons do not function in this land. They have faster reflexes than the average ogre, but the same strength level. They have a small brain, which might be the reason they answer to one individual in a group. Once you kill their group commander, they continue following their last order, until another leader comes along and countermands it."

"I examined the leader that accosted you. It must have been of the next level up in the hierarchy of the horde. It had a larger brain, and was stronger and faster than the others it was commanding. If we had to face only this example of the horde, it would make defeating them that much more difficult."

I invited Justin to stay for a few days, so that his troops could rest and recover from the battle at the tear. All his men would be well healed and ready for battle if needed. I called Peter to join us after the next meal period. Justin's mouth could not open more than it did when he saw Peter. We talked to Peter about launching some monitors to see what the world looked like, and what we might be up against if and when we walked in the Templar's world.

I said to Justin, "It will take some doing, but you will have to get used to the different races that are helping me out. If you cannot deal with it, then I will be unable to help you in your endeavours to free your world from the horde."

Justin replied, "It will take time for both me my troops to break centuries of indoctrination from the church, for right or wrong."

Peter said to me, "We have a few drones on Sir Justin's world. If you will come with me to the monitor room, I have images transferred from my world so that you can see what is going on."

Sir Justin looked angry, and said, "I take offence to the fact that some other races are watching my people. Everyone has some expectation of privacy in their own home. Only the enforcement arm of the church watches over people, and I do not agree with that either."

Peter replied, "We only monitor the outside of a dwelling. We have never looked inside any dwelling without the permission of someone of that world, and never without a good reason.

Justin nodded at Peter and said, "That makes me feel better. Thank you, Peter."

When the images came, we could see a lot of produce fields of different sizes, surrounding a castle in the middle. There were ten foot walls with fields of force extending another twenty feet into the air. The castle and town were surrounded by another wall, thirty feet in height, and a domed field of force covering the entire area. Justin explained that the shields of force protected the area from the energy weapons both sides of the conflict had control of.

We watched as the monitor worked its way south, where the grandly-manicured gardens and beautiful forest disappeared, leaving an area of desolation. There stood a huge mound, almost a small mountain, standing over two hundred feet high, and littered with openings. There was a steady stream of ant people going in and out, carrying in supplies and walking out empty-handed.

We could see a small town nearby, with people working in the fields harvesting the crops. The ants stood with weapons ready, watching over them. As we viewed the scene below us, one of the villagers made a run for it! He almost made it to the tree line before he was shot down. A couple of the ants dismembered him, and then, throwing the body on a cart, packed him into the ant mountain. Justin watched on in silent disgust. He looked like he was about to lose his last meal all over the floor.

Justin said, with a dismal look, "I had heard rumours that the ants ate all sorts of fruit and vegetables. as well as all kinds of meat. This obviously proves that the tales were true."

I placed my hand on his shoulder and said, "So it would seem, my friend. The sooner we go to your world and try to sort things out, the better it will be for your people."

I asked Peter, "Can you locate the portal, or tear, where these creatures have entered the world of the Templars? We need to close that first, so that reinforcements cannot come through to help the ones we are battling. Otherwise, they could overwhelm us just by their sheer number. It will be quite the task by itself anyway."

Peter replied, "It will take some time to locate it, but since my people are familiar with the energy overlap, it will be possible. A portal and a tear in the fabric of the worlds are two different things, and each gives off a different signature. We will look for a tear, since that is what brought Sir Justin here to this world. If that does not work, then we will look for a portal."

I asked Justin, "Would it be possible to have a couple of your mobile vehicles tow trailers? My guardians are going to raise a few eyebrows as it is. I do not want to bring our dinosaurs across to your world."

Justin nodded, and replied, "As long as you return the favour and transport my vehicles and troops to an appropriate portal where they can return to my world. They will not operate here in this plane of existence."

I arranged for the troops and several small dragons for long range communications, as well as six large dragons and Mercury. Once we were supplied and ready, we transported the Templar vehicles and men to a suitable site to set up a portal bridge to cross over into the Templar world. I was confident that my magic would work on Justin's world, as the Angel Michael had told me that I was to help him defeat the horde.

The site chosen was a small fortress located in the middle of a prairie area. The site could also be protected from outside interference. Enemies crossing over could be dispatched by archers on the wall surrounding the portal. The portal was placed in the middle of the fortress, visible on all sides from the protecting walls. A stone cairn was placed at the point where the portal was anchored in this world. Another would be erected on Justin's world, to show where it was located.

When we got set up, I opened the portal temporarily to the size of a football. Peter sent a monitor through to ensure there were no members of the horde nearby that could cause problems when we crossed into Justin's world. Peter confirmed that he had the monitor go up high enough that the area was visible for a mile around the portal entrance.

Peter said, "It appears that the area is totally clear. There are no visible signs at all of those creatures."

I smiled at Peter. "Thank you, friend rabbit. I will open the portal fully, and move Sir Justin's vehicles and the trailers across before we disconnect and move the ankylosaurs back across"

I signalled and the Elves and Yeti crossed into the other world, where they would spread out and hide in the brush to provide cover in case any enemy scouts showed up. I then directed that the vehicles and the energy cannon be brought across and deployed. I crossed over with the Templars, followed by the ankylosaurs with our two trailers, and a small contingent of dwarf engineers.

The engineers quickly set up the brackets that were designed back in the dragon world to attach the trailers to the two tank-like vehicles. They then set up the cairn in a design that Justin said would blend in to the normal of this world.

The Templar contingent set up outside of my fighters to give us a layer of protection if someone from this world happened to come upon us. Four of the elves brought in two bodies of dead horde members who appeared to be slightly different than those we had dealings with so far. These two appeared to be very slender, and I was advised that they moved with incredible speed, allowing them to avoid most of the energy weapons of the Templars. But since the elves were used to picking off raptors, there was little comparison in either's speed, and the elves made short work of them once they were spotted.

The scouts did not have the poison fangs that the warriors did, and just relied on their speed to get the information and rush back to pass on information to their leaders.

Justin looked impressed, saying, "We have never been able to capture any of these creatures in the past. Their speed has prevented them from capture. Looking at the brain case, which is enlarged, shows that they may be more intelligent than the average. We must take these two to the main capital and let the healer priests examine them. The more we learn of our enemy, the better."

Other than the two dead horde scouts, we passed a quiet evening. I checked the world to ensure my magic would work. I could feel the power flowing into me, as there appeared to be no one, or perhaps just a few, using the magic in this world. That could easily be explained by Justin telling me of how poorly magic wielders were treated, especially once the enforcement unit of the church got hold of them, believing that magic was evil and the purveyors were heretics.

It did not take much time before we reached one of the main thoroughfares, a large wide asphalt-like highway with walls along the side of the road and way stations every one hundred miles or so. All my troops were crammed inside the two trailers that we had brought along. They would not have been able to keep up to the high speed the vehicles were capable of doing on the main road.

THIRTY FIVE

Treachery in the Land of God

When we were a distance of a couple of miles from the city walls, Justin had the vehicles pull over and set up camp.

I advised Justin, "I think it is important that we get the support of Pope Jason. Otherwise, we will be in a state of constant bickering between the arms of the church. Only His Eminence can lay down a directive to all of the different branches to help us in our battle with the horde.

I took a small contingent of the People, including James, with me. We rode in one of the tank-like vehicles into the capital city to see the Pope. The People looked like normal members of the population of this world; they could blend in better than me if need be. I noticed that the road we were travelling on was bare of vehicles and had no side streets.

Justin said, "There are a few church roads in each city, which allow the anointed to travel faster and without encumbrance. There are no private vehicles in our land. We have transports for the commoners to get from town to town and some large vehicles for shipping food or finished products."

We approached the papal palace, where His Eminence, Pope Jason the Second, resided. As with the pope on my home world, he was closely guarded by a group of elite protectors, who took great pride in their duties and trained continuously.

There was a large parking lot with several of the tanks occupying the space. I asked Justin why they appeared to be of different colours. Justin advised that the cardinals controlled an area of the holy land and the slight difference in the colours of the tanks indicated each region, as well as the gold and silver indicating property of the papal house.

Sir Justin offered up the protection of his house, and outfitted the dozen of the People troops with his colours and the Templar markings of troops. James, out of pride, refused to wear anything other than his dragon guardian uniform, and as usual would not be swayed to be anywhere else than by my side.

As the troops exited the tank, I waited for them to assemble before I stepped out of the vehicle. The minute I was seen, the papal guards went on high alert, and an officer ran down to our group and challenged Sir Justin.

Sir Justin said, "We will wait here, but I feel His Eminence will want to meet our guest."

The guard officer replied, "I doubt the Holy Father will want to see this heretical wielder of magic, especially since he is also carrying weapons. He will probably order that he be killed on the spot! Why don't we save him the trouble and take care of this heretic right now!" He drew his sword and stepped forward as he spoke.

My men and Sir Justin stepped in front of him and spoke to the guard officer, "I have it from the most On-High authority that his life is blessed by The Almighty. Whosoever harms or ends his life is condemned to eternal damnation."

The guard officer signalled, and troops came pouring out surrounding us. Just before they came close enough to engage in battle, a shadow fell over the group and the Angel Michael landed in front of the guard officer, saying, "You obviously don't listen too well. I have shown myself to your men and you to prevent anyone from being cast into hell for harming this man." The guard officer just stood there for a minute with his mouth open, then closed his mouth and stepped aside, creating a path for us to travel.

The Archangel Michael led the way down the hallways of the papal palace. He strode with me, with a purposeful look on his face. The guards in the hallway stood to one side to make room for the angel, bending down on their knees and offering obeisance. Some were heard whispering prayers. They had never seen a real live angel before, and Michael's sudden appearance in the papal palace was one that would be remembered for centuries.

Two cardinals were seated before the Pope, and quickly stood as the group entered the audience chamber. Before seeing Michael, they ordered their household guards to seize these infidels and escort them to the dungeons.

Michael's voice filled the room: "Cease this nonsense and stand down before I punish you in the name of the Almighty." The only one who did not kneel down before Michael was the Pope, who remained seated due to his age, which appeared to be ancient.

Michael looked at the Pope and spoke. "This is the man whose forces, though strange in appearance, will free you from the horde. He is a God-fearing man who has been empowered by the Almighty with great powers."

Pope Jason the Second spoke in a slow, gravelly voice. "Yes, so you said when you came to my bed chambers the other night. Who am I to question the will of the Almighty? All men on this world will answer to you, Dragon Mage Jim, to help rid ourselves of this dreaded horde of creatures. We have never trusted the wielders of magic in this world until now. It will take time and much prayer for all the Christians to rely on you."

A travellers hostel, located just next to the papal palace, was designated for our use. The hostel was plain, but large enough to house the over one hundred of my elves, dwarves, and people. The Yeti chose to stay in the surrounding area outside of the wall of the holy city; the dragons stayed with them as well. The rabbit people, with the aid of the dwarf engineers, set up a small command centre in a clearing surrounded by trees, which also offered protection for the dragons to rest.

My warriors got more attention than Gizmo, who was nestled quietly around my neck, did. It was a quiet night and I slept soundly; so much so that I think someone spiked my food or drink.

* * * * *

I woke up in a dark dungeon, manacled to a stone table that had grooves cut into it to drain blood away (or so I assumed). Looking around me, I could see Sir Justin and James both laid out on tables themselves.

I said to James, "I thought you were supposed to watch over me. Looks like you fell asleep like the rest of us." James looked like a puppy who has been caught doing something wrong. Sir Justin woke and had a very colorful range of curses for so religious a man.

A cleric, wearing the black garment with a cross on it indicating the enforcement branch of the church, quietly walked into the room.

I strained my neck and said to him, "I would suggest that you free us, or else the consequences will be dire." The cleric did not say a word, but just continued pulling out various instruments of torture. "Don't say I did not warn you," I finished.

Several priests of the enforcement, wearing hoods to cover their features, walked into the room and started to play with the instruments of torture.

I looked at them and said, "I will give you a chance to repent and release us, before I send you all to hell."

The priest, who was obviously the lead in this pain party, addressed me. "You and your compatriots will be the only ones going to hell today! Once we are done, you will confess your heretical ways and embrace God."

I replied, "I embraced God in my heart many years ago. Have you not heard that Michael the Archangel vouched for me to His Eminence the Pope?"

The priest ripped off his hood in one swift movement and stared at me with a look of pure hatred. He said, "That was probably an illusion, or the use of a dark angel, which shows you are in league with the devil."

I was getting extremely agitated by this point and had no desire to be poked and prodded by these instruments of pain and mutilation. I concentrated on my body and began to heat it up, causing the pins on the manacles to melt, freeing me. While the priests stood there in stunned silence, too shocked to move as yet, I quickly freed James and Sir Justin. They both grabbed some poles from the side of the room and stood beside me—ready to fight.

The priests fled the room, and guards wearing the black of the enforcement arm of the church ran in with swords drawn and shields ready.

As the command was about to be given by the head priest to attack, a voice sounded from out in the hall: "Hold your ground or face the consequences!" A large contingent of the papal guard stepped into the room and placed themselves between us and the guards in black.

"By order of His Eminence Pope Jason the Second, you are commanded to step down and not interfere with this visitor from another world who has been blessed and vouched for by the Archangel Michael," the guard captain said. The guards gathered up the men dressed in black and escorted them out of the room under close watch. The guard captain asked Sir Justin and I, "Are you hurt? Do I need to send for a medical priest?"

I replied, "We are all fine. Your prompt response stopped any attack before it happened, and we thank you."

The guard captain nodded, saying, "His Eminence the Pope wishes to see you as soon as you feel up to it. Since there are no injuries, would now be a suitable time?"

I replied, "Yes, of course we will attend to His Eminence right away."

We were escorted to the Pope's private chambers, where he was lying in bed. Medical priests surrounded him with all sorts of equipment. It did not look promising. As we came close, he waived the other priests to stand out of earshot, as he wanted a private word with us.

Pope Jason said, in a raspy voice, "I am dying, and I am not sure I will be able to hold the next in line for the papal seat to abide by my promise of your safety. You must flee while life still holds me here, I see the angel of death watching over me, waiting for the right time to take me for the judgement of God."

I took his hand gently in mine, and felt his life essence slipping away, but it was not from natural causes. The Pope had been poisoned with the venom of the ant people. Since the healers of this world did not have any experience with this poison, they felt that his illness was from natural causes, as the Pope was very advanced in years.

I told Justin, "His Eminence the Pope has been poisoned with venom from the ant people. I can save him, but you must stop your healers from interfering."

Justin nodded and replied, "No problem. I know the guard captain on duty right now; he trusts me and will help us out."

Justin signalled the guard captain over and whispered in his ear. The guard captain nodded and left the room, returning in five minutes with twenty papal guards, who placed themselves around the bed, facing out. They were ready to prevent the healers from doing something foolish to prevent me from helping the Pope.

I reached into his body and poured strength into him, finding the organs that were shutting down, and cleaned the poison out of them. It took me about thirty minutes, and since my concentration was on the Pope, I did not even notice the arguments between the healers and Sir Justin. When I was done I was exhausted, and James helped me to a bench in the bedroom where I could rest.

The Pope climbed out of bed looking like a new man. His cheeks were rosy and his eyes were clear. He looked like a well-rested man.

He yelled at the healers, "That is enough! You could not heal me, but the stranger did, and you all want to crucify him as a demon! Now get out of my sight before I decide to do something nasty to you as punishment for your un-Christian-like attitudes."

After the healers left the room, the Pope walked up to where I was lounging on the bench, trying to get enough energy back to head to my rooms to rest in what was left of the day.

Pope Jason said, "Thank you my friend, you have saved me. I only wish there were some way that I could repay you. If there is anything that you want, just ask and it is yours. Right now I have to see if there is some way of ferreting out the attempted murderer and deal with him or her appropriately."

I replied, "Let me rest until tomorrow, and I may be able to help you find your attempted killer. The little dragons I have brought with me are capable of reading minds if they must. Reading the thoughts of those who wish to harm you would be a simple, but time consuming, process. I have six of the little dragons and trained interrogators who can find out the truth without harming the innocent."

Pope Jason said, "That would be fantastic! Thank you, Dragon Mage."

I walked under heavy escort back to our accommodations, where I could go back to sleep after tossing and turning for a couple of hours. I slept well, knowing that the rooms were well guarded by the papal guard.

The small dragons showed up early in the morning and were taken with dwarf interrogators and four papal guards each to protect them. They entered an area of the dungeons not far from where the torture chamber was located. Of all the priests and guards of the enforcement unit, only twelve of the priests were aware of what was to transpire once they forced a confession of heresy from the three of us. That way, they could call in a conclave of the Council of Cardinals and place a new pope into the Holy Seat to lead the masses. It was always about control. They could place the cardinal in charge of the enforcement priests, or at least put someone they could control in the position of power.

They did not like the fact that Pope Jason followed the teachings of the bible, truly believing what was written, and obeying the Word of the Lord. The twelve enforcers were to be beheaded the following morning, and were kept under heavy watch by the papal guards. The next morning we were asked to witness the dispensation of justice to the twelve traitors.

The executioner knew his job. He was right on target, and completed his task with one swift blow to each prisoner. The man wore a simple gray outfit, including a hood and mask to hide his features, so that no one could recognize him, which would protect him and his family from repercussions. When it was over, he would enter a room that had multiple doors, and exit after he had changed into his normal attire.

After this betrayal was dealt with, Pope Jason called for a meeting in his personal chambers. When we entered, there were cardinals from each of the sectors, as well as cardinals who were in charge of each of the special branches. I was introduced to each of the cardinals, including the new leader of the enforcement branch, who apparently had a more lenient approach. This would explain why he had never reached beyond the bishop level, as few would vote for him to lead the enforcement branch of the priesthood.

Pope Jason spoke slowly and deliberately. "I cannot thank you enough, Dragon Mage Jim. Without your assistance, I would have died. It shows that we can learn more from others outside of the church who are willing to worship God. I have given orders that the creatures of this world be left to grow and develop, as long as they do not cause any danger to our people. It will take a long time for the people to learn and push these prejudices aside, and wisdom to see and use the knowledge gained to grow with the land."

"There is a Templar knight who was involved in the attempt on our lives. He has been removed from power, and his troops are yours to use as you will. The troops are eager to prove their loyalty, and are willing to die in the service of God and the Holy Church. I am pleased to grant you knighthood, and place Sir Justin as your second in command to assist you in any way you need. Please kneel and I will knight you and give you a blessing as well, to protect you in your upcoming battles," the Pope finished.

The knight's dwelling was a mini castle in its own right. There were only two ways in to the compound, which made it relatively easy to protect if an enemy breached the walls of the city. With several knights in each city, it provided points of strength that could attack the enemy from different quarters. With the exception of the military road to the papal palace, there was no direct path to the center of the city where the religious hub was.

With the knighthood came a sword that supposedly came from the first Templars as they crossed over into this world. It was beautifully preserved, considering it was over six hundred years old, and was said to have powers endowed by God to defeat any evil.

THIRTY-SIX

I meet The Lady Amelia

W e moved the men that we had brought into the city with us to the estate of the disposed knight. We were greeted hospitably by Sergeant-at-Arms Thomas, who said, "Welcome, Lord Dragon Mage. Everything is in order. The lady Amelia will be escorted out of the estate by the end of the day."

I replied, "Take me to the lady of the house—Amelia. I wish to talk with her about the disgrace she is facing after the arrest of her husband."

I was escorted to the suite of rooms where the lord of the house and his lady lived. There were ladies in waiting running around, placing clothes in chests and having other servants packing them out to a waiting flatbed truck in the courtyard.

I ordered the servants, "Out; I will call you back when you are needed again." I then addressed Amelia, a tall blonde woman in her early thirties, who was dressed in formal daytime attire.

"Please sit, so that we can talk about your future."

She replied, "My ladies in waiting and I will be out of your hair shortly. It is my hope that my family will take me back, even with this disgrace hanging over me for marrying the wrong man."

I said, "You may reside in this house and in this suite of rooms for as long as you like. I do not have time to run a household this size; I need someone to run this place. I ask nothing from you, dear lady, and if you find an appropriate suitor, I will even provide a decent dowry to ensure that you have someone who will appreciate what you have to offer."

Amelia replied, "Thank you, My Lord—you will not regret your decision! I will run this estate like clockwork, without any issues to disturb you."

Amelia was all smiles as she stepped out to yell at the ladies in waiting to start unpacking and to get the main guest room ready for the new lord of the household.

As I walked back to the courtyard to help organize placement of my troops, Sir Justin stopped me and said, "That was well done, Sir Jim; truly a Christian move to welcome the Lady Amelia into your house. No one else would normally have taken her in, even her family, because of the stigma of being married to a man who was prepared to betray the holy church."

Late in the evening, the sergeant at arms called me to attend to the gate, as there was a group of robed beings of various sizes asking for entry. I brought Gizmo with me to confirm that they were friends and not enemies wanting in.

As I walked up to the man door in the gate, Gizmo said to me, "Elijah has sent them from the School of Mages and Companions to help."

I replied quizzically, "Why now does he feel I need assistance?"

Gizmo said, "More so to help the healers and technical priests explore other avenues of study that may lead them to new developments. They have fantastic developments in their fields of study, but have forgotten the old ways of healing. This would allow them to progress in different avenues."

The next morning, arrangements were made for the mages to meet with the priests to study and teach at the same time about the dragon world and its differences. I ensured that there were household guards escorting them and ensuring their safety from repercussions from the recent coup attempt.

Sir Justin took me out to the target range to show how effective the energy weapons of the Templars were. The field cannon was quite devastating to targets within range. The tanks had a shorter range, but were able to deal a hefty blow to targets. The hand-held rifles and hand guns that sent out a pulse of energy could disintegrate targets, but were useless against the ants, because their carapaces were shiny and reflected all but a head shot.

Fortunately, the same could be said for the armour of the Templars, so when it came down to it, the majority of the battle was hand-to-hand, with swords and such. It was the reason that the ants were slowly winning, as they were very much stronger. It took about five Templars to defeat one ant.

Sir Justin advised that the Templar knights and their soldiers prided themselves in constant training with hand weapons. This was passed down from generations, and so ingrained in what made up the Templar warriors that the training was maintained over the centuries.

They often sparred in the courtyard, so I told the elves that they could join in if they wished, as long as they did not hurt anyone too much. Once the best of the Templars was taken down, they were eager to learn any new tricks that could help keep them victorious in battle.

A search of the Templar world by the monitors and by the dragons was undergoing; so far with no results to this point. When I reached a point where I felt that the tear to this world from the ant home world must have healed itself, I heard from the dragons and Peter at the same time that the tear was still there. It was located a short distance from the anthill, which towered one hundred feet over the surrounding landscape.

Peter, at my request, dropped one of the monitors, with its sensors still working, along the path from the ant hill to the tear/portal, and waited. It was not long before one of the drones picked up the monitor and examined it. After conversing with one of the ant warrior commanders, it carried the monitor into the anthill.

There was only one visible way in or out, and that was at the top of the anthill. The smaller passages did not seem to lead to the main chamber and the queen. Past the constant flow of the creatures going in and out, I was sure there was probably another entrance or exit, if not more, situated at a hidden location. As the monitor was carried down to the queen's chambers, I looked at the maze of tunnels. As it got further into the chamber, the signal started to break up and soon became indiscernible, so we did not get a chance to see what the queen looked like; if in fact she was there at all.

I spoke to Sir Justin and advised him that I would deal with the tear between the worlds, but I needed to access several tanks for quick transport in and out of the adjoining area near the nest, or hill.

I said, "I am going to use the Yeti and the Elves to draw the ants directly opposite of the nest and toward them. The different groups will have a small dragon with each contingent, relaying information and directions, so that the ants will not be able to monitor any radio communication that you would normally use. We will take care of the tear as soon as we can mobilize the vehicles. My troops are ready to go at a moment's notice."

Sir Justin replied, "I only have six tanks, but I am sure His Eminence the Holy Father will be willing to provide any tanks that are needed. I will advise you tomorrow about his decision."

After an excellent meal and a conference with my commanders, in which we laid out plans for the near future, I headed to my bedchamber, with Gizmo curled around my shoulder.

As I approached my rooms, I found two Templar soldiers standing guard outside of my quarters.

As they snapped to attention, I asked them, "And what do I owe the pleasure of you gentlemen guarding my door?"

One guard replied, "By order of His Eminence Pope Jason the Second, a contingent of hand-picked guards to protect your person has been assigned for as long as needed, even to the point of returning to your world. These men have been trained extensively in the use of swords and spears, so would be able to manage in your world, where our technology does not function."

* * * * *

In the early hours, sometime after midnight, I was awakened by the sound of metal on metal, and cursing. I quickly strode to the door to my suite, tearing it open to see a group of the masked enforcement branch of the church fighting with the guards at my door. One of the guards was injured and the other was having a hard time fighting off the masked soldiers.

I lifted Draco and created a wall of air around the soldiers dressed in black. They were obviously from the enforcement arm of the church, as each of them had the silver cross over his breast. As soon as they realized that they could not escape, they began to froth at the mouth, and fell in a heap onto the floor. It was apparent that they all had taken poison so that they could not be questioned or tortured.

Since they were no longer a threat, I let the bubble of force drop, and gave the injured guard my full attention. I called for a healer, and as soon as one came to care for the wounded guard, I moved my attention to the dead enforcement clerics. More of my warriors showed up, ready for a fight that had already ended. I had them search the clerics to see if there was any information that could lead me to the instigator.

The search provided one thing of interest—a map showing the location of the room I was in, and the path to reach me without being seen by guards. If it were not for the guards at my bedroom suite, I may have been taken by surprise and captured, or simply killed in my sleep. It was apparent that there was an information leak in this household, since I had only been in the estate for one night. I spoke to the healer, who advised that the guard would be fine, thanks to my immediate care prior to his arrival.

I called Tomar and Neb to attend me.

When they arrived, I showed them the map and said, "I want to back-track this map to where it leads—to see if we could capture more black-dressed clerics before they had the opportunity to take a poison capsule." I wanted to gather more information in regard to who had sent them, and see if we could eliminate the source of these deadly orders.

Tomar said, "The dark elves will be ready to go within an hour."

I looked at the uninjured guard and asked him, "Do you want vengeance?"

He replied, "Yes, my Lord Dragon Mage. That would appreciated, if we can be involved."

I said, "Go and awaken the rest of the troops. Station the two weakest members here, to give the impression that I am still here for the rest of the night. I will be in the rooms waiting for your arrival, but be as quick as possible."

Sir Justin arrived with the papal guards within fifteen minutes, saying, "I am glad that I stuck around. I would not like to miss a good fight." Tomar showed up ten minutes later, reporting that the secret doorway was located, and the troops were making their silent way back, tracking the map to find out where it began.

I quickly caught up with the dark elves as they navigated down the tunnel. The way lead to a reception area belonging to the enforcement branch, in the papal palace.

The dark elves opened the doorway and silently placed themselves around the hall. On a command from Tomar, they stepped forward and knocked out the guards in this area. Tomar instructed his men to check their mouths for poison tablets and make sure they did not have any on them. They were quickly bound, and when they woke up, they were escorted by the papal guards back along the tunnel to the estate.

The doorway was closed, as if nothing had happened, and guards were placed at the estate end of the passage.

I told Sir Justin that the papal guard could be rough on the enforcement warriors, as long as they were still alive for questioning. The papal guards looked like wolves, their teeth bared in pleasure. The next morning while we were having breakfast with the lady Amelia, I spoke to her about having a spy in her household.

Amelia said, "My servants have always been loyal, unless someone is threatening family members in order to coerce information."

I arranged for all the staff to be questioned first, letting the dark-clad warriors stew for the day in the estate dungeons. It did not take long. Amelia's first lady-in-waiting turned out to be the leak of information, as her family was being threatened to be taken in and tortured until they confessed to be heretics and put to death. The lady in waiting did not know who the person was, just that he was a bishop in the enforcement branch of the church. That narrowed the suspects, but there were a lot of bishops in that branch, so finding the right one would be difficult. Proving it when they found him would even be harder, but I had some thoughts on that issue, which would wait until the suspect was found.

I got my papal guards to call the papal palace and arrange for an escort for the captured warriors. During the walk, Gizmo scanned their minds as they were walking down the main street with their heads bowed in shame.

Gizmo said, "The bishop's name is Conn, and he obviously does not feel the Pope is following the path of a good Christian. The warriors only know that they were ordered to watch the doorway for anyone uninvited who might enter the hall." The escort took the warriors, dressed in black, to the gate leading into the enforcement arm of the church, which was located in one area of the papal palace.

The bishop in question was standing at the gate, so I instructed Gizmo, "Try to read whatever you can from his mind, while I speak to him."

I said to the bishop, "It appears we have found some of your men who have wandered too close to where they did not belong. I am returning them to your care, bishop, in the hope that you can properly instruct them."

The bishop replied, "They appear to have been well cared for. I thank you for your gentle treatment." He then turned around and wandered away into his area of the palace.

I said to Gizmo, "I want him to disappear and be available for detailed questioning. He remains a threat to the Pope and to the government of this world. We cannot dispose of the ants without dealing with the in-house problems first. It is like the Inquisition here, with everyone afraid of the enforcement priests and their warriors."

Since it would be impossible to prove any charges against this branch of the church, another route must be used to gather information and informally punish the suspects, without the Pope being placed in an awkward position of dispensing justice. I did not want to face an enemy without someone I could trust at my back, and if Conn had anything to do about it, I could not trust that he would help me in any way.

Gizmo said to me, "The only thing I could read during the brief moments we were close is the fact that he is surprised that you were able to dispatch his clerics. I was able to read his plans for the evening, which include a, a – 'lady of the night?' And then he was planning on raiding a library, where he is going to place some forbidden manuscripts as an excuse to take the library down and torture all the staff. This way, the common man would fear the black-dressed priests."

I nodded, thinking that if one of the black dressed priests were able to get one of their cardinals elected to the papal throne, they could rule with a tight fist of fear. It would set back the start of democracy at least one hundred years, since the Pope was leaning toward setting up a government of the people, with the Templar knights overseeing it like a senate.

I, of course, had to explain to Gizmo about ladies of the night, or prostitutes, that were available for hire. Gizmo had a little trouble grasping the idea that women would sleep with someone they did not like for money. But of course, she just trusted my judgment that I knew what I was talking about.

I took a select group of my dark elves, including Tomar and Neb, placing ourselves around the address Gizmo had gleaned from Conn's mind. I walked into the common room of the bordello, and had a few glasses of mead while I waited. I passed the time flirting with the girls and pretending to be interested. When Conn entered the bordello, he headed up to a specific room without pausing to speak with anyone.

I headed outside, where we took out Conn's two bodyguards, who were waiting for his return from his tryst. When he came out of the building, we bound and gagged him, covering his head so he could not see where he was going. We took Conn to a barn in the farming area that surrounded the city. He was tied securely to a chair, with lights focused on his face so that he could not see the interrogators. Then his hood and gag were removed.

As soon as he could speak, he uttered some colourful curses. I was amazed that he knew these words and would utter them.

Conn said, "Do you know who I am, and what I can do to you and your family if you do not release me immediately?"

I laughed, saying, "You can guess who we are, but we are not from your world, so getting to our family would be impossible." I continued, "Not to mention the fact that you were in possession of books that are forbidden by your people, and you were seen going into a prostitute's room in a house of ill repute. I think there is a lot for you to answer to, Bishop Conn. We want to know who is behind these attacks on the dragon mage who has come under Michael the Archangel's and His Holiness the Pope's blessing!"

Conn said, "I am trained to resist torture, so you will not get anything from me no matter what you do."

I replied, "We will only ask you questions and listen to your answers, or lack thereof, to learn the truth."

The bishop did not say much, but I could see Gizmo paying close attention to him as the questions were put to him slowly, so that he had time to think of the answer, even when he did not respond vocally. Gizmo relayed the information to me as immediately as Conn thought of the answer. It turned out that there were only a few who felt the Pope was dealing with the devil and must be replaced.

The cardinal of the enforcement clerics was the source of all the scheming and back-room plotting to replace the papal seat occupant. When we were done with Conn, he was quietly executed by Tomar, and I burned the body down to a pile of ash, beyond recognition by anyone. The bodies of the two guards were disposed of at the same time.

Early the next day, I arranged for a private audience with His Eminence, Pope Jason the second. I explained to him the information that we received from the dark bishop, and that the cardinal was the leader looking to depose him from the Holy Seat.

The Pope said that he would delegate the cardinal and a select group of his troops to be on hand when we went to seal the tear between worlds. The cardinal would be on the front line and receive the most damage, having a chance to die with honour rather than face an executioner.

I thought the cardinal was going to have a heart attack in the main chamber when the Pope told him that he wanted to bring honour and a more positive appearance to the enforcement branch of the church. The cardinal obviously could not refuse the request, and bowed deeply, thanking the Holy Father for this prestigious honour.

The cardinal was dead before the next morning. His personal doctor advised that he appeared to have died of natural causes. Gizmo was with me when the healing cleric advised the Pope of this, and later told me that the healer suspected that the cardinal took his own life with poison.

As I prepared to embark on the mission to seal the tear between this world and the ant people's home world, Peter came to me with a few monitors to throw into the tear into the other world. I took a select group of my warriors, as well as Gizmo and the full-sized dragons who had come with me to the Templar world. Once the troops on the opposite side of the ant hill engaged the enemy and drew their attention away from the tear, I approached it and began to heal the tear between the worlds. When I had the tear down to the size of a dwarf, I threw the monitors through the tear and sealed it.

The ant drones who had been hauling goods to their world stopped in blankness and disorientation, waiting for orders about what to do, since their path was no longer there. We quickly left the area, and signaled the troops on the other side to fall back and withdraw. As we expected, none of the enforcement warriors and priests survived the diversion. I left behind a monitor to hover over the giant ant hill, to see how the ants would react to the loss of their gateway and what they would do.

Peter met me on the way back to the city, and directed me to the main monitoring station set up on this world at the portal site.

Peter said, "I want to show you the images we have received from the ant home world already." The pictures showed a pastured land, with much of the usable ground either in forest or developed into farmland. There were giant anthills scattered about one hundred miles from each other, as well as a huge anthill three times larger than the others, standing almost one thousand feet into the sky and covering a one-mile-radius at its base.

A plan was beginning to formulate in my mind. I suggested to Peter, "Search for a land that has little or no animal life on it, and is not populated by an intelligent species of some sort. I think that if we can communicate with the ant queen, we may be able to relocate them to a different world and save a loss of life on both sides."

Peter nodded and replied, "I will let you know as soon as I find something appropriate."

I requested and was immediately granted an audience with the Holy Father Jason. I explained to him what had transpired up to this point, and my thoughts on a possible nonviolent solution to the problem. Pope Jason agreed that this would be the best solution, if it could be managed. The troops would be organized and on stand-by to deploy at a moment's notice.

* * * * *

Peter came to see me the next morning and said, "A new world that fits your requirements has been found, and would be suitable for the ant people to settle in. A portal can be opened between this world and there. Now you have to figure some way of getting their attention without getting killed."

I said, "I agree totally. We will open the portal from the other world in the same location that the tear had been before. That way, it will entice the ant drones to walk the path and get their attention quicker."

Peter nodded his head and went to make the suitable preparations.

I stood silently, looking at the world that Peter had located, watching the area where Peter had opened up a portal back into the Templar world. It was only a matter of two hours before two scouts came through the portal and searched the immediate area. They obviously realized that they were not on their home world, and then went back through the portal. Shortly after, a large contingent of ant soldiers came through the portal and began an intensive search of the area, looking for visible landmarks to determine where they were.

My forces deployed in defensive positions, while I walked up to the lead warrior ant to speak with him. As I came into his line of sight, he had his troops surround me before walking up to me.

I said to him, holding my hands out indicating that I was not armed, "I come in peace. We have arranged for this world for your people to grow and develop. Take this message to your queen. If she stays on the world of the Templar knights, she will be destroyed, along with her entire nest. I await an answer from her as to what she wants to do. If any more people of that world are killed, then the nest will be destroyed."

The creature was a little hard to understand as he spoke, "I will pass the message to the Queen alongside of your body, man."

I replied, "You had better be more careful with your threats, or someone will get hurt from this meeting today."

The creature said, "I know not what you say about threats. I mean what I say about your body for the Queen."

The ant warriors stepped in to attack me while I stood there.

A flurry of arrows came flying through the air, dropping all of the ant warriors, with the exception of the leader of the group.

It looked around at the fallen warriors and said, "Your message will be passed on to the Queen, and I will come back to this location within two days to give you the answer." I just nodded as it turned around and slowed strode away toward the ant nest.

The creature was true to his word, and returned to the meeting place two days later at approximately the same time of day as the first meeting. I had an uneasy feeling deep in my gut, and I have learned over the years of police work and fighting with the marines to trust my gut.

It spoke to me and said, "the Queen will accept your offer of a new world, but she likes this one as well, as it has plenty of humans to use for labour. So we are just going to dispose of you and those that contest our control of this world. You humans do not stand a chance when it comes to one-on-one in a battle."

With that, the ant warriors started to stand up in the tall grass. I did a quick head count and quickly came up with a number of one hundred. It was a little daunting. They obviously felt that my troops and I were enough of a threat that they had to stomp us out as quickly as possible.

I said, "I will give you my answer as well, since I have no intention of being someone's slave to toil in the fields and build things for you." I waved my hand, and the dragons showed up and started to rain fire down on the ant warriors.

I told Gizmo to advise the troops to fall back and arrange for all available troops to surround the ant nest. I was going to deal with this issue myself, as I was getting pissed off. I was feeling the energy building inside me, ready to be released on these creatures. I could see bolts of energy going skyward, as the ant warriors were trying to shoot the moving dragons in the air above.

I directed the dragons to set up a perimeter around the ant troops, blocking them in so they could not leave the area to target my troops during their withdrawal. As they laid down the fire, I used the magic staff to create a two-level force field, one level encasing me and one encasing the total troops of the ants. Then I generated fire, increasing the heat around the enemy, and burning all of them, including their leader.

I was so angry, I stood there watching as the heat reached a point where the ants started to spontaneously combust. I increased the heat until the entire area was burned clear. The fire could no longer continue, as there was no air left in the large dome of force.

I stood there, allowing the heat to recede, looking over the area that held only ashes; no bodies or grass left.

I said to Gizmo, "I think it is time to rest now, while our troops gather at the holy city and prepare to move on to the next phase of our attack on the nest." I called Mercury, and we flew quickly back to our estate in the papal city.

I asked Amelia not to disturb me, as I wanted to get some well-deserved rest before talking to the Holy Father, Pope Jason the Second. I was spent from exerting the magical energy to dispose of the hundred and one ants. Wasn't that a movie? Oh wait—those were Dalmatians, I chuckled to myself. I nestled down in bed, comfortable in the knowledge that the suite doors were guarded by papal warriors who would die in battle rather than risk the chance of damnation for not complying with the Holy Father's orders.

* * * * *

I awoke with a start, as something soft and warm, with breasts, snuggled against me. I immediately knew it was the lady Amelia. I tried to ignore her, letting her press up against me. I rolled onto my back and let Amelia cuddle into me, feeling the warmth of her body next to mine, and drifted off to sleep peacefully. When I awoke to sunlight streaming through the window, Amelia was no longer there. I wondered what she saw in me, especially since I was not from her world, and my standing with the church was unknown. (Had it been a dream?)

As I sat there enjoying my morning meal, I noticed out of my peripheral vision that Amelia was spending a lot of time staring at me when she thought I was not watching. She made small talk about the upkeep of the estate and various things, including rumours about the new cardinal in charge of the enforcement clerics and how that was to change the way the common people were treated.

I called the papal palace to arrange for an interview with the Holy Father. The person at the other end of the phone advised that the Pope had left orders that anything would be put aside if I wished to talk to him. The phone system was a video type, which allowed for the person to see who they were talking to. I almost missed that on the dragon world, but it was only a minor inconvenience, so I just used it while I was here.

I walked with my personal papal guard, entering the papal palace and walking up to Pope Jason the Second's personal suite. As I approached the suite, the guards opened the doors to let me into the Pope's personal area, without even announcing me.

Pope Jason looked up and said, "Dragon Mage, thank you for your continued assistance in dealing with this evil enemy. I have been updated by Sir Justin as to your attempts to prevent further bloodshed by relocating the enemy to another world. It is unfortunate that they would take the offer and try to still remain here to take over the lands. It is further proof that the enemy is evil, and the only thing that surprised me is the fact that they shared their plan of world conquest with you."

I replied, "Your Eminence, they did not think I would survive to pass the information along to you. They intended to end my life immediately after the conversation was over." I explained to him that I needed the Templar houses to gather together and surround the giant ant nest, slowly closing the circle to prevent the ant horde from attacking in the surrounding area and kidnapping farmers as slaves.

Pope Jason said, "The Knights Templar are at your disposal. You have but to say the word and they will follow your direction. I will put the call out for them to meet at the nearest villages North and South of the nest."

It turned out that it would take a week for the furthest away to reach the area, so I had time to lay out a plan among my troops. I left the organization of the siege cannons and tanks with the troops to Sir Justin, who, being a Templar knight himself, understood their limitations.

I called Peter to transport my troops to the empty world we had offered to the ants. When they arrived, they would kill any of the ant drones and scout/warriors, then seal the portal again. That would block off any escape route, once we initiated the attack on the nest. Peter and my troops returned within two days, advising that the mission was a success, but we lost twelve warriors of different races in the process.

They brought the bodies back with them, and then used the portal to take them back to the dragon world, to be dealt full honours. I escorted the fallen back, and turned the bodies over to their clan for funeral arrangements.

THIRTY-SEVEN

The Queen and I

Then, I spent the night with Rose and Sylvia. I asked them what I should do about Amelia, since I was not yet an expert on this allowable plural marriage situation.

I thought about Amelia; tall, slim, blonde Amelia. The fact that she was making advances to me showed me that she was very interested. She was an impeccable dresser and extremely polite and wanted to make me happy. I was having a real issue with the fact that I now had two wives already. I did not know if I could handle three.

The women headed to the estate on the Templar world, to talk with Amelia to see how she felt and how they felt about her. As usual, I made sure there was a large escort of attendants and warriors to ensure the safety of the women. I received word that they arrived safely, without encountering any problems. Once they were in the papal city, I received further word that the ants had gone on the offensive and were surrounding the city.

I amassed a large contingent of warriors to stand by. I brought Flit with me. Once through the portal into the Templar world, I sent Flit to fly to the city to get Peter to jump from this world to the dragon world. Warriors and portal mages would meet him and set up a doorway to the Templar world inside the estate, where we could amass the troops and send them to attack ants from the inside of the city.

When I finally arrived at the estate on the Templar world, the citizens were crowded around the papal palace, asking the Holy Father for protection. I had Sir Justin call the troops in from the North and the West to allow the ants an out, so we could herd them in that direction. The warriors on the walls of the outer part of the city would rain arrows and energy bolts down on them, forcing them toward the East, where the ant nest was located.

With the mass of the army against them, and the weapon fire from the outer walls of the city, the ants were forced to pull back toward their nest. The Templar house troops joined forces, and spread out in a semi-circle, forcing the ants to continue their movement toward the ant nest. I was advised later that the troops and weapons reached their assigned positions and encircled the nest from a safe distance, laying down a slow barrage, which kept the ants close to the nest after they made some brief sorties toward the troops, which resulted in a lot of lost creatures.

The dragons I had brought with me to this world kept an eye out, and whenever they saw the ants grouping up for an attack, they would lay down a wave of fire. Within a day or two, there was nothing left for the ants to hide in, as all the cover was burnt down to ashes.

I was escorted to the site of the nest by Sir Justin's men and vehicles. Close up, the nest was a little daunting—it was huge! The only way I could see to resolve this issue was going to be to enter the tunnels and take out the queen, which would leave the ants without direction. This would allow them to be dealt with much easier.

I had the weapons and troops close their range just short of the nest. They continued laying down fire, to keep the ants inside the nest. I warned the warriors to keep an ear out for a digging noise, in case the ants started burrowing new tunnels for attack or escape. I left Flit to let my wives know that I loved them, but this was something that I had to do almost alone. I brought Gizmo with me, and she said that she would be able to channel power from the other, full-sized dragons, giving me access to more energy to attack the nest.

We started the attack at first light, while it was cool and the ants were less active. The battle started with the full-sized dragons laying down fire on top of the nest, to draw the protectors' attention away from the sides of the nest. The dragons were fast enough that a defender armed with an energy weapon did not have time to focus a shot before it was incinerated by fire.

Gizmo and I found one of the lower, side entrances to the nest. We proceeded down the tunnel encased in a globe of air for Gizmo and I to breathe, while laying down fire to clear the tunnel ahead of us.

There was little opposition barring our path, and I said to Gizmo, "I think we are expected visitors. I doubt that we will encounter much resistance up to possibly the queen's chamber. This is too easy so far. I expected much more of a fight up to this point."

Gizmo replied "I agree, Dragon Mage. The dragons are even reporting little or no shots being fired at them from the top of the nest."

I worked my way down to the center of the nest to the queen's chamber, which appeared to be unguarded. She was lying on a couch made up of animal hides and fur, and was adorned with bits of precious jewels all over her body. There appeared to be a half dozen males, richly adorned, standing several feet behind the queen. Their genitalia was visible, giving away their status. Six of the queen's warrior guards stepped forward and tried to attack me. Sensing that there was something more to this allowed meeting, I pushed them aside with a blast of force—just knocking them senseless for a short period of time.

I stood there waiting for the queen's next move. When the warriors woke, she spoke to them in their own language, which was a series of clicks and squeaks. The warriors moved behind the queen to protect the males, but left the queen unguarded. The queen finally spoke in English, in a sweet melodious voice that, although soft, carried across the chamber.

"I have underestimated you, Dragon Mage. The fact that I thought I could take what you offered and take this world too was foolish of me. My line will perish if we resist you in this battle. Is there a way that we can still take you up on your offer of another world to live in and start anew?"

I replied, "The day is not over yet, Queen. There is still a way out that will stop further destruction of the nest until your family is safely away. The nest will then be destroyed from the inside, leaving nothing left of your being here."

The queen spoke again. "Is there anything that you need from our people, to guarantee that this will occur? I am prepared to die for the nest, and a queen egg can be selected and allowed to mature to run the nest instead of me, when it is ready."

I replied, "That would not only not be needed, but a new queen would not know the lesson of this world, and make the same mistake you made initially. I only require that you and your guards be the last ones across the portal, ensuring that the nest is emptied."

The queen said, "That would be totally agreeable, Dragon Mage. You are the most understanding human that we have memory of, in the history of the nests."

I replied, "I will return shortly and let you know when we are ready to open the portal. I will have my people watching the path and protecting your withdrawal from this world, since the occupants of this world may not be as forgiving as I."

I turned around, keeping my shield of air around me, and walked calmly out of the nest. I instructed the dragons to withdraw, and had Flit communicate to the Templar knights and their men to fall back to the first positions they had held earlier in the campaign. When I returned to the command tent that had been set up, I called Peter to reopen the portal to the vacant world; then I confirmed to him that the ants were to be given a chance to leave this world. If they strayed or attacked the perimeter guard, they would be killed.

Early the next morning, the queen and her guardians were waiting outside of the nest, awaiting my arrival.

As I walked up to the queen, she said, "Welcome, Dragon Mage. I have instructed my drones and warriors, as well as the rest of the nest, to evacuate and go to the new world, which will allow them to build and expand. We are in your debt, Dragon Mage. Your name will be passed down through the generations and the queens to come, as a friend of the Formicidae people."

I replied, "Thank you, Queen. I do not like taking life if I do not have to, and I appreciate the fact that you see the wisdom to save your people and continue with grace and dignity."

The queen nodded, and said something in her own language to a scout who was standing by. It ran to the nest, and before long the warriors emerged, followed by the drones, carrying supplies and egg sacs.

As we got closer to the portal, I directed the troops to stand back so as not to cause the warriors to react to any perceived threat to the queen or her entourage. The evacuation of the nest went without a hitch, and the line running from the nest to the portal continued for the entire day. A scout came running up to the queen and communicated with her entourage, which spoke in their own language to the queen.

She looked at me and said, "The initial tunnels are dug to keep the eggs safe. We are well under way to complete the nest within a couple of sun cycles."

As the last drone crossed the portal, the queen nodded to me and disappeared through the gateway to her new world. The gateway was immediately sealed by my companion mages, and I dispatched the dwarf contingent to search the tunnels of the now-abandoned nest. I had the troops move into range to fire on the nest if needed, and then they stood by, awaiting the results of the search by the dwarf warriors.

The dwarf warriors reported back that the tunnels were all clear. There was no sign of anything or anyone left behind when the ants evacuated the nest. The Templar forces closed in within range and began a systematic destruction of the now empty nest, leaving only a pile of dirt and rocks where once the home of the ants rested.

I spent the night out in the field, and then headed back to the estate that had been gifted to me by the Holy Father. I sent the majority of the troops back home to the dragon world, keeping only a large enough contingent to provide adequate protection for myself, Lady Sylvia and Princess Rose. As I was standing there delegating the troops for sleeping quarters, a familiar shadow fell over me. The Templars in the open area of the estate dropped to one knee. I immediately knew who it was, so I was not surprised as the Angel Michael landed in front of me.

Michael said, "Congratulations on defeating the enemy. We were surprised that you did not eradicate the entire nest and its occupants."

I said, "I choose not to take lives if it can be avoided."

Michael laughed and said, "By the way, be wary of lady Amelia. She is a dabbler in magic and might be dangerous. She is an unknown quantity."

I thanked Michael and he took off again, disappearing into the sky. I was going to have to sit down with the ladies and discuss this new development with them. I was going to still let the ladies make the decision on who may or may not join our extended family. But first, I was going to get a good night's rest. I awoke in the middle of the night as the ladies crawled, on either side of me, into the huge bed. Their baby bumps were beginning to show quite a bit, but they cuddled with their backs to me, letting my natural warmth gently lull them to sleep.

I lay there, eventually falling asleep, but dreaming of tunnels and dark creatures grabbing at me and tearing at me. I awoke with a start, with daylight streaming through the window, as I lay in the bed alone. I climbed out of bed to get ready for the day and saw that I had scratches on my body in different spots, similar to where I was attacked in my dreams.

THIRTY-EIGHT

The Lady Disappears

Lady Amelia, Rose and Sylvia were absent during breakfast, which made me wonder. I passed it off to the women probably talking to Amelia privately, to feel her out about her intentions toward me. I sat enjoying my morning meal, amused by the fact that, instead of me doing any courting, Lady Amelia was being felt out by my ladies, to court me.

Suddenly, Rose and Sylvia came running into the room with a look of panic on their faces. Sylvia blurted out, "She is gone!"

I called the household guard, and was advised that Lady Amelia had been escorted off the estate by the enforcement arm of the church, on charges of heresy and witchcraft. I gathered my honour guard and headed to the papal palace immediately. I naturally took Gizmo with me, as she could read minds and gather intelligence on Amelia's whereabouts.

As usual, Pope Jason the Second was more than willing to interrupt any meetings he had currently going, in order to speak with me. When I strode into the room, I immediately saw the new cardinal of the enforcement arm of the church. He was dressed in the black of the order and was standing behind and to one side of the Holy Father.

I said to the Pope, "Your Eminence, one of my household has been taken without my knowledge by the enforcement clerics. I was not advised when they accused the Lady Amelia with heresy and witchcraft."

The Pope looked at the Cardinal with a questioning look, and asked, "Is this true, George?"

The cardinal replied, "I will look into it, but this is news to me, Holy Father. When I find out, I will advise you right away."

As we walked away from the papal palace, Gizmo spoke to me. "The cardinal was lying. He knows full well who she is and what she is accused of. Lady Amelia is safe at the moment—they are simply trying to scare her with their interrogation methods to get her to confess before they move to the next step. They will begin with the torture starting tomorrow, so we must move quickly if we want to rescue her before they start torturing her for a confession."

As soon as I returned to the estate, Sylvia and Rose were there to greet me with questions as to the Lady Amelia. I brought them up to date, and confided that I was not sure of the safety of my people on this world regardless of the Angel Michael's orders to the Pope about my safety. I directed Peter to escort all of my troops back to my world, and then I went to speak with the sergeant-at-arms about the troops who were part of the previous lord's household, and tasked with guarding the estate.

He said to me, "I speak for the men and their families when I tell you they would be grateful if you would take them back to your home world. With the history of the lord and lady of this household, it was just a matter of time before many of us would be taken in and forced to confess to crimes we did not commit."

I told him, "I need the men to stand at their posts until I return, or at dawn if I don't succeed. I guarantee your safety and that of your families on my estate on the dragon world."

The sergeant-at-arms answered, "We will stand guard until you return, regardless of how long it takes."

I then went to talk to Peter, and said, "I want a portal from here to as close to my stronghold on the dragon world as possible. If you need to set up a couple of portals to do so, go ahead. There will be women and children travelling with my ladies, and as soon as I return with the lady Amelia, I will need you to close the portal on little notice."

Peter replied, "It will be done as you wish, Dragon Mage."

I called Tomar and spoke. "I need you and ten of your best assassins for a mission into the papal palace and the enforcement arm of the church, to rescue the lady Amelia. I don't care about the clerics and their warriors. You may dispose of them as you see fit. I have reached a point where their lives are expendable."

Tomar asked, "When do you need them, Dragon Mage?"

"Two hours at the most," I said. Tomar nodded and ran off to get the men ready.

I asked Gizmo if she would come with me to lend her powers of reading minds and ability to locate hidden objects. I told her that it was completely voluntary, as I felt there was a great deal of danger if the guards were able to sound the alarm and get reinforcements.

Gizmo did not hesitate, but said, "I owe you my life, Dragon Mage, and I would not be worthy of the Dragon Mother's love if I did not help you."

Tomar and ten of his best men showed up, all dressed in black, and even had an extra black outfit for me. The outfits came with a hood attached, with eye holes only. I led the way to the secret tunnel leading into the enforcement area of the papal palace. We traversed the tunnel quietly, with only the light from my staff to show the way.

As we reached the other end of the tunnel, I signalled the dark elves to hold their positions, and I contacted Gizmo mind-to-mind. "Gizmo, is it safe to open the door and enter the papal palace?"

Gizmo replied, "There are roving patrols, but it will be clear momentarily."

We quickly entered the palace, and the elves spread out. They began dispatching warriors of the enforcement unit, and hiding their bodies in little nooks and crannies, where they would not be found for at least a few hours. Gizmo kept scanning the area, trying to locate lady Amelia. Tomar and Neb stayed with me as backup, keeping an eye out for anyone sneaking up on us or leaving one of the interrogation rooms.

Gizmo finally located the room that lady Amelia was in, and advised me that she had two clerics and two warriors in the room with her. The rest of the dark elves caught up with us, and we approached the door. It was bolted on the inside and two warriors stood outside the room on guard. Obviously, they felt that she was an important person to have confess her sins.

I nodded to Tomar and he, with the assistance of Neb, used throwing knives to quickly and quietly dispatch the two guards. They did not have breath to raise the alarm before they were dead from a knife in the throat. We propped a body up against the door and knocked. A small viewing port opened up. Whoever was on the other side looked at the dead guard, closed the portal, and then I could hear the door unlocked and opened inwards. I let the body fall, and stepped inside with the dark elves, quickly killing all the enforcement clerics and warriors.

Lady Amelia was lying on a table with a gag in her mouth, and her eyes were wide in terror. I removed the hood, held my finger to my mouth, and removed the gag from Amelia's mouth. She was so overwhelmed, she was silently crying for joy. I quickly removed the manacles and helped Amelia off the table. She tried to stand, but was too weak, and her legs gave out. I scooped her up in my arms and we made for the tunnel.

As we got to the tunnel entrance, I suddenly heard the bell tower ringing out, alerting the warriors that something was wrong. We entered the tunnel, and after we got halfway back to the estate, I could hear somebody coming down the tunnel behind us. I blasted the ceiling, causing a cave in, blocking the tunnel completely.

As we entered the courtyard where the portal was, I called the troops off the walls. There was no one left in the estate, with the exception of Gizmo and me. I directed Gizmo through the portal, with instructions to make sure everyone made it safely to my stronghold. I told her to leave me, and I would deal with the consequences of our actions.

I could hear the marching footsteps of the enforcement warriors coming down the thoroughfare, while I sat in a comfortable chair in the courtyard, awaiting my company. I had changed back to my dragon mage uniform/clothes, and sat enjoying a glass of cold mead. The warriors came to a halt at the front gate, and someone began yelling for admittance. They had a battering ram, and proceeded to break down the doorway—pushing in the gate that I had left unlocked—and fell flat on their faces.

They entered the estate with approximately one hundred warriors and clerics. An enforcement bishop walked up to me and demanded to know where the lady Amelia was.

I replied, "I was napping, and when I awoke, everyone was gone. I have not seen the lady Amelia since your people took her."

The bishop turned to the warriors and ordered them to search the estate thoroughly.

I poured myself another mug of mead and relaxed, while reports came back to the bishop that, true to my word, there was no one else in the estate.

Once they were done, the bishop looked at me and said, "You are under arrest for aiding in the escape of a known heretic and witch, the Lady Amelia. You will be taken for questioning."

I raised an eyebrow and said, "I don't suppose you are planning to tell His Eminence, Pope Jason the Second, that you are taking me into custody."

The bishop replied, "We only answer to God, and not the Holy Father."

They tied my hands behind my back and placed a hood over my head. It took five men to carry my staff, Draco. I could hear the warriors muttering about it being a cursed item.

They left the hood on as they strapped me down to a table, and I could hear them speaking amongst themselves about the fifty dead bodies found after Amelia was taken from their grasp. I was tired, so I must have dozed off and was snoring. They must not have appreciated that, because they removed my hood and slapped me in the face to awaken me.

I looked around me and could see the new cardinal of the order, sitting in a comfortable chair and silently looking at me. The bishop who had arrested me kept demanding answers to his questions. I just closed my eyes and pretended to go back to sleep. I opened my eyes as they began pulling out metal prods and branding irons, trying to burn me. They were hoping for screams of pain, but I disappointed them by thanking them for warming me up. Because of my dragon magic, fire was a friend and easy manipulated.

They then started pulling out other tools of torture: pincers, knives—a whole list of items that defied description. They started by lightly slicing my skin with a filleting-type knife, and then putting something that burned in the cuts. I would not give them satisfaction of screaming in pain, although the pain was getting close.

I glowered at the dark cardinal and said, "Now you have done it. I am getting a little angry, and you won't like me when I am angry!"

The dark cardinal chuckled warmly and said, "You let the evil enemy escape and you freed a witch from custody. I don't know how you made that apparition appear to the Holy Father, but that was done with the help of your master, the devil. God only has his angels appear to those worthy, and that you are definitely not!"

Just as the last syllable left his mouth, the room grew bright; too bright to do anything other than close your eyes.

As the light dimmed, I looked up, and there was Michael the Archangel, standing with a flaming sword. Everyone, with the exception of the cardinal, had been beheaded by Michael.

I looked at him and said, "I was about to deal with these idiots myself, but thank you for your assistance, my guardian angel."

Michael smiled at me and the shackles opened. He winked and said, "You will find that all the righteous prisoners are free, and all of the dark clerics and warriors have dropped dead and are on their way to hell—as I said would happen. I am taking this cardinal, who claims to be acting on orders from God, to be judged directly by The Creator. If he is forgiven, he will be back, but I do not think that will happen. If he has sinned beyond forgiveness, he will be cast directly to hell."

The cardinal was petrified with fear, as Michael grabbed his collar. They both disappeared.

As I got dressed, the door opened. An elderly man looked around the room and bowed to me.

In a shaking voice, he said, "All of the inquisitors have suddenly dropped dead, but we don't want to be blamed for their deaths."

I told him, "Gather all of those held for questioning. Meet me at the estate with all your families. I will take you someplace safe."

The elder bowed again and left the room, quickly gathering the others that had been held to get confessions of heresy by the enforcement arm of the church.

I grabbed Draco on my way out of the room, and strode to the gateway that led to the rest of the papal palace. The captives stood at the gate, which was locked and barred, preventing them from getting to the outside. I directed a bolt of flame to the lock, shattering it and blowing the door open.

I said to the people, "Be as quick as you can. I am going to leave a mystery to slow them down when they come from other cities." As the people rushed out of the area, I lifted Draco and concentrated, sending embers of fire to consume each of the corpses, leaving only ash and any jewelry behind.

I then walked into the personal rooms of the Holy Father, who was lying down for a nap. The papal guard did not wish me to enter the private rooms of the Pope. I knocked them down, stunning them momentarily, and walked into the room. As I approached the bed, the guards rushed in and grabbed me to pull me out of the room.

Pope Jason woke to the commotion and ordered the guards to stand down and leave the room. He then asked me, "What brings you to disturb my rest, Dragon Mage?"

"The enforcement arm of the church no longer exists. They took me and tried to torture me to say I was a heretic. Your newest cardinal was part of this plan. The Archangel Michael has killed all of them and freed their captives. I am leaving now, as I do not think this world is safe for me, after the enforcement arm of the church sends reinforcements from other cities to fill the vacancies. Should you need me, pray. I am sure that an angel can let me know my services are needed."

I walked slowly back to the estate to give the ex-captives time to gather in the courtyard, as I had instructed. When I arrived, I asked the elder if everyone was there that was coming.

The elder replied, "Yes, Dragon Mage, we are all here."

I opened the portal, but before I could direct them through, a large contingent of my warriors stepped into this world.

I said, "Tomar, secure the gate and watch for troops marching on the estate."

The elder and his people were escorted through the portal. The rest of the troops went with them to ensure their safety. One of Tomar's men whistled, and indicated that enemy troops were coming down the road. I quickly called all the men back, and we crossed the portal, sealing it behind us. I did not think the enemy had the technology as yet to create portals to new worlds, so we were safe for now.

When I arrived at my stronghold, my ladies ran to hug and kiss me. They expressed their love for me and were happy that I was safely at home.

Sylvia said, "Amelia is healing quickly, and has expressed her gratitude to you for saving her life." She smiled and added, "Rose and I, after talking with her, would be happy if you want to court her. Bringing her into the family would make us the perfect number. Godfrey and Elijah feel that Amelia has a large pool of power available to her, once she has been trained to use it."

I went up to the room that Amelia had been placed in with her ladies in waiting. She was sitting up in bed eating some broth, and when I entered the room she lit up like the proverbial neon sign. I sat down on the edge of the bed. Amelia's ladies were running around, with the eldest at a loss, because this was not appropriate behavior of any gentleman—sitting on the bed—never mind being in the ladies' bedroom at all.

"I came to check on how your recovery is coming, and also to seek permission to court you. I know that the Ladies Sylvia and Rose have spoken with you in regard to this world and its rules about relationships and wives," I said, holding her hand and looking deeply into her blue eyes. I looked admiringly at her, noticing that she was about five feet, eight inches in height, with golden blonde hair that went all the way down her back, falling just short of the floor. She was very slim, and had a beautiful smile, which lit up the room like a ray of sunshine.

Amelia said, "I would be honoured, My Lord, to be courted by you, and look forward to someone who would treat me with such care as I have heard you lavish on your ladies." I blushed, and Amelia laughed.

I excused myself, headed down to the portals, and transported to Elijah's stronghold. I called ahead to Elijah, and entered his chambers with no waiting needed. Elijah sent his attendants out of the room so that we could speak in private. I updated Elijah about what I had learned on the Templar world and my concerns about how things were run there.

I recommended that we not make any direct contact with this world for at least ten years, to give them time to grow as a society. I also advised Elijah that we had left several monitors, and Peter and his clan would monitor in case help was needed by the people. I still did not trust the enforcement arm of the church. If they took control of the church, it would be a nightmare, and the oppression would hurt the people greatly.

Now that the Templar world was dealt with, it was time to change focus and deal with the issues back on this world. I talked to Elijah about locating the home base of the Malum and focusing an attack on them, thereby removing the strong power base that Chavez was drawing upon. It would be advantageous if I could catch Chavez while he was at the Malum caves, because he always travelled alone when he went to see them.

I spoke to Elijah. "I am going to rest for a week and think about how it would be best to find the Malum caves and how to attack them, whether Chavez is there or not. It would be nice if we could deal with both of these enemies at the same time, but it is not vital. Either one could be dealt with on their own, without affecting the other. Peter has advised me that the monitors can be set on a person, following them as they travel, thereby keeping us updated on where that person is at any given moment. Of course we will set it on Chavez, as we can locate him initially easier than finding a Malum."

Part way through the night, I was awakened by something warm and soft crawling into my bed and snuggling against me. This time I did not resist temptation and allowed things to run their course with the lady Amelia.

* * * * *

The next morning, Amelia was gone. She spent the entire day with Rose and Sylvia. I could tell at mealtimes that they were all growing close. I told the ladies that this was the last time, as I did not believe I could handle more than three wives in my family.

Sylvia said, "We have had a long talk with Amelia, and she understands how plural marriages work in this world. This way, you will have a companion, as Rose and I are getting a little big for intimacy. We want you to have someone to fill your life with more love."

I replied laughingly, "I could have abstained until after the babies are born. I do have some self-control!" I looked at the ladies and smiled, shaking my head as I walked out of the room.

* * * * *

I sent an order out to all of the strongholds to search for a portal they might have missed previously. I knew there had to be a secret entrance to the caves of the Malum; something that would allow me to sneak in and surprise the enemy before they could organize a defence.

I went to Elijah's stronghold and up to the monitor room operated by Peter's people. I walked up to Peter and asked, "So how is the Templar world and the new ant world?"

Peter replied, "The ants are living up to their name. The new nest is complete, and they have begun harvesting the grasses and tilling the soil to plant new crops. As far as we can tell, there is a bit of an uproar on the Templar world. The enforcement arm of the church is putting up a fuss that the Holy Father had dealings with and assisted you."

I said to Peter, "Keep an eye on the Pope in the Templar world. He is a great man, and I would not like him to come to harm. If need be, we will have to stage a rescue on short notice."

Peter nodded, and passed the information on to his staff. I then left him to his work, and went to speak with the great dragon Elijah.

Elijah looked up as I walked into the room and said, "Greetings, young one. I hear that you have some concerns in regards to the Pope on the Templar world. Also, you are looking for a way to sneak into the caves of the Malum."

I looked at Elijah in mock dismay, and laughingly said, "I cannot keep anything from you! It is a good thing I am not planning a birthday party for you—it would never be a surprise."

Elijah roared with laughter at that comment.

I returned to my stronghold and spent the afternoon with Amelia, walking through the portal to allow her to see the huge marketplace in the main stronghold of the great dragon Elijah. I had to gently remind her a couple of times to close her mouth as she looked on in wonder at the different species of beings in the market, and how they worked to create wonderful works of art and jewelry with their hands.

As we were getting ready to return home, Elijah called and asked me to bring Amelia down to his chambers to meet him. I brought her into the room, where she stood frozen in fear, looking at this huge specimen of dragon before her. It took a little coaxing to get her to come close enough to Elijah to carry on a conversation with him. I used a spell to remove the fear from her mind, so that she was more comfortable with this gentle giant. Elijah asked me to leave the room, as he wished to speak to Amelia in private without interruption. Trusting Elijah, I stepped outside the chamber and the doors were closed.

Elijah's mind said to mine, "I promise to use no magic on her. I only wish to confirm what her intentions are in regard to our great dragon mage."

I shook my head and smiled. My extended family was asking Amelia what her intentions were! Usually it was the other way around; the prospective boyfriend/fiancé would be asked these questions by the father of the girl. Amelia was in with Elijah for over an hour. When she came out she was a smiling and walked over to me, giving me a huge hug and a kiss on the lips.

Elijah said in my mind, "I have given her my blessings, and explained about the great responsibilities that you have been tasked with. Her intentions are to support you in whatever you wish to do. Apparently her husband, who was executed as a traitor, left her with a dubious past that would not allow her to survive in the Templar world because of her association with the now-dead traitor lord.

She took my arm and we strolled back through the tunnels, back to my stronghold in time for dinner. It was a quiet affair with my ladies, which I thoroughly enjoyed.

Amelia, Rose and Sylvia looked at each other as if on cue, and then Rose said, "We have come to a decision, and are ready to welcome Amelia to our family if and when you have come to a decision, My Lord."

I looked at each of the women in turn, and responded, "I would be honoured to welcome the Lady to be my wife, as long as she is prepared to take her share, and be part of, but not in charge of my family."

Amelia was smiling as she responded, "I am aware of my responsibilities, and have had training in midwifery prior to meeting my late husband. I will be able to help in many ways, wherever my new lord husband may be."

I looked at my three ladies and said, "It is settled then. I am busy with other matters, and I will leave the wedding arrangements to you. I will add this, though—clear and concise. Although I welcome Amelia to our extended family, I forbid you to look for any other women to add to my life. If for some reason I change my mind, I will let you know well in advance. Is that understood?"

Rose smiled sweetly, saying, "Of course, my lord Jim, husband and love of my life." Batting her eyes.

I smiled back, knowing that I had little to say on the matter if they decided that I needed someone else in our family.

That night, as I settled in my bed, Rose and Sylvia snuggled in on either side of me. Amelia was apparently sleeping elsewhere in the suite of rooms that had been set aside for my use only. I quickly dozed off, comforted by the love of the ladies as they warmed my body with theirs.

Part way through the night, I awoke with the same nightmare that I had lately, running down dark tunnels with something unknown waiting for me. I heard a voice say, "Do not fear me, Dragon Mage. Free me, and I can help you fight the Malum!"

I sat up and moved around the sleeping women, getting dressed and walking down the hallways to go outside and clear my head. I went out and stared at the moon and the waves lapping down below on the beach. I reached out with my mind and called Flit, who was stationed at my stronghold. He flew up to the battlements.

I said, "Flit, I need you to fly to the Sea people and speak to Kleet and see if he will come here to speak with me."

Flit answered, "Do you need him right away, or can I rest for the evening before I fly to the villages of the Sea people?"

I responded, "No, my little friend, you may rest until morning—and thank you."

THIRTY-NINE

The Sea People locate the Malum

I t took about a week before a guard came to advise me that a submarine had just docked at the sea entrance of the stronghold. I went down to the dock to greet Kleet and his men. What surprised me the most was, the first being out of the vessel was one of the sea people elders, followed by Kleet and his men.

I bowed to the elder and welcomed him to the stronghold. Not knowing the diet of the sea people, I left the preparation of their evening meal to Kleet's men. I joined them in a meal, which I would describe as some of the best sushi I have had in many a year, even back home in my old world.

After the dinner was over, the elder spoke. "We have enjoyed our meal. Now tell me, Dragon Mage, how can we help you?"

"We have a rough idea of where the Malum caves are," I answered, "but we are looking for an entrance they may have forgotten about, or that is too hard to negotiate; one they may have ignored for centuries. The mountain range is near the ocean in the south. I would like you to search to see if there is a sea entrance to the Malum caves. It might be partially underwater, so that the entrance is not visible to anyone other than your people. If it cannot be located, there may be another way in, but I would be grateful if you looked, nevertheless."

The librarians of all the clan strongholds were also asked to search through their oldest volumes and see if there was any mention in them about the Malum and their caves. I also sent word to the dragon mother Neela, so she could have her ancient tomes searched for the same data.

Word was soon received back from the dragon aviary and the School of Dragon Companions and Mages, which led me to believe they had been looking in advance of my request.

Elijah said, after I called him, "I have been speaking to the Lady Neela, as well as the School, knowing that these two places had the oldest libraries in the world. It was my hope that one might have at least some information on the Malum."

I called Mercury, and we flew to the School of Dragon Companions and Mages, landing there late in the day. The building was well protected, and the walls surrounding the school had no gates. If you had not been invited and taught the opening spell or flew in, you could not gain entry.

An elderly mage greeted us as we landed in the courtyard. "Greetings, Great Dragon Mage Kai! We were told by The Eldest that you might be showing up to review our oldest ledgers."

The elder mage let a companion lead Mercury to somewhere he could rest, and showed me to a room that adjoined part of the main library in the school. The accommodations were simple but well maintained; the bedroom just had a single bed and a dresser. But the library was full of overstuffed chairs made for comfortable reading in quiet solitude.

The old books were placed in a large pile on a table, and the fire was roaring, filling the room with a warm glow. I sat and started to peruse the ledgers from centuries past. I handled each document with slow and deliberate motions so as not to damage the fragile pages. There were quite a few comments on the Malum and the damage they did, making the clans fear the dark and shutting themselves in to ensure the safety of their families during the long nights.

A scribe was in the library for any pages or documents that I needed copies of. I found some pages that showed a network of tunnels, which was believed to have been written by an escaped slave of the Malum before they could blind him. Notations made later indicate that this man was the one and only known escapee from the Malum. I handed the book to the scribe and told him what I wanted copied from the manuscript that I had been reading.

It took a week of reading the old tomes to go through all of the ones that the librarians had found. I called Mercury to advise that we would be leaving for the aviary the next morning. The scribe had completed copying what was purported to be a map of the Malum sanctuary. It did not show an entrance to the cave network, so the map was incomplete, but it at least showed something.

Mercury and I took off for the dragon aviary at first light, flying quietly through the clouds over the stormy seas. Mercury could sense that I was deep in thought and did not want to be disturbed. It was late afternoon by the time we reached the dragon island. There was an honour guard waiting for me, which led directly into the Lady Neela's presence.

She looked at me and spoke. "You look tired, Kai. I am concerned. You need to rest before you try to delve into the latest pile of manuscripts to find what you are looking for."

I suddenly felt the lack of sleep and the stress that I was under hit me. I started to stumble, and Neela grabbed me gently, pulled me into her soft nest, and placed me under her wing.

Neela said, "Sleep, and do not dream, my little Kai. I will watch over you and protect you. Nothing can intrude or harm you in this chamber."

Neela called the guard and said, "Triple the perimeter guard around this chamber and tell all the companions and guardians that I will not be disturbed or have any noise around my nest. Unless my life is in imminent danger, I will rest with my little Kai, and everything else can wait."

I don't remember having such a deep sleep—no dreams, no nightmares, no waking moments trying to go back to sleep. I awoke feeling full of energy!

Opening my eyes, I could see Neela watching me intently. I smiled at her and said, "Thank you, Dragon Mother. I needed that sleep. With your protecting watch over me, I am fully rested and ready to carry on."

Neela replied, "You are my little one, part dragon, part man. You fill my heart with love. You are of my nest and are special to me; that is why I try to treat you well."

I smiled, gave Neela a big hug around her neck, and went to find the library to do some more research on the ancient books. As I walked out of Neela's chambers, I found a librarian waiting patiently to take me to a smaller reading room, which was under guard.

This assortment of ledgers had more to do with births and deaths at the aviary, and contained a list of names of the dragons who had made themselves famous by their leadership or actions that stood in the service of the dragons. I sat down and began to go through the books.

I did find a story of how a dragon by the name of Rage had disappeared while looking for the entrance to the Malum caves. The writer of the story claimed that Rage had found an underwater entrance, with a tunnel leading up into the Malum caves. Rage had told the story to the chronicler, stating that he was going back to look into the entrance more closely. Rage never returned from the second sojourn into the caves of the Malum, and was believed to have died during his quest.

I returned to speak with Neela before I left the nest. She was in her chambers, ready to greet me as usual. When I entered her presence, she was in her usual position astride her nest and there was an elderly dwarf mage standing to one side. As I approached, the mage came to me and handed me a small bottle sealed and tied in such a way as it could be worn around my neck.

Neela said, "I had a vision that you will need this potion. It will bring back energy and vitality to any creature that is still alive. It will not bring back the dead, but those knocking on death's door can be brought fully back to life."

I examined the bottle, which was filled with a potion of red liquid, and placed it around my neck and against my body to keep the contents warm.

I asked Neela, "Did your vision give you any idea of when I am to use it?"

Neela laughed sweetly, "It would not be a true vision if it gave me all the answers."

I smiled at her and bowed deeply, before taking my leave of her presence.

Mercury was waiting patiently outside in the fresh air, all saddled up and rested.

I climbed up into the saddle and said, "Take us home, where we can rest while we wait for the next item of information I need, before we progress with our attack against the Malum and their servants."

Mercury leapt into the air, and off we flew to my stronghold on the east coast of the continent. As we got close, I saw a submarine pulling into the bay and sea entrance of the stronghold.

I immediately jumped off Mercury when we landed, and went down to the sea dock to welcome Kleet, and to find out what they had located—if anything—in their search for an ocean entrance into the caves of the Malum.

Kleet was brief, saying, "I have received word that there are some problems with large sea creatures around the villages, so I must return to protect my people. Here is a map of the coastline, with a possible cave that may lead you further into the caves. Unfortunately, we were only able to look at the part closest to the ocean. We did not venture further, but believe that areas underwater seem to lead west, in the direction of the caverns."

I said, "Thank you, my friend. Your assistance in this matter is greatly appreciated, and may aid us in attacking the enemy on its home turf. Go now to protect the sea people, so that no one is hurt. I will ponder this, as well as other information that I have gathered, before I decide what to do next. When you are finished at home, return here. I may need your underwater vessel to gain further entry into the caves." "I will call the great dragon and send dragons who can watch from the air and attack with fire to assist you".

Kleet bowed "Thank you; we are further in your debt". and he then immediately climbed back into the submarine, which closed up and quickly left the sea dock, headed to the villages of the Undine, and his people.

* * * * *

When I climbed back up to the courtyard from the tunnels, I was almost bowled over by Amelia, who jumped into my arms and covered my face with kisses. She was followed by Sylvia and Rose, whose greetings were just as warm, but less energetic.

Amelia said, "All is prepared for the ceremony, My Lord. We can have it performed whenever you are ready!"

I replied inquiringly, "...The ceremony?"

Sylvia spoke up. "To make her your wife, of course!"

I nodded, smiling, and replied, "As long as we can leave it to tomorrow, or any day other than today, as I need a bath and rest after this long journey."

Sylvia turned to her ladies in waiting and directed them to prepare a bath for the dragon mage, and a hot meal, as I had missed the evening meal. I was served in my rooms by Susan, the head of the kitchen. I made small talk with Fred and played with the drakes, who were beside themselves to see me.

Climbing into the hot tub of water and washing up, I almost fell asleep. Sylvia and Rose scrubbed me down to get at every nook and cranny of my body. I was completely relaxed as they helped me to my bed and crawled in beside me on both sides. I was soon fast asleep, not worrying about plans 'til the following morning.

I was awakened by James, who strode into the room with my formal dragon mage robe and clean clothes. While I ate my morning meal, Sylvia came in and braided my hair, which was getting quite long—almost down to my knees. I told Sylvia that I would need to cut it shorter in the upcoming days so that it did not get in the way if I were involved in a battle.

Sylvia disappeared after that. I presumed she was getting ready for the ceremony as Godfrey walked into the rooms, dressed in his finest wizard robes, to speak with me.

I looked him over and said, "You must let me get a tailor to make you some new robes, Godfrey. After two hundred years, yours are looking a little threadbare."

Godfrey just smiled at me and said, "I like to think of them as 'well-worn,' but if you wish, lad, you can get me some new clothes."

The ceremony was quick, with Sylvia and Rose standing by as witnesses, and Godfrey with James. Once the wedding ceremony was over, we all gathered in my rooms for a sumptuous meal, which was limited to leaders of the different companions, as well as my immediate family. This included Gizmo and Isaac, the little dragons whom I considered family.

The meal and celebration went well into the evening. Eventually, I excused myself and the Lady Amelia, my bride, as we headed to bed. We spent the night talking and slowly falling asleep in each other's arms.

FORTY

Assistance from On High

E arly the next morning, I was awakened by James, who advised me that Peter wanted to speak with me as soon as possible. I quickly dressed and went through the portals, to find Peter in the monitor room. The screens all showed the papal palace on the Templar world. It was surrounded by knights and clerics, all dressed in black, sealing in the palace so no one could come in or out.

I looked at Peter and said, "We need to arrange a rescue operation, through the portals, of Pope Jason the Second and his people."

Before Peter could reply, he was interrupted. Michael the Archangel suddenly appeared out of nowhere, and said, "That will not be necessary. The Most High has heard the prayers of thousands of believers on what you call the Templar world. If you watch carefully, you will see the wrath of God laid upon the dark priests. They have overstepped their beliefs and boundaries for the last time! Watch and see."

As we watched the monitors, I saw a flock of angels drop down amongst the dark knights and clerics. They were carrying blazing swords, and swinging them around themselves. They did not touch any of the dark ones, but all of the dark troops dropped dead as stones as we watched.

Michael looked at me and said, "This scenario is being re-enacted all over the world, wherever exist the ones who called themselves servants of god, and strove to weed out the heretics. Their methods of gathering confessions has angered Our Lord to the point where they had to be eliminated, ending their reign of terror."

I said to Michael, "It is good that justice has been done, and the people freed from under that oppression. Hopefully, the Pope will realize why, and be able to move on in a more positive avenue to help the people."

Michael said, "Yes, and by the way, this is for you—a gift for your services in dealing with the evil ones. It was the way that you dealt with them, fairly and justly, hopefully pushing them toward a more positive way in the future." Michael handed me a parchment. When I opened it, I found it showed a map of tunnels and caverns. I turned to ask Michael if it was, in fact, a map of the Malum caves, but he had disappeared just as mystically as he had appeared.

I thanked Peter for his help, as he was standing just staring at the place that the Archangel Michael had been standing. He finally just shrugged and went back to the monitoring of the screens. I took the parchment and went back to my rooms, pulling out the partial map I had found in the archives of the School of Dragon Mages and Companions. Examining the two documents, I could see that the partial map I had overlapped the complete map that Michael gave me.

The parchment showed one large entrance at ground level for entry into the caverns, as well as three others facing the same direction higher up—obviously intended for the Malum to enter or exit the caves.

The next morning, I brought the map back to Peter. I asked him to send a couple of monitors to verify the locations of the entrances to the caves. The map did not show any other entrances, which, I suspected, were hidden from view.

The monitors located the caves of the Malum. A circling pattern was set up to monitor the mountain chain, searching for other entrances that were not on the maps. The tunnels seemed to hit dead ends in certain areas of the diagram, which was copied and overlaid on one monitor. Any openings that were detected were added to the diagram. Most openings were too small to be anything else other than ventilation apertures.

I left the search to Peter, and wandered the stronghold for a couple of hours. Then I went to see Elijah.

As I walked into his chamber, Elijah looked up and said, "Welcome, my little Kai! Still having bad dreams?"

I replied, "Yes. They change slightly, but overall it has to do with dark tunnels and something chasing me."

Elijah replied, "I understand. It is something you must face. With your magic, you are very difficult to defeat by any opponent."

I thanked Elijah for his time and support, and then left. I walked slowly back to the portals and returned to my stronghold. My ladies were there to greet me, and told me that dinner was ready. I turned down the meal and headed to my bed.

Amelia climbed into the bed, cuddling up against me, and said, "I know you are troubled, husband. You do not have to talk. Just relax, and I will watch over you, protecting you from bad dreams. It is one of the things that my mother taught me before I was betrothed to my first husband."

Amelia started to sing softly, as she pressed her body against my back. I was soon in a deep, dreamless sleep. I slept the whole night away, resting as well as I did in the dragon mother's nest. Nothing disturbed me.

The sun shining into my room awakened me. I felt completely rested and ready to face the day, with whatever it developed into.

I called for all of my companion leaders to meet me in my chambers for a meeting to organize an offensive against the Malum. I organized the archers from all the races; I believed they were the best ones to deal with the Malum, as they were an airborne species. The ground troops were organized to form a number of guard contingents, to protect the archers from attack by ground troops.

Because it would take them a week to deploy in the area of the Malum cave homes, I advised them that I was not ready to get them in place yet. In the meantime, I dispatched several Ankylosaurs troop transports to go to the School of Dragon Mages and Companions. They were to go under escort to pick up all of the mages who were ready to provide healing and fire to cover for the companion troops when they arrived at the Malum caves.

In the meantime I had Peter focus a monitor on Chavez, to ensure that we knew where he was at all times. Chavez knew something was up, as he was strengthening his guards around the capital city and abandoning smaller outposts that did not require Orcs in the posts, or the posts were not of strategic worth, so were abandoned—leaving the gates wide open.

I did not attempt to interfere with the movement of the orc troops, knowing that the more orcs who moved into the capital city, the more their resources would be stretched to the limits. I received word from spies in the capital city that the murder rate had escalated astronomically. The orcs were never known for their good sense, and old rivalries between the different clans had been stirred up again, ending in murder and all-out battle between the clans.

I decided I would give them more time to stew for a while, letting the rivalries build up; causing issues amongst the orcs, and tearing at the fabric of the command structure. It appeared that Chavez was just letting things run their course, not interfering with the strife. I wondered if he was weaning the weak orcs out of the mix, and letting only the strongest and most powerful warriors survive.

FORTY-ONE

Templar World revisited

S ince the mass destruction of the dark-clad enforcement arm of the church, which was trying to take over the world and the church at the same time, I decided it would be a good time to take my new bride back to her home, where I could meet her parents. I arranged to shower her with jewels and lovely handmade gowns, and I also arranged for appropriate attire for myself—as befitting a knight of the Templar world.

I went to speak with Amelia and tell her of the surprise I had arranged, She squealed with joy, jumping into my arms and showering me with kisses.

I added, to Sylvia and Rose, "You can come along as well!" They both broke into grins until I spoke again. "The trick is that they must not know all three of you are married to me on this world. It is not that I am ashamed of my three lovely brides, but polygamy is frowned upon on the Templar world. You will be introduced as friends of my court, with powerful husbands that were unable to come with you. That way, no one will look down on you as servants, and will understand your station. Go prepare yourselves for the trip!"

I could hear the ladies giggling like schoolgirls as they gathered clothing and other things that they needed. I was concerned that, because of all the ladies-in-waiting in attendance, there might be gossiping about our multiple marriage, which was a common thing on this world. I asked Susan to talk to the ladies in waiting about not talking to outsiders. I sent Gizmo and a dwarf interrogator to determine if they were honest and could be trusted to keep to themselves, or at least gossip in such a way that they would not be believed, or even that whom they were talking to would think they were at least exaggerating.

I sent a contingent of guards and engineers to work on fixing up the estate, especially since I knew the gate had been damaged by the attack of the dark clerics. Once the building was secured and access protected, staff came across to ensure everything was cleaned and the estate was pristine by the time they finished.

The estate was staffed by dwarves and people from the dragon world. That way, there was always someone there that I trusted; maybe if I kept the estate I would hire locals later, when there would be no problem with possible spies. When the women and I arrived at the estate and got settled, I arranged for two chests of gold and jewels to be sent with the sergeant-at-arms of the estate to Amelia's parents' estate. I sent a well-written letter with the chests, explaining that this was a dowry for the lady Amelia's hand. I explained as well that since I had wed her already, they were welcome to visit the estate, and if not completely satisfied she was happy and well taken care of, they could take her away with them.

Before they were to arrive, I arranged for a visit with the Holy Father, the Pope. Pope Jason welcomed my entourage into the audience hall.

He said, "I presume you know what has transpired in the last week. With the passing of all of the dark clerics, it is like all the people are able to breathe a deep sigh of freedom. I have turned the coffers of the enforcement arm of the church back to the cities where they were located. Negotiations are ongoing about having a lower government made up of those voted in by the people of the city, with a higher level of lords to ensure that frivolous laws are not passed."

"By the power invested in me by the Holy Church, I give your union with the Lady Amelia my blessings. May you be happy, and may she be a good and supportive wife, caring for your needs and the needs of your household first and foremost."

I bowed my head down as he blessed Amelia and I. Later, my ladies and I had a private meeting with the Pope in his chambers. His guards were instructed to step outside, because Pope Jason felt completely safe in my presence. I explained to the Holy Father about plural marriages on the dragon world, following in the old testament traditions of multiple wives and concubines.

The Pope did not hesitate, and gave his blessings to all of the ladies saying, "May the Lord bless and keep you safe, and may all your endeavours to wipe out evil on any world be successful."

I thanked the Holy Father, and we walked back to the estate. I saw couples walking in the streets, holding hands and dressing in brighter colours, which would not have been allowed when the old enforcement arm of the church was watching over things.

The ladies were watching, taking in all that was transpiring around them. Lady Amelia kept up a running commentary, pointing things out and explaining the changes that had occurred in the last little while. I could tell that the women were getting along exceptionally well. It would make my life so much easier than if they did not get along.

The next day, Amelia's parents, Lord and Lady Jonah Strongwind, showed up to meet her new husband. I personally greeted them and rolled out the red carpet, treating them like royalty.

Jonah was staring at the amassed troops of the different races, light and dark elves, dwarves, and the small dragon Gizmo draped on my shoulder. It took several minutes before his attention turned back to me, and I greeted him formally, after having my staff escort his luggage and his personal staff to a suite of rooms put aside for he and his lady.

Amelia advised that her father did not approve of her previous husband, being leery of what he might be capable of, which turned out to be true. It apparently was an arranged marriage, and Lord Jonah did not have the money to say no to a generous dowry. I left Amelia with her parents to get reacquainted, as she had not seen them for several years. Her previous husband had not allowed her to have any communication with her parents, possibly fearing that she may tell them too much.

Susan outdid herself, preparing a sumptuous evening banquet for Amelia's parents. Pope Justin showed up at the gate and invited himself to dinner at the estate. Lord Jonah was beside himself in excitement, as even a man of his stature would seldom even get close to His Holiness.

During the meal, I turned to Jonah and said, "As you know, I do not live in this world of yours, and I plan on taking Amelia with me. I have here documents transferring the title of this estate into your family's hands. I have no need to reside here. I may visit on occasion, but have no intention of staying, as the dragon world is my home now."

Lord Jonah replied, "Thank you, Sir Jim. Your gifts, including this estate, are more than enough to carry the name of my family through tough times. You have my word that you will always be welcomed here and it will be a safe place to rest. With all of your wives." Jonah winked at me. I would like to speak with you later on a matter of a personal issue—alone, without anyone listening in."

After the meal was completed, Jonah and I entered a private lounge off the dining area. I dismissed the staff, telling them I would call for something if I needed it. I instructed James and a couple of trusted companions, Blaze and Blade, to not let anyone disturb us unless the estate was under attack.

Jonah sat down with a glass of brandy in his hand, staring into the fire for a few minutes, before he turned to look at me and said, "First off, I must tell you that Amelia is not of my bloodline, or that of lady Strongwind. Her mother was executed by the enforcement clerics as a witch and heretic. The child was left down by the river, for God to decide her fate. My wife had a stillborn daughter about three months prior to this happening, and she was inconsolable. I sent a trusted man to find Amelia where she was, and bring her into our household and the Lady's arms. It was like my wife had a second chance at life. She perked up and was ready to live for the child and herself."

I replied, "You have said nothing up to this point at which I would second guess my decision to wed your adopted daughter. I love her, and I doubt there is anything you can tell me that would dissuade me."

Jonah continued, "Amelia began to exhibit strange abilities starting at the age of six. Her nanny caught her, on several occasions, apparently talking to animals. That would be normal, but the animals seemed to understand her and would obey any direction that she gave them. Then she would greet them and heal any injuries that they had. The nanny had been with my family for many years, and kept the information to us alone; she did not gossip with anyone."

I said to Jonah, "I had an inkling that was the case. As you are probably aware, I am known as the dragon mage. I have powers over fire and other elements. The fact that your daughter has powers of her own only makes me more fond of her. In my world, she will be cherished for her abilities and be kept safe from enemies. I have learned that magic is not evil, but the purpose that it is put to can be good or evil. You have nothing to fear for your daughter's safety. Does she know she is adopted?"

Jonah replied, "No, we have kept that one thing about her past from her. We were going to tell her during this visit, but wanted your permission, as her husband, to speak with her on this private matter."

I laughed, saying, "The way I was brought up, women are individuals and have their own opinion, either in agreement with their husbands or not. You may speak to her on any topic you wish, without my permission, in the future. Stay here and I will gather your lady and Amelia, so that you may speak with her in private without being disturbed."

I stepped outside the door and asked James to find the Lady Amelia and her mother, and to bring them here to this lounge. When they arrived, I got up to leave.

Jonah said, "Please stay, Lord Jim. I realize, with your intuition, we have no secrets, and I believe that you are the best match for Amelia."

Jonah and his lady explained how Amelia had come into the family, and as much about her deceased mother that they were able to glean from her old village. At several points during their narration, Amelia broke into sobs, and leaned into me for comfort.

After all was said, and Lord Jonah and his lady went off to their rooms, Amelia looked at me, with her eyes reddened by crying, and said, "I understand if you wish to annul our marriage and leave me here to deal with Christian justice, whatever it may be."

I said, "I am no saint, Amelia. You are welcome to my bed and my life. I have no intention of leaving you alone. The fact that you have some undeveloped magic talents intrigues me even more."

I gave her a big kiss and a strong hug, letting her have time to herself to think. I spoke to Sylvia and Rose, letting them know what had transpired, and they advised that they were going to spend the night with her and comfort her as she dealt with these new revelations.

I slept fitfully, dreaming of dark tunnels and being pursued by something. I must have yelled out in my sleep, suddenly coming awake with Amelia cuddling me and comforting me until I drifted off, asleep again. I awoke when the sun was shining in through the window, realizing that I had overslept into the late morning. James came in to check on me, noting that I was slowly waking up. A few minutes later, all the ladies came in, bearing a tray heaped with baked goods and fruit plates. They sat on the edge of the bed around me, and we enjoyed idle chit chat as we ate the morning meal.

I asked Amelia, "How are you doing? Have you spoken to your parents yet this morning?"

With a smile on her face, Amelia replied, "Yes, I have spoken to my mother and father. I am feeling fine, knowing that I am loved as much as if mother had borne me herself. I want to try something that I have wanted to try for years, but I was afraid of the consequences if the church found out. I know you have stated that you will protect me, but I wanted to check with you before doing this."

I looked at her curiously and asked, "What did you have in mind, my little princess?"

Slowly and quietly, Amelia said, "I want to call a creature that has not been seen for a long time, as it has been hunted almost to extinction. It may be violent. I have heard rumblings of how dangerous it might be, and I would like you, my husband, to be there to protect me in case things do not turn out the way I wish."

FORTY-TWO

Gryphons and Doorways

We travelled outside of the city, almost to the old post where the portal was protected, enabling entry into the dragon world. I had a large entourage of guardian companions, as all three of my ladies were with me. I had the troops spread out, but they were under orders not to fire unless I directed them to. I then gave Amelia the green light to do the summoning.

Amelia stood there. She looked up at the sky and held her hands out, showing that she was not armed, and was not a threat to whatever she was summoning. I watched the sky, and soon saw a dark speck growing in size as it grew closer. When the creature came to a landing, I recognized it as a Gryphon, a mythological beast—part lion and part eagle. I stepped beside Amelia and faced the Gryphon, bowing to it in greeting.

It spoke in my mind: "Greetings, Dragon Mage. I have heard about your adventures in this world. My clan is being hunted to extinction. We do not have any place to go, unless you will let us use your portal into another world; a world where we can grow without being hunted down by humans."

I replied, "If I have your word that you will not hunt the intelligent species on my world."

The gryphon said, "My name is Nebulon. As head of my people, I guarantee that we will not hunt any that are intellectual unless they are enemies and you give your permission to do so."

I bowed to Nebulon and said, "Gather your clan. We will open the portal to the dragon world, where you can live. If that does not work out, we can find you another world that is more suitable, and then open a doorway for you to use. When you are ready, send an envoy to the little fort down here, and we will open a portal near your nests. That way, you will not have to risk the safety of the young ones by travelling to the portal down here."

Nebulon said, "Agreed. We should be ready in six sleep cycles. At that time, I will send an envoy to this portal gate."

With that, he flew off toward the sun and the mountains in the area.

I looked at the departing Gryphon and then at Amelia, and said, "I sensed a bond between you two, although nothing was said about it by Nebulon."

Amelia answered, "I have vague memories of an imaginary playmate, that was perhaps not so imaginary."

I smiled at her and reached over to give her a big hug. We headed back to the estate, where we would prepare to leave this world and return to the dragon world.

* * * * *

We gathered together in the courtyard to say our goodbyes to the Lord and Lady Strongwind. I brought over the old guards and staff of the estate to work for the Lord and Lady. I knew this would help them to feel comfortable being back in their home world, while still being faithful to me if I had reason to return to the estate.

I had placed the portal in an archway, where I also built a couple of sturdy doors, so no one could accidentally enter the dragon world. The door had to be unlatched and open to allow passage to my stronghold on the other side. I advised Lord Strongwind that this would be the only portal. If I was needed or they wished to visit their daughter, they could do so by simply opening the door and walking through to another world.

I brought Mercury with me through this portal. Once all had gone through, he and I took to the air to fly to the nesting area of the Gryphons. They had sent an envoy the day before to the outpost, who relayed the information to me, and then closed up, leaving through the portal there and sealing it behind themselves.

Mercury was in a bad mood this morning, grumbling about not trusting these 'bird cats,' as he called them, and suggesting that we should have brought more troops or dragons for reinforcements in case of trouble.

As we approached the nesting site, two young males flew up as if to challenge us.

I looked sternly at them and said, "Nebulon knows we are coming. He has arranged this. Why are you even considering getting in the way?"

One of the young Gryphons said, "Apologies, Dragon Mage, but there is a hunting party coming up the mountain side, and we had to be sure you were not part of it."

I landed with Mercury and instructed him to locate the hunting party and do a little burning from the sky, to slow them down while we got the hatchlings and mothers to safety through the portal.

Mercury said to me, "All right! A chance to play. I will teach them a lesson they will not forget, Kai."

I strode past Nebulon, and started the incantations and concentration required to open a new portal. Once the portal was open, I had Nebulon stand by while I stepped through to ensure there was no danger on the other side.

I had hit the target location exactly where I wanted. On the dragon world side were two contingents of archers and a contingent of dwarf warriors. I had the dwarves stand by to intercept anything other than the Gryphons from entering the world, and I brought the archers with me back to the Templar world. I explained to the commander of the archers about the hunters and the fact that I did not want to kill them outright, but merely injure them to the point of giving up their task. Holding them back until all the Gryphons were safely across the portal would be satisfactory.

The archers were true to their commander, aiming for legs and arms, downing about one third of the hunters before they started to fall back. I walked down to where the archers were and tested the wind, which was fortunately blowing in the direction of the hunters. I then laid down a wall of flame, which burned down the mountainside and forced the hunters to flee for their lives.

Once the last Gryphon was through the portal, I pulled the archers back and doused the fire with my magic. I was the last one through the entrance to the dragon world, ensuring that none of my troops were left behind, and closing the aperture behind me. I spoke to Nebulon briefly and then dismissed the troops to return to their posts.

Mercury and I flew back to Elijah's stronghold and I filled him in about the latest venture in the continuing travels of Kai the Dragon Mage.

I told Elijah, "I have to quit doing these excursions! They are pulling me off track from the tasks at hand. I need to concentrate on the Malum issue before I can help other worlds or people, but first I must help my adopted world.

I went back to my stronghold and my ladies, relaxing and scanning the maps I had acquired, which I believed were ancient—from the times before the Malum became enemies of the dragons. If it were not for the fact that I had so much on my mind, it would have been really enjoyable spending time with Sylvia, Rose and Amelia. I also spent time playing with Matilda and her kin. A new little batch of drakes was there to play with and I was advised by Fred that all of the mating pairs had birthed healthy litters. Fred was doing an awesome job of taking care of the drakes and doing the initial training.

Matilda was so overjoyed that her whole body was quivering with joy whenever she saw me, and especially when I spent time with her. Once Bonnie and Clyde were done nursing, I had them with Sylvia and Rose, with Matilda guarding Amelia and me. I knew that the drakes would not let anything happen to the ladies, or die protecting them.

My nightmares grew in detail so much so that I woke up yelling most nights, and had to be comforted by whoever was spending the night with me. Since the ladies spent time with me in turns, they were better rested than I.

I recognized some of the symptoms, and knew I was suffering from Post-Traumatic Stress Disorder. It did not surprise me, as I had been through a lot in the last year and a half. Much had occurred during my time here. I had had a baby on the way, but lost it because of who I was, and I now had three women who relied upon me for protection and guidance. I went from being a simple police officer to a powerful wizard, whose opinion carried a lot of weight in this world.

I had become crippled and then saved by intelligent dragons, whom I could speak with in my mind; had found and rescued at least two species from extinction; and had made friends and enemies in this short time. The enemies did not just hate me, but wanted me dead, and the friends would die for me. This was a heavy burden to bear, and I did not know what the solution was. But the sooner I dealt with this matter at hand, the better I would sleep at night.

I received an invitation to see the Lady Neela at the crèche on Dragon Isle. I immediately asked Mercury to get ready for a journey, and he advised that he would be ready at first light. I climbed aboard Mercury with a little travel pack, and we flew off into the sky. We arrived late in the day at the aviary, and the guardians who greeted us said that the dragon mother thought it would be best if I rested for the evening before seeing her the next morning.

FORTY-THREE

Attack on the Malum

I walked into the dragon mother's nest room and bowed to Lady Neela, waiting for her to start speaking to me.

Neela looked at the host of guardian companions and servants and said, "Leave me with Kai. What I have to say is for his ears only. No one is to interrupt us for any reason. Kai will advise you on his way out when I have finished with him."

Neela waited until everyone but she and I were out of the room and the doors were closed, with guards to prevent anyone disturbing us.

She said, "Kai, come close to me and I will share with you another vision that I have had in regard to your upcoming battle with the Malum."

I responded, "My ears and mind are open to whatever the Great Lady has to tell me, especially if it will help me in facing the Malum and Chavez."

Neela said, "This is what I have dreamed of in my vision Kai. If you go with companions, they will be killed and so will you. You must go alone—but fear not! In the darkness you will find an ally. It will be one who will need the potion I have given you, but one who will be greater than any you can take with you. The Caves are in darkness, but your staff will light the way and keep most of the dangers at bay. You must study the maps and know them by heart, for if you are distracted and need to view the maps, you will miss small dangers that could hinder—if not stop—your venture."

I bowed to the great dragon mother and said, "Your insight and visions will make my attack on the enemy far more likely to succeed."

I slowly walked out of the chambers and told the companions and servants that they could again enter the chamber to assist the dragon mother. Mercury was waiting all saddled up, and it was but a moment before we took to the air again.

As we were flying over the ocean, Mercury said, "Well, what did the mother of dragons have to tell you?"

I replied, "I don't know if I should share with you Mercury, as you will not like what she said to me about her vision of the attack on the Malum."

Mercury replied, "Yes, there is no point sharing with me unless the vision includes me. I probably do not want to know, because if I do not like the vision, I might try to talk you out of it."

* * * * *

It was early evening by the time we reached my stronghold, and a hot meal was ready for me. The ladies joined me, having waited to eat until I arrived. I sat down after the meal was cleared, and had all the staff leave us alone. Then I explained to my ladies in detail the vision that the dragon mother had, and why I had to venture into the Malum tunnels alone. It took a little bit to settle them down, as they were quite upset about me going unaided.

Finally, I held up my hand and explained that this topic was not open for discussion. All three of the women stormed out of the room in anger!

I sat there watching them walk out, muttering to myself, "Women! Can't live with them sometimes, can't live without them." I walked out of the room and headed to my chambers and crawled in my much-too-large bed. It was going to be another long night of nightmares, but without one of my ladies to comfort me.

* * * * *

I lay in bed for a couple of hours, as sleep eluded me. I finally dozed off, dreaming of tunnels and giant spiders and being grabbed by something that pulled at me. I woke up with a start, yelling in my sleep as I usually did. James came in and checked on me to ensure that I was all right. I did not bother with breakfast the next morning, and left directly through the portals to Elijah's stronghold.

I walked into Elijah's chambers without checking in advance, and growled at the companions and guards to leave us alone.

They looked at Elijah, who nodded his head, and they left us alone.

I explained to Elijah about the dragon mother's vision, and how my wives took it to heart. I explained to him about worrying that there would be a great loss of life if I took warriors into the caves with me. I told Elijah that I wanted to have men surround the area around the entrances to the Malum caves that were obviously visible.

I called for my leaders to arrange for phase one of the attack on the home of the Malum, but I wanted to know first when Chavez was there, so as to kill two birds with one stone. They would be expecting a frontal attack, as I did not believe they were even aware that the tunnels could be accessed by the ocean entrance. It was either that, or there was some sort of trap set along the way into the main part of the Malum caves.

I advised the warriors to set up in the areas surrounding the mountains of the Malum, but to be secluded, camouflaged, and out of sight of anyone using the road leading to the caverns. Once Chavez reached the area, the cordon would be closed, preventing him from leaving unless he was flown out of the area by the Malum. Elijah did not think that would be likely, as the Malum were of slighter frame and lighter, so were not capable of carrying Chavez.

I knew that it was just a matter of time, since Chavez had not left the capital city and gone to the home of the Malum for a while. I sent Flit to get a submarine from the Sea people to come to my stronghold and stand by to transport me to the undersea entrance to the caverns. I waited for three weeks before receiving word that Chavez had left the city to go to an unknown location, which later proved to be the Malum caverns.

As soon as Chavez entered the caverns, the troops set up a perimeter around the openings, setting up a blockade, and drawing attention to themselves. They had instructions to fire their catapults and seal the tunnel entrances that were visible. The Snow people set up outside of the capital city, with instructions to intercept and eliminate any groups of Orc warriors who left the city.

FORTY-FOUR

Into The Dark

A s soon as I heard that Chavez was headed to the Malum caves, I boarded the submarine and headed to the cove where the underwater caves were to be found. The submarine navigated the tunnels that were filled with water, coming up after a dip in the passageway and surfacing into an area that had air in the chamber. There was a stone pier, but no lighting in the area. When I got out of the vessel, I saw dead light globes.

Reaching out, I powered up the globes that showed the dock area. It was obviously an ancient access to the tunnels. There were barrels and boxes stacked at one end of the dock, and everything was covered in dust and cobwebs. I could not see any footprints or cleared areas in the dust to indicate that anyone or anything had been there recently. I felt like I was in a grave.

I had this sick feeling in the pit of my stomach, as my nightmares came back to haunt me. I shook it off, and prayed that Lady Neela's visions were accurate. As I stared down the dark tunnel, I was aware that there was no noise at all. I felt it was time to turn up the heat, and called out to Elijah to pass on the command for the troops to start the bombardment of the visible entrances to the tunnels.

I decided to wait for a couple of hours, staring into the inky waters sloshing against the stone jetty. It was not long before I started to hear a distant booming coming through the tunnels. I could also feel intermittent vibrations as the missiles struck home. Elijah told me, via our link, that there was a large contingent of orcs storming out of the main entrance to attack the catapults. I had prepared for that contingency, and the archers and ground troops were able to dispatch the orcs, with only a few of our men falling in battle.

With the entrance blocked by debris from the catapults, the occupants of this place would either clear up the tunnel entrance or be looking for another way out to remove Chavez to safety. I started to walk down the dark tunnel, touching light disks as I passed, which caused them to glow dimly. It was like leaving a trail of breadcrumbs to lead me back if I needed a way back out. I continued to hear the distant booming as the catapults continued their bombardment.

I entered into a large chamber, whose walls disappeared into the darkness. I could hear scrabbling in the blackness. The first thing that came to mind was spiders. I shuddered in fear and loathing. Suddenly there was a blast of flame, which spread out in an arc and passed over me. Of course, with my powers of fire, I was untouched. But, I could see several newly crisped spiders that were the size of bears. This was followed by the sound of chains and the crunching of something eating the spiders.

I cast a spell, throwing up into the air a globe of light, which I directed to the ceiling of the cavern, where I could see extinguished light globes. As the chamber began to brighten up, I could see the chains leading to something in a heap on the floor. I walked up to the heap, and was engulfed by fire from a dragon's breath. I just stood there, waiting for the dragon to finish, before walking closer.

I said, "Greetings. I am the dragon mage Kai, and I am here to attack the Malum and the evil wizard Chavez."

A weak voice responded, "Kai, I am the dragon lord Rage. If you would do me the favour of ending my existence on this plane, I would be honored."

I responded, "Would you rather die in battle than just lie there like a piece of meat to be cut up and left to rot?"

Rage replied, "Unfortunately... I am too weak to put up much of a fight."

I looked at him. He was huge—probably the largest dragon I had ever seen in my travels of this world.

I said, "I have a gift for you from the Great Dragon Mother Neela. May I approach you, Great Lord Dragon?"

Rage nodded, and I walked up to him and emptied the contents of the vial that Neela had given me into his mouth. I watched in fascination as his emaciated body filled out, and strength returned to the great dragon. I smashed the shackles holding him prisoner and he shook violently, shaking off the chains holding him in place.

Rage said, "Thank you, Dragon Mage. I am ready for a little payback to the Malum for keeping me alive in these horrid conditions, and I am now ready to fight for my freedom."

I explained to him about the lighted tunnels behind me. I told him that, if he wished, he could swim to safety and then fly to the dragon crèche.

Rage said, "I would be without honour if I were to slink away from a fight. When I can kill a few Malum, it will be worth dying in battle."

I nodded to Rage and started to walk down the tunnel deeper into the mountain. Rage slowly followed, since his muscles were stiff from lack of use.

Rage startled me a couple of times as we walked down the tunnels, burning some creature with his dragon flame before I even noticed the danger. The tunnel started to curve uphill, but remained large enough for Rage to walk up it comfortably. I continued to light the globes as we passed when I saw ones that were intact. There were quite a few that were broken, in a deliberate attempt to keep the tunnel dark.

Part way down the tunnel system, I found some sealed portals surrounded by dragon script. This made me wonder if at one time this was an old home for the dragons before they separated and one branch devolved into the Malum.

I looked at Rage following behind me, his eyes alert for any movement in the tunnels, and asked, "Do you know where these portals lead to, Great Dragon?"

Rage looked at me momentarily before he went back to scanning the tunnels and said, "No, I don't think the Malum or their servants are aware of the existence of these portals. They probably think of them as just closed-up tunnels, with graffiti written by some servant on the walls. The Malum are so full of themselves that they do not grant much intelligence to the lesser races, especially since they only pick the simplest of subjects to blind and use as servants. And it would be difficult for a blind person to notice the script on the walls, because it is higher than their reach."

Looking at the inscriptions closely, Rage muttered to himself for a couple of minutes before looking at me again and saying, "It appears that one goes to the dragon island crèche, and I am not sure, but the other appears to go to the School of Dragon Companions and Mages. I think it best, for the time being, that we do not open these doorways. They could be used by our enemies to access vulnerable locations, especially in the event of a surprise attack."

I nodded, and continued on along the tunnel until we came across a stone plug blocking the tunnel. I examined the plug, which must have been designed as a doorway to protect from intruders coming through the ocean access tunnel. I believed that the plug was also in place sometime before the doorway portals were sealed, to be able to isolate the Malum tunnels.

I looked back again at Rage and said, "Do you remember which way the plug-like doorway opens? We can push on it, forcing the lock."

Rage replied, "I think it slides into a side niche, if my old memory has not failed me."

I prepared to blast the edge opposite of where we felt it was to open. Rage stepped forward, grabbed the edge, and pulled. I could heard squealing, as whatever was holding the plug closed gave way under Rage's phenomenal strength.

I chuckled at Rage, "Show off."

Rage chuckled back at me, bowing his head to acknowledge the compliment. I could hear shouting and weapons being drawn, as the guards at the plug gate prepared for battle.

I was ready. I placed myself near the opening gap leading further into the Malum fortress. As soon as Rage had the opening wide enough for me, I stepped through and created a wall of flame, which overwhelmed the guards as they stood. They did not even have enough time to scream in pain as they were overcome by the intense fire.

Rage looked at me and said, "Spoilsport."

I laughed and replied, "There will be many more for you to play with as we progress through the tunnels. I did not want to waste your power until we came upon some Malum."

Rage considered me and said, "You are a truly worthy battle companion, with your power and fearless attitude. The tunnels are larger from here on. Climb onto my back and we can fight these puny orcs as one."

I climbed up onto Rage's back and used my legs to hold me in place behind his head. From this point on, there was a constant battle with guards. A few of the blinded servants were cowering against the walls, out of the way. The amount of heat that I could generate was even hotter than what I normally would be able to spawn outdoors, as the passageway walls contained the heat. This made it hot to the touch for orcs further along from the initial attack point.

We worked our way to the entry area to the caves, where I could hear the continued pounding of missiles hitting the area, causing rock to break free and fall, partially blocking the tunnels. I sent a message to the troops to cease fire for the time being so that Rage and I did not get crushed by falling debris.

As we got closer to the guards and workers, they did not even look up to notice us standing there. I leaned forward and whispered in Rage's ear, saying, "Time to cook them, my friend." Rage let a blast of dragon fire go sweeping from side to side, filling the whole area with a wall of flame.

I suddenly noticed guards trying to sneak up behind Rage and let loose with bolts of energy to destroy him. Either they ran out of guards or the guards were keeping a low profile so as not to be cooked by the dragon and dragon mage. We turned toward the central chamber. The Malum were there in compartments that opened up into a central chamber. The Malum, according to Rage, were a communal race and preferred to stay together as much as possible. Rage did not know what the count of the Malum was, but knew they would be in that chamber, young to old, male and female.

We finally came upon a great door that blocked the entrance into the main chamber where our target, the Malum, were. I looked at the door. which was covered in dragon script. It was not even scratched by any attack spells that I could manage. It was a beautiful piece of ancient hand crafting and dragon magic, seemingly impenetrable to magic or manual force.

Rage said, "The script on the gate is an ancient form of the dragon tongue, many centuries old. Let me study it for a little while. I may be able to decipher the password, or spell, which will open these gates. While Rage was reading and scanning every inch of the gate, I called the troops to advise that the front gate was secure and they could move the troops up to clear and open the entrance to the Malum caverns.

I must have fallen asleep, because the next thing I remembered was Rage nudging me awake. Rage said, "If I recall when you introduced yourself, you said that you were the dragon mage?"

I replied groggily, "Yes I did, and yes, I am the dragon mage."

Rage said, "Good. Then we can open the gate easily. If you look at the door, there is a handprint marked on either side of where the doors join. You simply have to state your name and title, and the gate will unlock itself, allowing us to enter the center chamber."

I stood up and brushed the dust off my hands. Walking over to the door, I could see the handprint location.

I placed one hand in each spot, and incanted, "I am the Dragon Mage Kai, also known as Jonathan Isaac Martin. I demand entry to this place in the service of the dragon clans." I could hear clicks and grinding as beams slid themselves out of the way. The doorway slowly came open, allowing Rage and me to enter the Malum chambers.

Just before the chamber opened up, there stood Chavez, a slight glow of power surrounding him.

Chavez looked at me and Rage and said, "Last chance, Dragon Mage. Kill this old fossil with you and you can join my forces and rule this world with an iron fist. I will even let you keep your wives and you can rule half the kingdom—answering to me, of course. You must realize by now that the dragons are just using you as a tool. You will never leave here alive. You may succeed in your battle, but I guarantee that you will die in that encounter."

After I spit on the floor of the cavern, I looked at Chavez and responded, "I would rather die with honour at the side of this fossil, as you call him. I have given my word to the dragons to take down the Malum. Also, I think Rage here has a score to settle, and what kind of friend would I be if I did not help him?"

Chavez sent a blast of energy at me. I held up Draco, which had been equipped with Pater's crystal. I barely felt anything other than a slight push, as the staff absorbed the magic cast by Chavez. Chavez stood there with his mouth open, surprised at the fact that his spell did not even faze me. He then cast a more powerful spell, which I felt a little more. I cast a huge bolt of energy, which threw Chavez one hundred feet back, back into the darkness of the cavern.

Rage and I walked into the chamber and I pulled out a light globe from my pack, charging it and casting it high into the air. I could see globes spaced around the chamber on each level. I cast the spell and the globes started to lighten the whole cavern up. I could hear the squealing of the Malum, as they did not like light at all. Rage roared in anger and started to climb the walls of the chamber, breathing fire and lashing out at the Malum, who were having trouble with all the light in the chamber.

I stood in the centre of the chamber and concentrated on casting a powerful fire spell, causing a whirlwind of fire to spin around me. I did not worry about Rage, as he, like me, was fireproof. I poured everything into the spell, enveloping the entire chamber like the inside of a kiln. I realized that I was putting too much attention into the spell when I felt a sharp pain pierce me from behind.

I turned to look at Chavez, who was standing there with a smile on his face. I angrily lashed out and threw Chavez to the far wall with such force that I could see blood coming from his mouth and nose as he slumped down to the ground. I turned and concentrated on the fire, spreading it so that it filled the entire chamber. As I passed out from pain and blood loss, I could hear the screams of the Malum as they were incinerated in the fire.

I smiled as darkness began to envelop me, knowing that I had at least ended the curse of the Malum from continuing and endangering my family. I knew the dragon clan would care for my family, ensuring that my children would be protected and taught properly. I was happy that I had least died in battle fighting for what I believed in.

I heard glass shattering and the top of the cavern was suddenly lit up. Apparently the top of the cavern was glassed in, and the glass had been painted black to block out any light. Rage flew down and grabbed me, and then flew out of the cavern, headed somewhere I was not aware of, as I blacked out again.

I found out later that a large group of dragons entered the cavern after Rage left, and searched everywhere to ensure that all of the Malum were destroyed, as well as their troops.

FORTY-FIVE

Sick Bed

The next thing I remember was lying in my bed, with friends and family looking over me as I woke.

Godfrey was there and said, "Do not talk, just lay there. You were very close to the edge of death. As it stands, we do not know if you will make it, Dragon Mage. You were pierced by a magical blade, and part of the tip was left inside of you. It is travelling toward your heart. We are doing all that we can to slow or stop the piece of metal from killing you."

"You must lie there quietly, focusing your energy on surviving this evil presence inside of you. The longer you last, the more likely we can find the proper spell to rid you of the blade tip," Godfrey said.

Godfrey cleared the room of everyone but my wives, who spent some time holding my hand and caressing my brow with a cool cloth. The girls left me to try to rest, as I lay there trying to fall back asleep, but afraid at the same time that I would not wake again. I started to fall asleep again, when I felt a strong breeze in the room. I opened my eyes to see Michael the Archangel looking down at me.

I said, "Next time, knock first. I am lying here getting ready to talk to your boss about how rude you are."

Michael laughed, saying, "Good one, dragon mage. Hold still. This is going to hurt like a son of a gun."

He reached his hand down over my chest and looked like he was concentrating. I suddenly felt intense pain, as I could feel something moving inside of my body. Obviously, Michael was drawing the piece of blade out of me.

I started swearing like a trooper, and gasped, "Complaint number two Michael. Your bedside manner really sucks, and you could have made this a little less painful."

Michael just laughed.

Godfrey and James burst into the chamber with weapons drawn, ready to attack. I directed them to stand down and weakly said, "Godfrey, James: meet the Archangel Michael, who just removed that poisoned tip of blade from me. So that is why I was cursing—because it hurt like hell."

Godfrey looked at Michael and bowed. "Thank you for saving the dragon mage. As you must be aware, he means a lot to me."

Michael said, "He is also considered quite highly by Our Lord. It is not his time to die. He still has things to do that he cannot accomplish if he is deceased."

With that, Michael faded away—disappearing completely within a matter of seconds.

Godfrey said, "Now we can focus on the infection. Once we defeat that, you will be well on your way to recovery."

I lay there in the bed, fading in and out, soaked through the sheets and blankets with sweat. I don't remember how many times someone came in to change the sheets. But I do remember that my three brides must have been taking turns scrutinizing me, because each time I awoke, one of them would be sitting beside me, watching me like a hawk.

As each day passed, I began to feel better and better, knowing that I was in the best hands ever, and that Godfrey was doing his best to heal my injuries. I asked James if there was any word on Chavez. I was hoping they had found his body somewhere in the great chamber where Rage and I attacked the Malum.

James said, "We have searched every inch of the caverns, finding bits and pieces of body parts and a lot of ash. But we have not found anything that we can trace to Chavez for sure. I am sorry, Dragon Mage."

I lifted my hand to stop him, and said, "Do not fret, James. There is nothing you can do. Either Chavez was there in the ashes or not. Send some portal mages in with troops to determine where those two sealed portals lead to. I expect an update as soon as possible."

James nodded, and stepped out of the room to arrange for my requests to be fulfilled.

I knew I was healing, but at this point I felt as weak as a newborn T-Rex. My beautiful ladies kept a close eye on me, and I knew James was feeling a bit put out, because watching over the dragon mage had always been his job. The ladies shooed him out of the room whenever they were there, so they could spend time with me alone.

The next time James and I were alone, I said to him, "Do not take offence, James. They just care for me as much as you do, and want to be close to me without the distraction of someone else in the room."

James replied, "I understand, Dragon Mage, but I feel that your safety is in my hands, so that no one can hurt you further while you are weak and cannot defend yourself."

* * * * *

After a couple of weeks, I was able to sit up. They carried me to a spot in the sun, where I could relax and continue my healing. It was like a déjà vu moment. I could see a large dragon flying to the balcony that I was lounging on. I knew this dragon from a distance, since I had never seen a great dragon of this colour in my time on this world.

Rage came to a landing on the balcony and said, "Greetings Kai. It is good to see you healing well, and finally out of your bed, even if it is only for a few hours. I had been imprisoned in that horrible darkness for longer than I can remember. If you had not rescued me, I probably would not have lived much longer, as I could feel myself slipping away. Too bad I almost ate you before you could tell me who you were."

I had to laugh. "It is good that you did not eat me. I would have given you such a bad case of heartburn you would have regretted it for a long time!"

Rage laughed loud and hard. "I made the supreme mistake of trying to take on the Malum by myself. Being a headstrong young dragon lord, I thought I was indestructible. Ah the folly of youth! I should have known better than to take on the Malum by myself, even though their numbers were less than when you and I tackled them."

"Elijah spent a lot of time berating me for my actions, even though he was happy to see me. Older brothers can be a real pain at times, but he was more than glad to see me again, alive. I could feel his happiness, even as he chastised me for my mistakes."

That was an interesting development—Elijah being Rage's big brother. When I was up to it, I went through the portals to see Elijah.

"Greetings, Eldest Dragon. I hear you are a little upset with your younger brother."

Elijah replied, "Yes. You have done something that was unexpected, as usual, Kai. For that we are grateful. I speak not only for myself, but for the entire dragon clan."

I said, "Whether you believe it or not, the help that I have given now and in the past has simply been a matter of being in the right place at the right time. I was not a believer in fate until recently. Things just seem to happen everywhere I go."

Elijah said, "Be careful around Rage. He is impetuous, just like he was when he was young. Rage is one of those who does not like to follow orders or suggestions from his siblings."

I laughed at these comments, and responded, "I say this from experience: not too many like to listen to suggestions from their siblings or their parents."

I thanked Elijah for his time and headed back home to my stronghold and my waiting bed. I skipped dinner, still feeling a little weak from the poisoned blade, and fell asleep quite quickly. When I woke part way through the night, Sylvia and Rose were snuggled in on either side of me. I dozed off quickly, feeling safe and warm with my family beside me.

FORTY-SIX

Big Changes in Capital City

W hile I was enjoying a hearty breakfast, James strode in and said, "It was difficult to open the portals in the Malum caverns. There were a few enchantments woven together to make it challenging to open, even if you knew the proper spells. When the portals were finally opened, they led to secret entrances to the dragon crèche and to the School of Dragon Mages and Companions."

Information began to trickle in about the capital city, which was still under the control of the Orcs. There was total chaos, with different houses fighting each other, since they believed that Chavez had been killed in the battle of the Malum caverns. Honest citizens of the city were hiding behind locked doors and barred windows.

Well, so much for resting and recuperating from my injuries! I was needed to restore order in the capital city and ensure that the loss of life was kept to a minimum.

I sent out a call for troops from all the strongholds to meet outside the nearest stronghold to the capital city. I took my select companions with me and met the troops outside of the stronghold. They would wait and follow six hours behind my men, with Ankylosaurs hauling siege weapons and supplies.

I took elves and the snow people, who were experts at stealthy movements, to get as close to the city gates as possible without being seen. There were three gates into the walled city, and all three were heavily guarded. Each gate was guarded by a different clan of orcs, which was beneficial for us in case they did not yield the gate to my men, as the different orc clans did not communicate with each other.

I had the snow people divided into three groups; one to attack each of the gates at the same time. Not only would surprise be on their side, but most orcs were scared silly of the yeti. Each contingent would have elven archers with them to hold the gate until the dwarven warriors could move forward, take the gates, and hold them.

I walked up to the main gate with James and six elven warriors, all wearing traveling cloaks. As we approached the gate, we were challenged by the gate guards. Gizmo was wrapped around my neck, reading the minds of the gate guardians.

Gizmo said, "They do not suspect anything, thinking these are just some elven merchants coming to the city to arrange trade."

As the guard captain approached, the snow people came out of the tall grass around the entrance and attacked the guards. I raised my staff and sent a small fireball in the air to signal the troops at the other two gates to attack and take control of the entrances. The troops at the gates were unprepared for any confrontation, and were quickly killed or captured. We waited at the gate until the dwarves came up and took charge of the gate.

Troops dispersed and took control of the walls, removing any archers that may have posed a danger to the troops on the ground or dragons in the air. Once we had control of the whole perimeter of the city, I called and a full dozen dragons flew in from where they were waiting.

Rage showed up, tagging along with the other dragons, and said, "I thought you might need an extra hand, Kai, so I followed my young brothers here to help."

I laughed, "As long as you don't burn the city down out of frustration! We are going to deal a bit with politicians, and they tend to get to the point very slowly."

Rage laughed at that and said, "I will do my best, Kai. I promise not to burn the city, but I cannot say the same for the occasional orc who makes me angry!"

It took a couple of days before we were able to round up all of the clan leaders, and get them to sit down at a meeting in what used to be Chavez's castle. They were outnumbered two to one by my companions, and one leader had already tried to kill another leader and take over that clan. The room was large enough that we also had three full-sized dragons overseeing the meetings.

I looked at the orc clan leaders and said, "The large red dragon in this room is the Great Dragon Rage. He has little patience with your people, since they were part of his imprisonment in the hands of the Malum for over one hundred years. So if you make him angry, we will just sweep up your ashes and start with your second in command."

I waited for a few minutes as the orc lords muttered amongst themselves, then I stepped up and said, "We are going to institute a chamber of lords to make decisions for the people of the city. There will be other race members from the community to act as advisors. If you think that you can rob them blind by taxes or strict laws, know now that we will be overseeing everything to ensure that you are treating your people and those that conduct business in the city fairly."

One older orc lord stood and said, "Thank you, Dragon Mage, for our lives. It was feared that this was simply a reprisal for following the orders of Chavez. We are deeply aware of the history of bad blood between our people and other races. Now that Chavez is no longer around to force us to do evil deeds, we look forward to earning the respect and friendship of the races in this world."

In closing, I said, "We will leave a small group of dwarf elders, who will be in an advisory position only to guide you in the right direction You are used to running your operations in a military manner, with Chavez being the commander. It is my hope that we can put everything behind us and move on to a peaceful co existence."

All the troops withdrew from the city. Fortunately, the loss of life incurred by the orcs was minimal, and we were able to leave with little hard feeling between the combatants. The citizens of the city were quick to realize that the war was over, and people were crowding the streets and markets again as if nothing had happened at all.

I took my time heading back to the stronghold with the troops and the Ankylosaurs transports. I felt it was important to spend some meaningful time with the troops to show my support and encouragement. They had successfully taken control of the capital city with a minimum loss of life. I knew that historically, commanders who spent time with and showed support for their men did better, and troops were more willing to lay down their lives, if necessary, for those commanders.

FORTY-SEVEN

Devastation

I t took a week of travel before the walls of Elijah's stronghold came into sight. As I strolled through the gate, Peter was waiting. He had a somber look on his face, and seemed upset.

I said, "Peter, there is something wrong. I can see it in your face."

Peter replied, "It is not something I can discuss here. I would prefer to discuss it in the monitor room, as I want to show you something."

As we walked into the monitor room, Peter's assistants stepped back to give us room in front of the main monitors. What I saw was scary. Cities had been reduced to rubble, and the streets were bare.

I asked Peter what it was that we were looking at.

Peter replied somberly, "It is your old home world, Dragon Mage. The people in all the major cities have died, and there are few left alive in the rural areas. Death is travelling in the air, and it is just a matter of time before all life on this world is gone."

I tried to seem impassive as I asked Peter, "Is there anything we can do to save the remaining people, so that the human race can survive?"

Peter replied, "Yes. We have found a world that is pristine. There is no intelligent life on this new planet, but the land and wildlife are the same as what was on your old world—minus the technology. If you could cross the portal and gather your people, we could activate another portal and lead them to safety."

"The trick will be to get them to believe me. I have been away for almost two years now, and surely thought of as dead," I said, deep in thought. "Is my old home town still intact? If so, there might be someone there whom I can convince of the truth."

Peter replied, "Yes. The whole area that I have been told you worked is intact."

"I need a portable monitor station, so that I can show the person who I know needs to be convinced to move the people through the portals to safety. I will also need a contingent of dwarf engineers to build a town for them to live in while they get their bearings," I said to James, who nodded. He then left the room, so he could organize the engineers to build a large town to house the people when I finally brought them over to this new land.

Peter advised me that a poisonous cloud was slowly spreading over the continent, and that the temperatures were dropping in extremes that were killing fauna and flora all over the world.

Peter and I set up a portal halfway between the farms in the area and the town. I walked to town, with Gizmo in her usual place, wrapped around my neck, to comfort me.

Peter handed me an amulet and said, "This will enable you to draw on the magic of my world, even if you are on a world with little or no magic present."

* * * * *

I knew where sheriff Malone lived with his wife, and I knew he would at least listen to what I had to say; he had always been open to new ideas. I walked to just outside of his house and waited. Malone usually let the dog out in the evening, and then stood by to enjoy the fresh air and quiet solitude. I waited patiently until Malone was about to go back inside of his house.

I cleared my throat, and Malone whirled around, saying "Who's there?"

I replied quickly, "It's Jim. I've come back on a rather urgent matter—that being saving your life and that of the people of this area."

Malone responded, "You know more than I do, Jim. We've lost all communication with any of the larger cities. We still don't know what's happening out there, but I'm guessing you're gonna tell me." He added, more slowly, "...also, I would like to know where you've been the last two years, and where the patrol car you had disappeared to, as well."

I knew he was joking, as he could see Gizmo hanging around my shoulders.

I asked him, "Are you going to invite me in to hear my story, or do you want to take a walk to where I can show you more evidence of what is happening in this world?" Malone stood silently appraising me and then said, "I think a walk is in order, so you can show me what evidence you have."

I waited while he ran inside for a minute to grab a jacket and tell his wife that he was going for a meeting and would be back later. As we strolled down the wooded path, I filled Malone in on what had been happening in my life up to this junction in time.

Malone suddenly stopped and said, "I might have disbelieved you, if not for your pet dragon around your neck."

Gizmo piped up and vocalized a comment in English: "I am no one's pet, and the dragon mage never lies."

Malone walked along with his mouth wide open, which changed to a smile as he shook his head, casting sidelong glances at Gizmo and me from time to time.

Malone's amazement did not die down as we approached the small station set up by Peter's people in a quiet area in the woods, where few people travelled.

Malone stared at the rabbit people, and looked at me quizzically, saying, "I take it this is just another of the different creatures you have encountered in your travels?"

I replied, "Yes, but that is not the reason you are here. These people have come up with a remote viewing system—kind of like low orbit satellites—which can monitor the entire world. They brought my attention to something I am going to show you, and then I have a solution to help."

The room was packed with monitors and a couple of large lanterns that were generating magical energy into the room. No one would notice this unless they were users of magic.

I nodded to Peter, and he explained simply how the monitors worked. He then showed Malone the devastation of the large cities all over the world.

I looked at Malone and said, "I think, from researching the issue, that the Big Powers have finally done it. They dropped nuclear bombs on each other. When the nuclear winter sets in, there won't be anything left alive."

Malone went pale. I brought a chair for him to sit on, as he buried his head in his hands. When he looked up, he said, with hope and worry written on his face, "You said that you had a solution to the end of the world."

I replied, "You have six months to gather as many people as you can, as well as seeds, livestock, etcetera. We will open a portal to another world, wherever you think it can be protected. I can arrange some transport from another world that owes me a great deal. I have also arranged for a large town to be built as we speak, where you can shelter until you are ready to spread out. It will be without a lot of power, so you can leave most items behind. The library, hospital and central buildings will have solar and wind power, and the building will be able to be upgraded when you have time. The area will be warmer, and the winters milder, so it won't cause any hardships. There are a few predators, but nothing larger than the mountain lions or large wolves you might encounter here."

I continued, "I need you to vacate the Sheriff's Office for a couple of days. Peter's people will set up the monitoring station and train a couple of men from another level, where they look exactly like the norm of everyday citizens. They will help you keep the people you are gathering safe. We can start moving people and livestock to this other world within one month, when the town will be finished. I have dedicated a very large contingent of engineers to build it."

Malone said slowly, "Why are you doing this, Jim? I appreciate the help and the chance to save my family, but I am—as always—cynical, and I want to know what you want."

I replied, "This was my home world. I want to save whomever I can. It's just the same reason why I chose to be a police officer. I am needed in other worlds to combat evil, and in a sense have not stopped helping those who are victims of evil."

Malone nodded and said, "I'll clear the office out and tell the staff that its being fumigated for pest control, Here's a key to the back door of the office. You can start first thing tomorrow. I'll round up the three men in town who have ham radios, and start broadcasting a message about having a safe haven from the radiation and a chance to restart anew."

I said, "I'll be back in touch with you as soon as the town on the new world will be ready. If you need me, the monitor station can send me a message that I will receive almost immediately. The transport and support troops will arrive when the town is ready. They will also surprise you, as they are a group based upon the Templar Knights. They have modern technology, but are very adept at hand to hand combat. Take care, Sheriff Malone, and be well. You know where I will be if you need me."

Malone replied, "Thank you, Jim, I'll follow up at my end. I look forward to a day where we can sit down and talk in detail of your adventures."

Malone was led away by one of Peter's guardians, who ensured he made it out of the woods without losing his way or tripping on roots.

The following morning, Malone was true to his word. The office was vacated. We walked in after I checked to ensure that no one was there. We had two of the technology clerics from the Templar world trained and ready by the end of the day to run the system.

Malone came into the office alone to see what was being done. He was greeted warmly by the two clerics, and ended up spending a lot of time while they explained what they were monitoring. They had launched six more monitors to keep an eye on the surrounding area of North Fork.

FORTY-EIGHT

Moving a World

I went to the Templar world and requested an audience with the Holy Father. It was only a very short time before I was surprised when he came to the estate to see me, rather than have me travel to the papal palace. After the Pope arrived, the servants practically tripped over themselves running back and forth to ensure that he was comfortable. This was a real honour for the estate, as the Holy Father rarely left the papal palace.

I said to the Pope, "I have need of some troops to assist and protect settlers who must leave a dying world for another world, where they can start anew. Also, I will need some transports they can keep for moving people and supplies to their new home."

Pope Jason the Second said, "What I have available is yours to use. Sir Justin has commented that he owes you his life. He would jump at the chance to reciprocate your aid. He also has a brother with another estate. They will both send men. I will give you all of my transports, which I will replace with new, so that you can keep the ones you have been given. The troops and transports will be ready for you within a week. Also, I am sending you clerics from the technology arm of the church to set up this town you are building for the emigrants to the new world."

I thanked him and allowed Lord Strongwind to have the honour of hosting the Holy Father. I stepped back as several friends of the Lord were invited to share a meal with the Pope. I went back to the dragon world, to my stronghold, and into the arms of my lovely ladies.

I spent the next two days spending time with Sylvia, Rose, and Amelia. I went shopping with them for baby items and trinkets, to show how much I loved them all. It was nice to rest and not have to worry about anything at the moment, now that the evil wizard Chavez had been dealt with. If Chavez was still alive, he would be severely injured. It would be a while before he became a threat again.

A pair of dragons had volunteered to oversee the building of the new town. I did not have to worry, as they dealt with all the minor questions that always percolated up during any construction. I just had to sit and wait for any more details as they trickled in, and deal with issues as they arose. I received word that the Templar Knights were ready to deploy. Arrangements were made to open a portal to the new unoccupied world, and then another portal was set up to transport the knights to my old home world.

I showed up on the new unoccupied world, where Sir Justin had set up a camp outside of the town. It was almost done, with the exception of the wall around the town to protect it, and some garden areas that were set up for some of the townspeople. A couple of large barns were also set up for cattle and pigs.

I asked Sir Justin, "So—are you ready to help my other friends from the world I originally came from?"

Sir Justin replied. "Yes, of course. But—what has happened, that you must move people from their homes to here? I must admit, this is a beautiful world."

I answered, "The powers that be had developed a weapon so destructive that it kills thousands of people when it is used. Their enemies also had the same type of weapon. They each have threatened for years to use the weapons. There came a time when someone made a mistake and one thing led to another, and these weapons were unleashed by all sides. Because the weapons were used from all sides, millions of people were killed. The land is poisoned, the weather is getting worse, and soon the poison will spread to the survivors, killing everything and everyone in its path."

Sir Justin was aghast. "How could they do something like that? I do not understand the evil behind such decisions."

I replied, "It is a case of thinking that their weapon was the ultimate deterrent. They thought that if they had it, no one would be stupid enough to use it. So obviously, someone was stupid enough. They paid the ultimate price, because they were the first target of their enemies."

Sir Justin shook his head and walked back to his troops and their small camp, waiting on orders to start. I set up the portal and stepped through with Gizmo and a small group of guardian companions.

As I entered my old world, one of the clerics I had left to monitor things came running up and said, between gasps of breath, "Military men have showed up and have taken charge of the town! They are talking of shooting the sheriff and all the law enforcement officers, and initiating something called marital law."

I said "that's martial law" and directed the cleric back through the portal to bring Sir Justin through immediately, with the troops ready to deploy. I then told James to go back to the dragon world and bring my troops through right away to deal with these soldiers. I wanted little dragons and interrogators, so we could weed out those just following orders or those who were there with their own agenda.

Sir Justin was through the portal and deploying his men around the portal in defensive positions within minutes. My troops began appearing within half an hour. They set up with the Templar soldiers in the perimeter.

I talked to Tomar and said, "I want you and your dark elves to locate all of these soldiers and monitor them. If they are violent or commit any attacks on the citizens of this town, you have permission to dispatch them quietly and quickly."

Tomar nodded and took off at a run, with his men following suit.

The next morning dawned cool and damp; cloudy, with the occasional sprinkling of rain. I watched from close by as all the police officers and the sheriff were escorted to the center of town. A firing squad was lined up to shoot them, but I had a surprise up my sleeve for these so-called military men.

An officer wearing captain bars called out, "Ready...aim...fire!"

Before he got to "fire," I cast a spell, shielding the police officers and the sheriff from the bullets.

Once they had stopped firing, they looked surprised, as Malone and his men just stood there. I stepped out and walked up to the captain.

I said, "I think that is just about enough of this self-justice—killing men for no reason."

The captain responded, "And who do you think you are, friend?"

I looked at him and said, "For starters, I am not your friend. You will lay down your arms and surrender—or die. You have thirty seconds to decide."

The captain drew his pistol in response and pointed it at me to shoot, and then he dropped dead with an arrow through his throat. The rest of the men with him dropped their weapons and put their hands behind their heads. The Templar troops drove down the road and spread out, rounding up the rest of the close to one hundred men who made up the military contingent. I came over to Malone and the men cutting their bonds, and stood by while all the military men were brought to a temporary camp for a quick debriefing. The dwarf interrogators and the little dragons processed the troops quickly, with only twenty of the officers being held in custody.

I turned to talk to Malone, saying, "Are you ready to start moving livestock and some of the people across the portal to the new world we have set up for you? I think we need to advance the timetable a bit to clear the town, in case someone else shows up and can be screened for ill intentions."

Malone replied, "We can round up cattle, pigs and poultry from the farms, and get them and a herd of sheep from the next town over through the gateway with their handlers."

"I want all the law enforcement families, as well as medical families, moved for their safety. I know you will sleep better knowing that your family will be in safe hands, away from any chance of violence or radiation," I said, looking at Malone.

He nodded and began issuing orders to the men, directing a transport to each residence to pick up a vehicle's worth of furniture, food, and personal items.

The Templars knew what I wanted, and they moved quickly and efficiently. The families were relocated to the new world without any issues, and settled down in new lodgings. The engineers had finished the town, and had left the updates to the Templar clerics who specialized in technology. The clerics had finished with a few homes, where the families were relocated to.

While people got ready to travel, I loaded the transports with the contents of the local library and school, to be transported to the first library that had been built on the new world. The transports were going back and forth full time, with the exception of two, which were held back for emergencies. I pulled the soldiers that we had cleared as only following orders, and we asked if they were aware of any other battalions on their way toward this safe zone. They denied any knowledge, but stated they would stay behind until the last ones were through the portal.

As Malone was saying goodbye to his wife and children and grandchildren before they went ahead of him, I walked up and handed Malone two vials of an amber coloured liquid.

Malone looked at me quizzically. "What is this, Jim?"

I replied, "The new world needs a strong leader who will be around for a long time to guide the people. This vial is for you and your lovely wife. It will make you feel young again, and you will live for at least another hundred years. The reason there are two vials is because I know how much you love your wife, and this way, both of you will live long and fruitful lives."

Malone began to tear up. He tried to cover it up with humour, saying, "Thank you, Jim. I appreciate your thoughtfulness by including my significant other in your plans." Then he reached across and gave me a huge hug, which was a side of him I had never seen before.

In the weeks that followed, people from other towns and cities who had heard the radio messages began to show up. They trickled in, both as family units and as individuals. I was cautious, and had the interrogators screen them to ensure that we were not sending a mass murderer or psychotic through the portal.

I took a group of healers to the nearest hospital with transports, and Malone introduced us to the hospital staff. They were reluctant at first, but when the healers began treating the sick, clearing at least half the patients in a day and stabilizing the rest for transport, the staff were eager to learn and help evacuate the hospital.

At the end of the thirty-day period I had quoted to Malone, the weather started to deteriorate. Radiation levels were higher, and a bitter cold was setting in. Malone and I were the last ones to cross the portal, which I left open for another six months. A camp was set up to screen anyone who came to the new world, complete with a contingent of dwarf guards, interrogators and little dragons, as well as healers to treat the sick or injured.

I spoke to Malone as we walked toward the new town, "There are a lot more people we have managed to save than I thought there would be. The dwarf engineers will be back to start building another city one hundred miles away, so that you are not on top of each other. There will be a rail line between the two cities for trade and emergencies."

Malone smiled and said, "You have done so much for all of us, Jim. You will be remembered well after you pass on. I hope I am able to fill the boots you have left for me to fill. I'll do my best to make you proud of me."

I replied, "As you used to say to me, I never give a job to someone who I know will fail. I know you're capable of the job, sheriff. If you need help at all, go to the monitor room located in the capital building. It will have a call button, and I will be sought out to answer or aid you in any way I can."

"We are looking for a large library in one of the major cities, so we can recover books and whatever can be salvaged to keep history alive. We are also looking for museums, to save culture as well. When we have located anything intact, I will contact you to help in saving what we can. I have no intention of keeping anything, but will give it all to you to archive here on the new world. Also, engineers will be here for a year or two, helping to build farmhouses and barns, to help with developing infrastructure," I said as I walked with Malone.

When I returned to Elijah's stronghold, I instructed Peter on what I was looking for on my old world. He advised that they would search amongst the ruined cities for the buildings that I described to him. As it turned out, the entire U.S. Library of Congress was intact, along with the majority of the capital city. My guess was that they used a neutron bomb, which killed people but left buildings more or less intact. I talked to Peter, and we were able to send a monitor into the building through a broken window. It was cloaked, so not visible to the naked eye.

The building inside appeared clean; there were no signs of any bodies or survivors in the area. There was a small amount of dust that had blown in from the outside through a few broken windows, but nothing else.

I took my wives with me to visit Malone.

I said to him, "I need your help with art and books of value to help you in your quest to advance civilization in this world. I want you, and several people who have experience, to travel to the Library of Congress and several art museums that are still intact, and select what you think would be beneficial for generations to come. In the meantime, my wives can visit and help around your new home to get your family settled."

Malone looked at me quizzically and said, "Wives? What happened to the single man I knew? Never mind, I would be more than happy to accompany you and get what we feel would help the people."

I said in reply, "The dragon world believes in multiple marriages—kind of like the Old Testament, especially when it comes to a man of power and prestige, so that his greatness can be spread through the generations to come. Those are their words—not mine! The women get along fantastically with each other. Two of them even picked my latest bride."

Malone just stood there appraising me with a smile on his face. He shook his head, saying, "Just let me know when you're ready to go, and I'll gather the librarians and a couple of art critics who showed up after fleeing the radiation. Thank goodness for your dwarf friends who have started building another town. We were beginning to get crowded in the two new towns they had already built."

I called the Templar Knights to gather and prepare to travel with me to the old world. I also sent a message to Elijah, asking for all the librarians who could be spared to help sort and catalog all the books and records that were taken.

Peter offered to send fifty of their knowledge gatherers to document and copy all the books. He showed me a couple of machines the books had to be passed through, to record the entire book without having to copy each page separately.

FORTY-NINE

The Library

I left Malone and all the troops behind when I stepped through the portal, directly into the Library of Congress. I created a bubble of force around the entire library, pushing the contaminated air out, and drawing clean air from the portal. I then stepped back through the portal, and called the Templar knights to deploy and search in and around the library for any hostiles or injured victims.

Once the area around the library was cleared, Malone and his people came through, followed by the dragon companion librarians, and Peter's rabbit people with their equipment. The Templars searched from the top floor down. As soon as one floor was cleared. the librarians and rabbit people moved in and started selecting books to transport to the new world. They started in the rare book archive, with such things as a Gutenberg bible, and other rare volumes that were important to human history.

One of the Templar guards ran up and said, "We have found people in the vault area in the sub-basement. They closed the door when they saw us, and won't come out to even speak with us. Malone and I went down to the vault. I stood back and let Malone yell through the vault door until it was opened a crack, and he then stepped in to talk to the occupants.

I said to Gizmo, as she lay around my neck, "Keep monitoring Malone and what is going on inside the vault. If there is any sign of trouble, I will rip the door off its hinges to protect Malone."

Gizmo replied, "Everything is calm. Malone is making you proud, explaining where he will take them to safety and about the healers that we have available to help the sick and dying."

The vault door opened within about ten minutes. Malone introduced me to the group leader, who, although his clothes were tattered, was obviously a police officer.

The Templar warriors, under my direction, began helping the fifty people that were crammed into the vault area to waiting transports to be taken to the new world. About a dozen of the people had to be stabilized first, as they were in critical condition. I spent all night treating the most sick, so they would survive the relocation.

I was exhausted by the time I finished getting the last patients ready to be moved. Six healers showed up, and went with the transports to ensure that they were completely taken care of in the new world. We spent a week selecting the best books that would assist people to progress in the new world. Then we left the building, leaving things that would not be of any use to Malone's people.

I spent the next two weeks with the art critics, picking through museums for anything of value, including some works from famous painters.

When we finally headed back to the new world, there were at least one thousand people, from all countries, who had been saved from the nuclear winter. We were very careful to screen out anyone who might be a threat to the new government that was forming under Malone's direction.

It turned out that Malone's wife was getting along famously with my wives. She had a very open mind, after it was explained to her what the mores of the dragon world were. My ladies had helped getting everything organized and comfortable for their family.

When I closed the portal to my old world, I left only two monitors, which flew high in the air and kept an eye on the devastation. If there were any survivors, eventually they would surface to get supplies or equipment. Depending on their actions, we would decide if we wanted to contact them or leave them to their own designs.

FIFTY

My babies are born

N ow that all the major incidents had been dealt with, it was time to relax and recharge my batteries. Both Rose and Sylvia had their babies on the same day, surrounded by healers and helpers, skilled at bringing healthy babies into the world. The women delivered within one hour of each other, which at least allowed me to be witness to the birth of each of our babies. Rose had a boy named Kai, and Sylvia had a girl she named Kaleigh. Both were healthy, and the deliveries went without a hitch.

I felt full of energy and pride. I had never had any children with my first wife on the old world. Rose and Sylvia were aglow with feelings of love and joy. I could see their happiness, because in their eyes I had given them the most ultimate gift they could ever want. I could see, though, that Amelia was just a little bit jealous. Obviously, she and I would have to work on that! But practice makes perfect, and I planned to practice as much as I could.

I got a call from Elijah to meet him at his chambers in his stronghold.

I walked in and said to Elijah, "What now, old man? I feel like I have been run off my feet. As soon as I deal with one problem, another one arises."

Elijah responded, "Yes, I know, Kai. But you are so capable in dealing with any of the major issues that we rely on you. Without your strength and power, the possibility of success would be greatly reduced. We have been searching the worlds for signs of our dragon brothers who are being kept in the slavery of wizards. Yes, this is the same world the dragon clans escaped from. There is an old manuscript which says that the dragon mage will free our people from captivity."

I replied, "And, of course, you have found the world you originated from?"

Elijah said, "No, not yet, but we have narrowed the search down to a manageable number. We hope to find the world within the next two weeks, at which time we will let you know so that you can help the clans."

As I walked out of the meeting with Elijah, I thought that it was typical of the dragon mentality. Don't ask, just tell what was needed, without expecting a negative answer. I smiled as I headed back to my stronghold to be with my growing family.

The search took longer than Elijah had thought, giving me more time to rest and be with the ladies and the two newborns. Elijah contacted me, advising that they thought they had found the wizard world where dragon clan members were kept as servants, or slaves, to their masters. I talked to Peter, who immediately launched multiple cloaked monitors to scan this world.

I walked the battlements, watching the moons rising and giving the twilight that weird glow, which caused the woods to emit an eerie luminosity—almost surreal. I wondered what this new development would bring to light. The last two years had been a constant battle, and now I was being tasked with helping to free the dragon clans from servitude on another world.

I was feeling very tired, and knew I wouldn't have as much time to spend with my new family as I needed. I was looking forward to the day when I could rest for more than a few days at a time, and spend my energies directing the troops, instead of having to be quite so hands-on for all the matters I had to deal with.

But I would not have traded it for the old life I would have had in my old home world.

CHARACTER INDEX

Amelia	Widow of disposed Templar knight, and third wife of dragon mage Jim
Adam	Leader of Diamond clan
Adoronac	Dragon Guardian of the North and provider of counsel to the dwarves
Anax	Elven wise man elder, who, in passing of old age, declared Jim an Elf friend
Argentum	Caravan leader (dwarf). Travels south part of world, trading
Betel	Young dragon lord, taking charge of Quartz clan
Blaze	Dwarf warrior, incorporated into companions on clan edict
Blade	Dwarf warrior, incorporated into companions on clan edict
Bonny and Clyde	Breeding pair of drakes that stayed with the dragon mage
Cerebus	Dwarf mage, spy for Chavez.
Chavez	Grand Wizard, leader of the government and one badass dude

Companion protectors from the People:

	John (Cpl) Frank (Cpl), Bill, Joe, Fred, Samson, Kevin, Karl, Larry, Lionel
Conn	Bishop of enforcement clan, who disobeyed papal order
Creditum	Dwarf caravan leader and trader. Extremely honest
Dagger	Commander of Dark Elf jail

249

Domar	Eldest of Dark Elf clan
Dragon Council	Three dragons: Adam, Joshua, and Zachariah
Drake	Type of flightless dragon; about the size of a large mastiff back home
Elijah	Eldest Dragon. Decision-maker and chooser of dragon mages.
Envoy	Snow People contact person between the Sea People and his people.
Fire-Tongue	Dwarf warrior, incorporated into companions on clan edict
Flit	Small dragon lord, known for speed and stealth.
Fred	Drake handler
George	Dark Cardinal of the enforcement branch of the Catholic church
Gizmo	Also known as Lady Gizmo, small dragon
Gladius	Elven warrior, head of one of the Elf communities that welcome Jim as a friend
Godfrey	Ancient wizard, wise in the ways of all types of magic (other than dragon magic)
Ice Storm	Yeti (Snow People) advisor to the Bronze clan in the north
Ice Wind	Yeti (Snow People) dragon mage companion
Isaac	Small dragon, husband of Lady Gizmo
James and Joshua	Twin brothers of the People, sent to act as Jim's escort and servants
Jason	His Eminence Jason the Second, current Pope in the Templar world of high technology, who has little use for magic.
Jeremiah	Leader of Bronze clan
Jonathon Isaac Martin	Full name of Jim, also known as Kai, the Dragon Mage

Jonah Strongwind	Lady Amelia's father, a lord on the world of the Templars
Joseph	Village Elder at one of the People villages
Justin	Knight of the Templars, tasked by the Pope with keeping order and peace
Kali	Young dragon, guide to Dark Elf clan
Kai	A young fledgling dragon who dies. Also name given to Jim by dragon clan when dragon spine is used to cure him. Also name given to Jim's first-born son from mother Rose
Kaleigh	First-born daughter of dragon mage Jim from mother Sylvia
Kleet	Guard captain for the Sea People
Lazarus	Dwarven dragon clan wizard trained to control portals to other worlds
Lomar	Elder Dark Elf from forest community
Malum	Descendants of dark dragons. Bat-like creatures that do not like light at all
Matilda	Eldest female and Leader of Drake pack
Michael	Archangel sent from On High to assist Dragon Mage Jim in his quest
Midnight	Pitch-black dragon Seeker of things from other lands for Mother of Dragons
Mercury	Dragon descendant of Elijah, dragon mage companion and mount
Malachi	Leader of the Gargoyles, who call themselves the Stone People
Morlack	Detachment commander for Orc encampment in the North
Mortimer/Anthony	Dwarven merchant in Capital City, front for Assassins' Guild, and later, ally for the dragon mage.
Neb	Large Dark Elf who was taken under **Tomar's** wing

Nebulon	Gryphon, head of the clan of this mythological species
Neela	Eldest breeding female dragon, Keeper of the Creche and aviary on Dragon Isle, who gave Jim the name of Kai
Otis	Peace-seeking soldier of the Orc army
Pater	Dragon: the father of all dragons, dating back to the beginning of recorded dragon history
Peter	Four-foot-tall rabbit from another dimension (The Watchers, who monitor other worlds), possessing magical powers.
Rage	Red dragon, younger brother to Elijah
Raphael	Small dragon, traitor to the dragon clans. Spying for Chavez in exchange for power and money.
Rawlings and Smith	Detectives from Scotland Yard; sent to question Jim while he was in a Liverpool, England hospital in his world.
Reee	Great explorer of the Undines (Sea People)
Rose	Elven princess. Elite warrior, second wife of dragon mage Jim, mother of Jim's son Kai
Samuel	Elder of The People (normal humans)
Shree	Elder of the Sea People (Undines)

Companion protectors from the Snow People (also known as Ice People):

	Yeti: Snow Flake, Ice Runner, Snow Ball, Snow Storm
Spirit	Fire salamander. Pet of dragon mage Jim
Susan	Fred's mother, in charge of the kitchen at Jim's stronghold

Sylvia	Lady Sylvia. Dwarven widow, first wife of dragon mage Jim, mother of Jim's daughter Kaleigh
Thomas	Sergeant-of-Arms at dragon mage Jim's new estate on the Templar world
Tleec	Great writer and historian of the Undines (Sea People)
Tomar	Assassins' Guild senior and most experienced killer
Torlak	Orc wizard
The Voice	Elder Yeti (Snow People, or Ice People), leader and friend to Elijah
Would-be Assassins:	John, Luke, Mark

ITEMS OF MAGIC

Draco

Magical Staff made of bone of ancient dragon, carrying strong dragon magic

Golden ring of Strength

Gift from The Voice of the Snow People

Kritico

Elven wine: keeps your head clear, but warms your body and spirit

Mithril mail shirt

Gifted by dwarves of the Northern clans

Mithril Vambraces (arm braces)

Gift from Adoronac, to focus magical power

Orb of Pater

Magical orb containing a crystal that steals power from the enemy and protects the bearer

Pendant

Intricately carved necklace, showing carrier as Elven friend

Plain ring of Invisibility

Taken from wizard Torlak

| Texas Ranger Silver Badge | Gifted by Creditum, the Dwarf merchant: Family heirloom, kept for over two hundred years. Seems to emanate energy to the wearer, giving him more endurance. Belonged to Jim's great-great grandfather, who disappeared from his world over two hundred years ago. |

ABOUT THE AUTHOR

Timothy was born in Chilliwack, BC in a military family. Even at a young age, he found his escape by reading science fiction and fantasy books, taking him to a place where he could dream of being a hero.

Upon completion of school, he started his career as a RCMP officer. After much success and 25 years of service, Timothy is now retired. He suffers from Post-Traumatic Stress Disorder and finds that writing gives him an outlet, helping him deal with this debilitating disorder.

This is the second novel in the Dragons & Dinosaurs universe continues with his wishes to share his passions for this genre of fiction with others.

He now resides in Grand Forks, BC with his wife of 35 years and his service dog Hunter. You can reach Timothy at timothysdragon@ outlook.com

Printed in the United States
By Bookmasters